Praise for

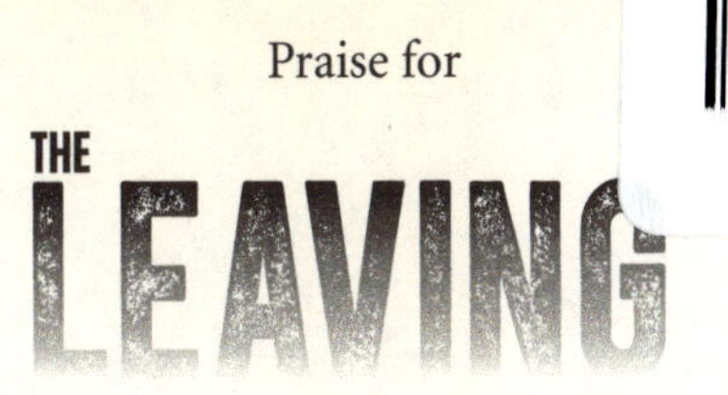

"Altebrando hides a meditation on memory and identity inside a top-speed page-turner." —E. Lockhart, *New York Times* bestselling author of *We Were Liars*

"As heart-stopping as it is heartbreaking, *The Leaving* layers a wildly strange suspense story over a lovely and unexpected narrative of grief, loss, and the struggle to imagine a future in the shadow of the past." —Robin Wasserman, author of *Girls on Fire*

"A twisty, *oh no she didn't* thriller that keeps the surprises firing, but also a thoughtful reflection on what really makes us who we are." —Bennett Madison, author of *September Girls*

"Bold, inventive, and engaging, *The Leaving* leaps straight off the page." —Beth Kephart, author of *Small Damages* and *This Is the Story of You*

★ "This is no mere thriller; folded into this compulsively readable work are thought-provoking themes." —*SLJ*, starred review

★ "A twisting, harrowing story." —*Publishers Weekly*, starred review

"Will keep readers engaged from beginning to end." —*Booklist*

"A bit of romance, a bit of pathos, a bit of science fiction, and a bit of ripped-from-the-headlines trauma." —*BCCB*

"A twisting and turning mystery that will grip readers." —*Kirkus Reviews*

BOOKS BY TARA ALTEBRANDO

The Leaving

The Possible

TARA ALTEBRANDO

BLOOMSBURY
NEW YORK LONDON OXFORD NEW DELHI SYDNEY

First published in the United States of America in June 2016
by Bloomsbury Children's Books
Paperback edition published in June 2017
www.bloomsbury.com

Bloomsbury is a registered trademark of Bloomsbury Publishing Plc

For information about permission to reproduce selections from this book, write to Permissions, Bloomsbury Children's Books, 1385 Broadway, New York, New York 10018
Bloomsbury books may be purchased for business or promotional use. For information on bulk purchases please contact Macmillan Corporate and Premium Sales Department at specialmarkets@macmillan.com

The Library of Congress has cataloged the hardcover edition as follows:
Names: Altebrando, Tara, author.
Title: The Leaving / Tara Altebrando.
Description: New York : Bloomsbury, 2016.
Summary: Six kindergartners were taken. Eleven years later, five come back—with no idea of where they've been. No one remembers the sixth victim, Max. Avery, Max's sister, needs to find her brother—dead or alive—and isn't buying this whole memory-loss story.
Identifiers: LCCN 2015037730
ISBN 978-1-61963-803-7 (hardcover) • ISBN 978-1-61963-804-4 (e-book)
Subjects: | CYAC: Mystery and detective stories. | Memory—Fiction. | Identity—Fiction. | Missing children—Fiction. | Kidnapping—Fiction. | BISAC: JUVENILE FICTION / Mysteries & Detective Stories. | JUVENILE FICTION / Social Issues / Strangers. | JUVENILE FICTION / Love & Romance.
Classification: LCC PZ7.A46332 Le 2016 | DDC [Fic]—dc23
LC record available at http://lccn.loc.gov/2015037730

ISBN 978-1-68119-403-5 (paperback)

Book design by Kimi Weart
Typeset by RefineCatch Limited, Bungay, Suffolk, UK
Printed and bound in the U.S.A. by Berryville Graphics Inc., Berryville, Virginia
2 4 6 8 10 9 7 5 3 1

All papers used by Bloomsbury Publishing, Inc., are natural, recyclable products made from wood grown in well-managed forests. The manufacturing processes conform to the environmental regulations of the country of origin.

For Liz, who was taken too soon

The lights hurt my eyes and Mommy is crying and not looking at me. I am on her hip, with Woof-Woof between us.

I am wearing my monkey pajamas.

I am supposed to be in bed.

But Mommy and then Daddy came into my room and turned on the light and said, "Sweetie. We just need to do this thing. It's important. Then you can go right back to sleep."

Daddy scooped me up and I grabbed Woof-Woof because he goes where I go, especially if it's someplace important.

Max isn't here.

Max isn't in his fireman pajamas.

Today was his first real day of kindergarten and he didn't come home.

I don't know why and I am afraid to ask because that is why Mommy has been crying.

It started at the bus stop.

The bus came, but Max wasn't on it.

I want to ask "Is Max dead?" as Daddy puts me in my car seat.

But I don't want to because I don't know what dead means except that it's bad. Maybe kindergarten is bad, too? Maybe it takes you away and makes moms and dads sad.

The lights that hurt are on big cameras where we end up. In front of a big building that looks like it is made of gray LEGOs.

They make night feel like day.

They make me feel weird about my pajamas.

There are men talking into big microphones and I haven't seen my Minnie Mouse microphone in a while and it seems like my toys have started disappearing. Did Max take them with him?

Men are talking.

Like grown-ups with rules.

Then Daddy is right next to me and Mommy—with a microphone, lollipop-close to his mouth. Fishy camera eyes are pointed at us.

He is saying, "Please, bring back our son. Bring all the children back, unharmed."

A woman screams, "My daughter said she was going on a trip, to the leaving . . . does anyone know what that means?"

And Mommy looks at me, like she's only just remembering that she's holding me, and I squeeze my thighs around her tight so that now I can lean toward the microphone, and the world gets quiet, so I say, "I really want Max to come home."

Mommy lets out a sound I have no word for and pulls my head into the space between her head and her soft parts and pushes through all those shoulders and elbows and arms.

Woof-Woof is gone and I think about screaming.

Then I do.

My father says, "Here," and he has Woof-Woof.

I grab him and hug him and his brown ears smell like sleep and apple juice and my thumb that I suck and I say, "Woof-Woof, I thought I lost you," and he has these two eyes that are stitched out of thread and they are wide apart and I know he's not real but for the first time ever, he looks so very sad.

So sad that it hurts to look at him.

I find Mommy's shoulder and find my thumb and close my eyes to make it all go away.

DAY ZERO

Scarlett

Like being ripped open, midnightmare. Breathless, in the center of a scream.

Her hands went to the knot on the blindfold at the back of her neck. It was tied tight. It hurt her fingers to undo it.

Then her eyes were freed.

Night.

Heat.

Palm trees.

"Where are we?" A girl.

"What's going on?" A boy.

She turned.

Saw the others.

Saw him. His name was . . . ? Something with an *L*?

He took off running after the van, screaming, "Stop! Wait!"

One taillight out. Tires screeching. Gone.

Lucas. His name was Lucas.

And hers?

They'd gotten out of that white van, just a moment ago. Three rows of seats. Ripped leather upholstery that dug into her thigh.

She had spent the journey fighting sleep—or something—and working hard not to tear the blindfold off.

He'd said not to. It had been important to behave.

"Where are we?" A girl—

Sarah?—

screaming.

"Who *was* that?" Adam—his name was easy, biblical—paced. "Who was driving?"

She studied him—his skin light brown, darker than the others'—then his clothes.

Black shirt.

Black jeans.

Sneakers.

Then Lucas's.

"Scar?" He was staring at her.

What scar? Where?

Oh.

Scarlett.

Her name was Scarlett.

"You okay?" He came closer.

She studied her own clothes. Swallowed to wet her throat. "Why are we all wearing the same thing?"

"I think I'm having a panic attack," Sarah said. "Oh my god. Ohmygodohmygod."

"Just calm down"—the first words out of . . . K . . . K . . . K . . . *Kristen's* mouth.

"**WHY SHOULD I CALM DOWN?**" Again, Sarah. Screaming.

Something was poking Scarlett's hip.

Two of her fingers slid into her right jeans pocket, found a folded piece of paper. Took it out. Unfolded it.

"What's that?" Lucas asked.

Lines, this way and that. "A map."

The others dug through pockets. They all had maps.

Her eyes found a red-inked star on hers and saw her nails were also red: worn and chipped, like blood leaking out of her cuticles.

"I think this is a map to my house," Lucas said. "Thirty-three Locust Place."

"Mine's not ringing any bells." Kristen flipped to the other side of her map, and back. "Maybe I got the wrong one?"

She wasn't chewing gum, but Scarlett pictured her that way. Always chewing.

Scarlett turned. A slide. Some swings. A gate.

A thought about a cracked tooth, a boy.

Had it been Lucas?

No, but . . .

Her feet had orders.

Marched toward the playground.

Stood at the center on the springy blacktop.

A warm wind woke an old swing. It squeaked and swung a ghost child.

"I've been here," Scarlett said to no one.

The others came in, too.

She stopped at a red horse on a springy coil, the kind you sit on . . .

. . . and rock.

Sarah was all panic. "Why don't we remember *where we live*?"

Good. Question.

Better question: Why don't we remember . . . *everything*?

The horse's eyes spied. Crickets pulsed. The wind whipped palm trees into whispers.

The world folded in.

This was the Cliff

of Scarlett.

No idea how she'd gotten here.

The path behind her was wiped clean.

She *knew* the others . . .

. . . and she could not think of a thing they'd done before . . .

. . . this.

Her mind clicked its blankness at her . . .

/
/
/

. . . three times.

"We must have been drugged," Adam said. He was taller and more muscular than Lucas but somehow not as confident.

"Does anyone remember who was driving?" Lucas asked. "Or where we were when we got into the van? Were we all at a party or something?"

Heads shook.

The wind died and the swings froze, a still photograph.

Adam said, "I don't remember . . . *anything*."

"It has to be a drug. It'll wear off," Lucas said.

Another car drove by: extra lights under the body and bass-heavy music blasting. Scarlett's heart rattled and settled.

Probably drugs.

If not that . . .

/
/

. . . what?

Sarah was shaking her head. "I don't understand what's happening." She walked in small circles, rubbing her hands together.

"We should go home." Lucas held up his map. "Someone will know what's going on."

"What if it's a trap?" Sarah's eyes were drowning.

"Why would there be a *trap*?" Kristen looked like she was about to hail a cab or hitch a ride. Anything to get away from them.

Adam said, "Why should we trust whoever dropped us off here and gave us these?" He wagged his map around.

"There's no point standing here talking about it, is there?" Kristen bent, retied her shoelace, and then stood. "I guess I'll see you guys around."

She started to walk off, but Lucas grabbed her. "Wait. Just wait."

"Why?"

"We should have a plan," he said. "We should, I don't know, get our story straight."

"*There is no story*," Kristen said. "The story is we have no idea what's going on. So let's go home. What else is there to do?"

"We'll go, yes." He released her arm; she rubbed it. "But let's meet back here tomorrow night, like eight o'clock. Just to make sure we're okay, just to make sure we've gotten some answers and snapped out of it, whatever it is."

Scarlett was running into dead ends, circling back on herself.

o n
She was n n i e r.
l a

Cycling back, again and again, to a memory of riding in a hot air balloon—happy, unafraid.

So, yes. *Definitely* drugs. *Had to be.*

"Somebody will be able to explain," Lucas said. "Somebody will know what happened."

"What if we can't get away tomorrow?" Sarah's circling was surely making her dizzy. "Maybe we should go to a hospital and get checked out."

"No hospitals." Lucas shook his head. "Meet back here. Tomorrow night at eight. Okay? And if that doesn't work out for whatever reason, we try the next night, same time."

Sarah stopped circling.

Everyone nodded except Scarlett, who looked at her map again.

That red star.

Was the address familiar or just . . . generic?

"Scar?" Lucas said.

There was something between them.

Something . . . extra.

Something . . . else.

"Tomorrow night." Him, again. "Okay?"

Lucas

He couldn't walk fast enough, pushed his calf muscles to the limit, stretched the very definition of walking.

Not good enough.

Started to run.

Slowly at first—a jog—then faster, his sneakers slapping the pavement hard and loud.

Faster and faster.

The red star promised answers.

Relief.

Sleep.

But he had to stop, bend, breathe, because the world spun.

He was standing perfectly still, but he was on a carousel—

WHITE HORSE GOLDEN REINS

A BUBBLE-GUM-PINK TONGUE.

He was being carried around and around while the

SUN BLAZED OFF THE OCEAN, LIKE WHITE FIRE.

He was holding on for dear life and loving it.

He closed his eyes, shook his head and arms, started to walk again, focusing on a point far ahead to try to fight dizziness.

It was annoying, the spinning.

CAROUSEL HORSE CAROUSEL TONGUE
CAROUSEL WHITE FIRE

What carousel?

He had no time for it.

He took off again, overshot the address he was looking for and had to double back, winded, to find the old red trailer house.

But between there and here, there was . . . what would you even call it?

A sculpture park?

A monument?

Hundreds—no, thousands—of rocks formed a pathway that his feet started to follow. To the right, the path divided off toward a rain-collecting pool. To the left, some kind of tunnel, and ahead, more spiraling walkways and stairs and bridges. It felt ancient. Sacrificial.

Like built on bones.

Still.

Red star.

Answers.

He kept walking, then spotted a figure way up back on the slope: a man in a lighted hat holding a chisel.

His father?

Had *made* this?

Was *still* making it?

"Dad?" he called out, hearing his uncertainty and confusion, and the figure in the distance turned. Standing on a tall platform of stone, the man took his hat off, dropped it, and squinted into the night.

"Ryan?" Sounded confused.

"No." Ryan was . . . a boy? A brother? "Lucas."

"Is this some kind of joke?" Now angry.

He started to approach, and Lucas called out, "Not a joke!"

Why would he be joking?

The man inspected him from the top of a ladder-steep set of stone steps—"Oh my god, Lucas!"—and started to run down, and then he slipped and, as if in slow motion, tumbled and bumped and then landed—headfirst—with a dull smack on stone.

Lucas ran to him. "Dad!"

And bent to help him up.

And lifted his head. "Dad!"

And it was all warm and black and all over his hand.

"No." Lucas stood, backing away. "No-no-no-no-no-no."

Then, one more try: "Dad!"

Only the hum of the night: distant cars, tree frogs, a far-off motorboat. The sound of it echoed inside him, his body hollow.

He stood, ran to the house, pounded on the door until it opened.

Ryan.

But not a boy: grown.

"Call an ambulance," Lucas barked. "NOW!"

"Who the hell—"

"Just do it!"

Then back to the body, ear to mouth.

Hands to chest.

Pumping.

Then, a minute later, Ryan: "Get away from him! What did you do?"

Hands grabbing Lucas by his shirt, hauling him to his feet.

FISTS, ARMS, LEGS,
A PAIN IN HIS JAW.

"It'smeLucas," between gasps.

They froze.

Ryan stared. "*What* did you say?"

"It's me . . . ," he said again. "Lucas."

Why would his own brother not recognize him?

Then hands again, pushing him back and back and back and his bones hitting stone and Ryan saying, "Where have you *been*?"

And their faces inches apart, Lucas's skull pressed to the wall and spit from Ryan's mouth in Lucas's eye when he said, "Where could you *possibly*"—Lucas now sure his head would crack—"have been?"

AVERY

The phone rang—the clock glowed a red *12:45 a.m.*—but Avery wasn't going to get out of bed for the landline. It was probably just Dad, all messed up about time zones, on day one of a business trip out west.

And anyway, it was spring break.

The plan was to sleep as late as she could and then make her way to a lounge chair by the pool out back and spend the day there, watching boats go by in the bay. She'd practice for auditions next week and maybe invite Sam and Emma over to hang out and swim. Whenever her dad was away on business, Avery liked to pretend that their house was hers alone. With her mom usually sleeping or shopping, it was pretty easy.

Mom probably hadn't even heard the phone. She was a "deep sleeper." Right next to her pill bottles.

But then it rang again and again. Avery heard her mom groan and then say, "Hello?"

Then silence.

Then "Oh my god!" like out of a horror movie.

Then more "Oh my gods."

Avery kicked off her comforter and went to her parents' room, where her mom was on her knees by the nightstand, crying, saying, "No, not yet. I should go. I should get ready."

"Mom?" Avery crouched down, bracing for some kind of bad news about her dad.

A plane crash, maybe? Car accident?

Get ready for *what*?

Mom looked up and smiled and clutched the phone to her heart. "They're back."

Avery's grandparents had just taken a trip up to New York, but that hardly seemed worthy of a wee-hours phone call. "Who's back?"

"Your brother," she said. "The others." Then she pushed past Avery and said, "I'm going to be sick."

"But—?"

Avery had years ago stopped imagining it would ever happen and certainly hadn't pictured it happening this way: her holding her mom's hair as she retched up nothing at all.

"Where are they?" Avery actually looked around the room. The shower dripped once. "How?"

"That was Peggy." Her mother wiped her mouth with the back of her hand. "She said Kristen showed up at the house and said they're back. They're fine. She doesn't remember anything—she said none of them do—but they're fine. They turned up with just the clothes on their backs." Then, with her eyes wide and wild, she said, "Ohmygod, I can't believe it. I seriously can't believe it. Can you believe it?"

Like a crazy person.

Again.

Avery followed as her mom walked downstairs and through the kitchen and stopped to fix her hair in the mirror that hung beside a massive floral arrangement—mostly sunflowers that Rita had clipped from the front yard and then gotten an earful from Mom about. Her mom then turned and opened the door, and Avery half expected her brother to be there, too shy to knock after so many years away.

What would he even look like? Would she like him?

They don't remember anything?

He wasn't there.

She and her mom stood out on the porch for a while, looking up and down the quiet road. Eventually, they sat down on the top front step, still in pajamas, and waited.

Scarlett

She walked and walked, panic receding some.

Her mind was a void.

But . . .

. . . drip

. . . drip

. . . into it

. . . glimpses.

Her loop *u n w i n d i n g.*

That house over there had a small pond in the backyard, she knew—where frogs hung out; she'd played there . . . with that same boy from the playground.

That road led to the beach, where there was a long walk to water.

By the time she stood where the star was, she thought,

Yes.

This was where she lived.

Had lived?

This was *home.*

A pale-yellow shingled house built up on tall wooden stilts.

A fence of white crisscrossed wood that ran down both sides.

An old turquoise car parked under a carport made of more crisscrosses.

Angry fists of hard grass punching up out of the sandy front yard.

There'd been a pink plastic flamingo in that garden right there at one point. Right at the base of that palm tree.

But not now.

The whole place looked storm beaten and crooked, like if she closed her eyes she could see wild winds, diagonal rain.

She knocked.

Nothing.

She knocked again, more loudly, and a light went on inside.

A middle-aged woman with a long bleached-blond ponytail opened the door. Her shirt: a hot-pink polo with a tiny stitched white lantern and the words LAMPPOST BAR AND GRILL. "Can I help you?"

/

/

/

/

She was *almost* a stranger.

But her voice was familiar, and her scent—cigarettes and vanilla—felt right.

"Mom?" The word felt weird in Scarlett's mouth, garbled and foreign.

And everything around them froze—some sort of cosmic snapshot—and the air seemed to shake.

The woman trembled and her hand went to her mouth. "Oh my god, Scarlett?"

Then *screamed*: "SCARLETT?"

Scarlett nodded, half wanting to deny it and not knowing why.

And the woman grabbed her and collapsed into a hug.

Then stiffened and pulled back, eyes scanning the yard, the road. "Come in, come in," she said. "Before someone sees."

Ten minutes later, the woman had finally started to calm down, had finally stopped crying and rubbing Scarlett's hand—too hard, with her thumb—and asking, "Is it really you?"—who else would it be?—and "Are you okay? Are you hurt?" and more.

She was fine, Scarlett had said, over and over.

She hadn't been hurt.

She hadn't been abused.

"Not that I remember," she added now. "That's the thing. I don't remember anything."

"Are the others back, too?" The woman was closing the blinds, drawing the curtains.

Looped again now.

Back in that hot air balloon, the heat coming off the flame, making the air

w a v y, unsure.

"How do you know there are others?" Scarlett asked. "What happened? What's going on?"

The woman stiffened. "Are they back or not?"

/ / / / /

"Yes, but no one remembers anything."

The woman seemed not *as* confused. "Well, that's common."

What could that possibly mean?

But then Scarlett looked at the papers on the table beside the sofa where she was sitting. *Paranormal Underground* magazine. *UFOlogist Monthly*. The cover of *Open Minds* had a story called "ETs and Religion."

"Do you think we were abducted by aliens?" Scarlett asked.

"You got any better ideas where you've been all this time?" the woman asked with a bit of an edge.

All.

This.

Time.

A person doesn't accumulate that many magazines in one night, or even a week.

"How long was I gone, exactly?" Scarlett asked, slowly, as a series of revelations clicked into place.

She had never before sat on this couch.

She had never before seen the cat that had peeked out once but was now hiding under an armchair by the television.

"You really don't know?" The woman shook with tears. "You don't *know*?"

????

????Know???????

??????????????? what?

The woman sat beside her on the sofa, took up her hand again. "You all disappeared eleven years ago."

Scarlett pulled her hand away; the room spun around her.

One spin.

Two.

Three spins.

Four.

Who *was* this crazy person?

Five spins.

Sixseveneightnineten spins.

You couldn't be somewhere for eleven years and not remember.

"I always believed they'd bring you back." The woman put her hand to her heart and eyes toward the sky. "That we were chosen for this special thing for a reason."

It was closing in on 2:00 a.m., according to the clock on the dining room wall, and Scarlett felt her body starting to shut down.

Like the lights going off in a large building, wing by wing, fuse by fuse.

Legs—*clunk*—out.

Lungs—*clunk*—out.

Head about to shut *down*

down

down.

She very suddenly wanted only to sleep. "I need to lie down."

The woman said "Of course," then wiped away tears and said she had to call some people, to tell them the news. "Steve's never gonna believe it," she muttered. Then she went into her bedroom with her cell phone.

Scarlett lay on the couch, but it smelled of cat, so she got up and went down the other short hall to where she knew her room had been.

And still was.

Exactly as she had left it?

The life-size cardboard cutout of Glinda, the good witch, from her *Wizard of Oz*–themed fifth birthday party.

The purple hanging canopy adorned with butterflies and ribbons that created a little nook in the corner.

The My Little Pony stickers on the wall.

They seemed familiar.

She liked the feeling.

She wanted to run.

Scarlett stretched out on a cupcake-print comforter—on her back, fingers laced over her belly, as if in her own coffin.

A mobile made out of wire and puffy plastic princess stickers hung from the ceiling.

She stared at it and tried to remember something.

Tried to remember anything or everything.

Long stripes of blue, green, red, and yellow, with black stripes in between.

The feeling of floating away, possibly forever.

The wonder of it all, of a bird's-eye view.

Unable to sleep after maybe twenty minutes of lying there and drifting through the sky . . .

Clouds . . .

A flock of birds

Below, a river.

Or . . . ?

She got up, went down the hall, through the living room, and out onto the terrace off the dining room. The beach—the Gulf—seemed to whisper an invitation, so she went down and across the patio and through the gate and stepped out onto the sand. It was cool and soft beneath her bare feet. Down to the right, the shoreline was rainbow-speckled, hotels aiming colored lights into the night. The *boom-boom-boom* of a far-off dance party tempted her. She could run there—*that* way—until she found it.

Found him.

Wait.

Who?

Lucas.

Or she could fold into the crowd like she belonged there, maybe disappear again through some dance-floor trapdoor.

The water was calm, lakelike. Putting her feet into the warm surf, she looked down at her toes.

When had they last felt the ocean?

Eleven years?

Then looked up at stars.

Aliens?

Really?

So very many stars.

She didn't think she'd visited any but what-did-she-know-not-much.

No wonder her mother had had so many strange questions—"Can I check you for scars?" "Are you still a virgin?"; probably other people would, too. Maybe answers would come. In time.

Or maybe it was better to forget.

Because didn't this qualify as a happy ending?

There's no place like home even if home smells of cat dander and ashes and desperation.

Right?

Lucas

First came the ambulance then the squad cars then the bad news was confirmed—his father was dead—and next the questions.

"Do you have ID?"

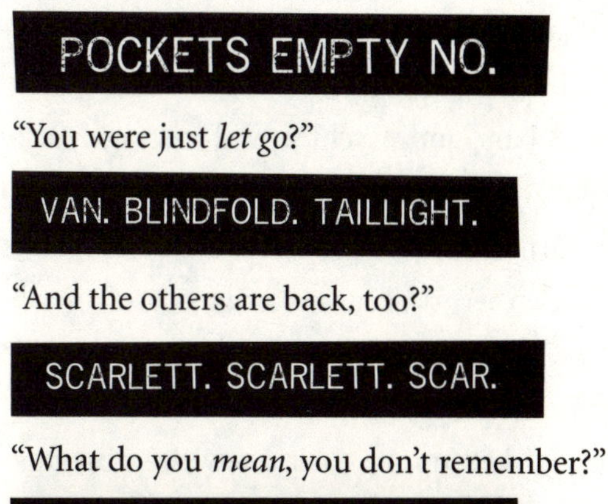

"You were just *let go*?"

"And the others are back, too?"

"What do you *mean*, you don't remember?"

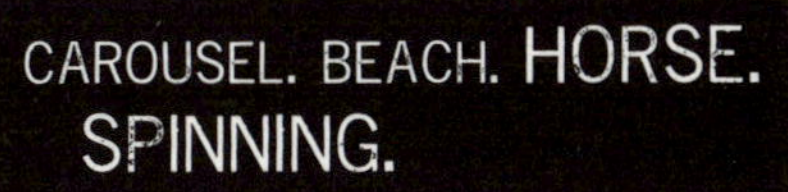

The back of the police cruiser was, at least, quiet as they rode through town—Fort Myers Beach, Florida, he'd discerned from signs. The sidewalks bulged with college types out barhopping. Cars crawled through the main intersection in town, even at 2:00 a.m.

They were stopped in front of an aging hotel called the Tiki Tower, where the parking valets wore leis; totem poles flanked a fountain lit with blue and green spotlights. A group of girls in a white convertible were stuck in the same traffic but in the opposite direction. They all had long ponytails, and bikinis under their tank tops, and they were singing along—poorly, drunkenly—to some pop song Lucas didn't know. Two guys walking on the opposite sidewalk stopped, red plastic cups in their hands, and one of them shouted, "Ladies! Where's the party?"

So this was what he'd been missing.

Eleven years, the cops had said.

Two-thirds of his life.

It didn't make any sense.

He had to make sense of it.

The car started to move again and passed a massive inflatable water slide on the beachfront side of the road, and then a bunch of tourist shops, and restaurants, and bars, and psychics, and massage parlors, and then, finally, they went up and over a steeply arched bridge. The view from the backseat turned into rooftops and distant marinas, and so Lucas closed his eyes; there'd been a shirt in one of the shop windows that read: SUN'S OUT, GUNS OUT.

What did that even mean?

As the speed of the car picked up, he took a few deep breaths of warm, briny air.

He felt *free.*

The feeling was new.

Or maybe old?

He felt his body preparing to weep, but felt it fighting, too.

Why so much fight?

His father was dead.

Why *not* weep?

The car stopped, the door opened, and he was pulled out into the precinct, and then escorted through the main hall. All eyes on him. Most of them . . . what? Suspicious? Confused? Surprised?

He was put in a room alone.

Locked in, actually.

Was he accustomed to being locked up? Used to being alone?

He had to have been imprisoned.

Right?

For eleven years?

The room started to spin, so he sat down.

THE HORSE. TEETH YELLOWED, CHIPPED.

He let his head fall to the table, forehead first, heard the door click open.

"You okay there?"

"I will be," Lucas said. "When I get some sleep. And some answers."

"Answers?"

"Answers." Lucas looked up.

A middle-aged detective who'd shaved what was obviously a balding head now sat across from him. He was thinner than seemed healthy, and something about his mouth seemed British, but he had no accent. He said, "I never thought I'd see the day."

"What day is that?" Lucas asked.

"I'm Mick Chambers. I was the lead investigator when you all went missing." He folded his hands together on the table in front of him. "I figured by now you were all, you know . . . dead."

Lucas reached down and checked his pulse on his wrist with two flat fingers. "Not dead."

"Yes." Chambers shook his head and smiled. "I see that." Then he leaned forward, cleared his throat. "This whole thing? The Leaving? Pretty much ruined my life."

"And that's supposed to be my problem?" Lucas didn't have to put his fingers back to his wrist to know that his pulse was quickening with irritation; the cops on the scene had called it that, too—The Leaving—right before cuffing him. Would they give that whole mess a catchy name, too? The Cuffing?

"No," Chambers said matter-of-factly. "But this is all *very strange.*"

"You have a reputation around here for being a master of the obvious?" Now he could almost feel the tapping in his wrists, blood boiling from the inside out.

Chambers smiled again, wider this time. "Listen, Lucas. I don't need you to like me. I honestly *couldn't care less.* But I got guys who are going to be banging down that door right there in about ten seconds. FBI. Younger guys. Hungrier guys. I may not even end up as lead on this case and there's not a lot I can do about it, so let me just ask you something."

"Fire away," Lucas said.

"If you were me, and there were a bunch of kids who were abducted years ago, and when they came back—just showed up—they said they didn't remember anything—about *ten-plus* years?—would you believe them?"

He pictured the others.

Wondered whether Scarlett was having a better homecoming.

How could she not?

Was she his . . . *girlfriend*?

"Would you?" Chambers pressed.

"Probably not."

"And if one of them was at the scene of an *accident* the very night he happened to come back, and it turned out his father was dead, would you believe it was an accident?"

That free feeling was now officially gone. "I *didn't* kill my father." Then with raised voice: "Why would I kill my father?"

"You might have your reasons. I have *no idea* who you actually are."

"*I*"—Lucas leaned forward—"am the person who's going to figure out what happened, figure out who did this." His blood seemed to cool at the idea of it.

"Oh, yeah?" Chambers stood. "Well, good. You be sure to give me a call when you've got it all sorted."

Knocks on the door came right before it opened, and two men flashed badges.

Chambers said, "He's all yours" and left.

AVERY

Avery flushed the toilet—she'd held off as long as she could out there on the porch—and washed her hands, then stopped in the hallway outside The Shrine and decided to call Sam, who was her boyfriend. Why was she always reminding herself of that? It was possible she needed reminding because he was her *first* actual boyfriend and the concept was still fresh. More likely, there was another reason, but she wasn't ready to admit that quite yet. He might not even pick up so late—or was it so early?—but this was the sort of thing you woke people up for. Especially people who were your boyfriend.

As the line rang, she went into her brother's room and lay down on his Scooby-Doo bedspread. Apparently he'd loved that show—and supposedly she'd watched it with him, but she didn't remember; when she'd gone back to watch some episodes a few years ago, she'd found Shaggy annoying.

"Hey," Sam said sleepily when he answered.

"Hey," she said beneath a sky of glow-in-the-dark constellations.

"Everything okay?"

"They're back." She'd spotted the Big Dipper on the ceiling. "My brother and the other kids."

"*What?*" That quickly, he was wide awake.

"Well, *he's* not back." And there, the Little Dipper. "Not yet, but we've heard they're back."

"No way," he said.

"I know." The bed smelled lonely. "My mom's sitting on the front steps. Waiting. She heard that they don't remember anything."

"How is that even possible?" Sam said.

"I have no idea. It's all just . . . crazy. Right?"

Sam had only moved to Fort Myers a few years ago, so he didn't really understand *how* crazy it was, not having lived through it all the way everyone else had. Not the way she and Ryan had. Sam had seen the movies, but that was all.

Avery didn't actually remember much about the day it happened; she'd been only four years old. But she learned everything she needed to know eventually.

For starters, her parents had given her endless lectures about strangers—they still did—and why she should fear them, because she didn't want to end up like her brother—abducted by some crazy guy and held hostage somewhere or, worse, killed or sold on some foreign sex-slave black market—did she? And, "Sorry, Ave, but we're not sugarcoating this for you. This is your reality. The world is a horrible place. The Bogeyman and Slender Man may not be real, but there are worse, real things to fear. And not just guns and ISIS but quiet, messed-up people who can take a bunch of kids and make them go poof."

When she was old enough, she went online. She knew about the small bus a few people saw behind the school that day and that the bus company claimed no knowledge of it. She'd read about the search parties in all the nearby swamps and on beaches, the accusations thrown at the school security guard, the lawsuits filed against the school district and the bus company (her parents had initiated the claims), and the suicide, a few weeks later, of the school principal. She'd also read countless supposedly moving profiles of each of the kids, which said dumb things like how they loved music and sports and playgrounds and princesses and all had sparkling personalities.

Of course they did!

THEY WERE FIVE!

Avery had even been on TV the day it happened. She'd watched that clip once, then never again. Her four-year-old self, clinging to her once-beloved Woof-Woof and saying, "I really want Max to come home."

Brutal.

Now she was impatient for him to get on with it.

She said, "What do you think is taking him so long?" and knew it sounded ridiculous.

Scarlett

Back up on the terrace, the woman—her mother, her *mother*—was waiting for her, holding pajamas.

"The night before you disappeared," she said, "you told me you were going on a trip. Your exact words were that you were going 'to the leaving.' Do you remember that?"

Scarlett closed her eyes.

/

/

///

/ /

"I don't." She opened them. "And we just disappeared? Like . . . how? Did you look for us?"

"Of course!" Now looking tight, defensive. "It was the first real day of kindergarten."

"What does that mean, 'real day'?"

"The first day all the kindergartners went to school. They do a staggered start, with some of the kids going one day and then the rest another day. So it was the first day *all* the kindergartners were there together."

"And?"

"And at the end of the day, you weren't on the bus you were supposed to be on. People *say* there was a bus at school—like a small one, a short bus—that you all got on, but they never found it, but I knew right away it was something else. Some people spotted a craft up by Venice."

"A spaceship?"

"Yes, ma'am."

The wind blew a few strands of Scarlett's hair into her mouth, and she pulled them away. "Do other people think that? Aliens?"

"Everyone has their own ideas. Come on. I'll show you."

Soon, newspaper clippings were spread out on the dining room table. Article after article about the mysterious abduction, many of them beginning with lines like, "Just months after a school shooting that took the lives of fifteen children, another tragedy has rocked the town of Fort Myers Beach."

Awful.

But not her problem.

In a photo array, she recognized her younger self among the "Victims of The Leaving."

"They called it The Leaving?"

The woman—

Her *mother* nodded and showed her a glossy page ripped from a magazine. "Because of what you said, yeah."

Reading from the page . . . *directed by* . . . *starring*. "There was a *movie*?"

"There've been a couple. None of them any good."

Scarlett reached for her own hair, pulled it. "We were *five years old*! We didn't *leave*."

The . . . *mother* stared at her for a minute, then reached out and put a palm on her cheek. "I always knew they'd bring my baby back."

Scarlett said slowly, "*We got out of a van tonight. A van.*"

Her mother snatched her hand away—"You should rest"—then started gathering up the articles and returning them to a folder on the kitchen island.

But Scarlett was looking back at those photos of the victims . . .

. . . and counting,

and . . .

"Wait."

Six photos.

One of her.

Then Lucas.

Kristen.
Sarah.
Adam.

She pointed at the last one.

More confused than even before.

/

/
/

"Who's Max Godard?"

Lucas

He hadn't even wanted to go back to the house, but that was where the agents dropped him and he didn't have any better ideas.

A light above the front door sensed him and turned on, and moths seemed to materialize just to flit in its light.

The door was locked, the inside lights all off.

He knocked.

Then again, more loudly, when nothing happened.

Then again.

There were three cars parked beside the house.

Knocked one more time and the door swung open.

She had blond hair and her eyes were too far apart and her T-shirt—the only thing she was wearing, legs long and tan—read BRUNETTES HAVE MORE FUN. She stared at him for a moment, then called out, "Ryan?"

They waited.

A moth flew at her and she ducked. "So you're the brother."

"And you are . . . ?" he said.

"The girlfriend." Her stare was unflinching—unnerving, really. "Miranda."

"You think I could come in?" he asked.

"I don't know . . ." Then louder: "Ryan?"

A voice from down the hall: "Let him in."

Lucas stepped past her and into the living area just as Ryan appeared and sat on the couch. Lucas sat at the other end. Miranda inserted herself between them.

"I don't even know what to say." Ryan rubbed his face with both palms. "What *happened*? You escaped? What?"

Lucas mirrored his brother's gesture. "I guess we were let go. There was a van that dropped us off. We had maps to help us get home."

"Why now?" Ryan was shaking his head. "Where were you? Who had you?"

"I don't know. I don't remember anything." Lucas looked at his brother for a long minute and thought Ryan's eyes had the exact same color and tilt as the ones he saw reflected back in mirrors, though he couldn't remember the last time he'd looked in a mirror.

"Well, who was driving the van?" Miranda asked.

"I don't know! I can't explain it. It's like we woke up on the van right before we got off."

Ryan was staring at him. Then he said, "I really have no idea what to say to you. It feels unreal. And now Dad . . ."

Dad.

Dead.

Didn't even know how to feel.

Losing something that had already been lost.

"I didn't kill him," he said. "You have to believe that."

"I don't know what to believe," Ryan said, now covering his face with his hands, shaking his head. "It's . . . *insane*! And I guess I have to call people and . . . what do I even say? 'Well, there's good news and bad news. Lucas is back but Dad's dead.'" Then he looked up and said,

"Actually, who do I even have to call? Dad's parents are dead. Mom's parents are dead. They were both only children. So I guess cross 'making phone calls' off the list."

They had no one?

"I go for a bunch of tests tomorrow, so maybe someone can figure out what's happening." Lucas leaned forward, head tilting down, the dizziness starting up again.

CAROUSEL OCEAN GOLDEN HORSE TEETH

He tried to push past or through it. "They took blood and all, to check for drugs in my system. Because I actually do have one really vivid image stuck in my head, and I don't know if it was a hallucination or what's going on."

"What?" Miranda perked up. "What is it?"

ROUND AND ROUND

"Riding on a carousel by the ocean."

Ryan stood up. "You remember a *carousel ride*? But not who took you for *eleven years*? What about me? Do you remember *me*?"

FIGHTING BASEBALL WRESTLING RUNNING FROGS
KIDS SUN

"Do you remember Mom?"

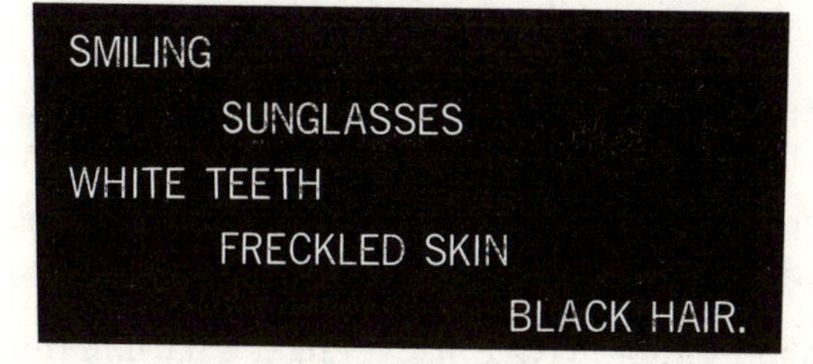

"And Mom *dying*?"

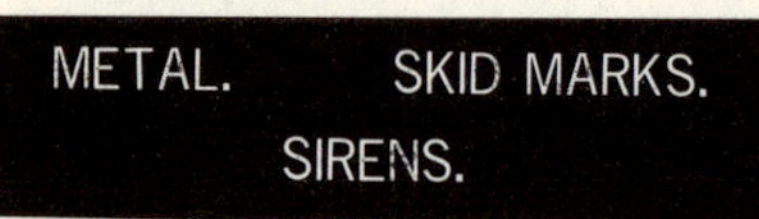

"Do you remember Dad? Because I barely remember him before he went off the deep end with the rocks, myself."

Lucas couldn't form an answer.

The rocks.

The deep end.

Off it.

HORSE TEETH NEEDING POLISHING.

"What is it?" Lucas asked. "The rocks."

"That's Opus 6. Dad's life's work. His 'song for the missing.' He said he was going to keep building it in tribute until you all came home."

"I don't understand," Lucas said, vaguely recalling that his father had been a builder and dabbled in sculpture. "Six?"

"For the six of you."

"No." Like someone was manually spinning his brain. "Five."

"Who didn't come back?" Ryan asked.

"How should *I* know?" Lucas near-screamed.

"This gets better by the minute." Ryan shook his head and stood—"I always thought I'd be happy to see you"—and left the room.

After a moment, Miranda said, "He'll come around." Lucas lifted his head.

She turned to face him squarely, stared at him as if through clear glass holding back some exhibit of oddity on the other side. "You really don't remember *anything*?"

She waved a hand in front of his face, like it might wake him from a trance.

“I’ll get sheets for you,” she said finally. “There’s a room down that hall.”

“Thanks,” he said. “I need a shower.”

“There’s towels on the shelf behind the door.” She walked off.

The water wasn’t hot enough to wash away the day.

The skin beneath his right hip bone burned when he turned to face the showerhead.

He looked down.

Saw blood.

Black ink.

Angry, puffy skin.

Had to sit down, afraid he might pass out.

Had to take a few deep breaths.

Then looked again.

And saw this:

AVERY

The sun arrived right on time, at least, and nosy-body Mrs. Gulden took her yippy dogs out for their early-morning walk and stopped at the foot of the circular driveway. "Everything okay?"

Avery smiled and waved. "Yes! Beautiful morning!"

She should call Ryan, to see whether Lucas had come back yet, but they hadn't spoken at all these past few years—not since Avery had started high school and decided to try to reinvent herself and stop letting the past be such a part of her life.

They should probably call Dad, too, but maybe it'd be better to wait until it wasn't a really ungodly hour out west, or to wait until her brother was actually there.

The mailman came and put a bundle in their pelican mailbox, but neither Avery nor her mom went to get it. Mom didn't even get up once to put real clothes on or make coffee or use the bathroom or answer the phone, which rang a lot more than usual.

When it was a normal time, Avery went inside and popped some bread in the toaster—texting Emma about the weirdness while she waited and getting suitably shocked replies like:

OMG

and

WHAT???????????????

She brought her mom a piece of toast with jam. "You should call Dad," she said.

"We'll call him together"—she frowned at the toast—"when he gets here."

A van turned onto the street, and for a second Avery actually wished it was the Mystery Machine—Scooby-Doo and his crew could crack the case for sure—but no, of course not. It was a news van.

Avery really should have called or at least texted her dad.

He needed to get on the next plane home.

The phone rang and, this time, it somehow sounded more urgent. Avery ran over and picked it up, hoping it was her dad, and if not him at least someone who could explain the delay. "Hello?"

"Avery?"

"Dad."

"Is it true?" he asked. "They're back? I just got a crazy call from Adam's father. Something about us needing to get in front of this, in terms of the news."

Avery's mom came to the open doorway, hope lighting her shiny eyes.

"Some of them are back, yeah," Avery said into the phone. "But no sign of Max yet."

Her mom sank to her knees on the foyer rug and began to sob. Avery saw a flash of her mother's fleshy white thigh inside her robe and had to look away.

"I'll get there as fast as I can, Ave," her dad said.

"Move mountains."

Avery hung up and went to her mom and knelt beside her, pulling her robe closed and then easing her into a stiff hug; her mother had turned mannequin, unfeeling.

Right then a reporter reached the front porch, trailed by a camera guy, and said, "Tell us your story. Why do you think Max is the only one who didn't come back?"

Avery used her foot to push the door shut and pictured the days ahead. The endless news coverage, the weird-sad looks she'd get from neighbors and everyone at school next week. She'd be famous, but not in the right way. Mannequin Mom would end up in the hospital again, quick-sanding into depression, and Dad would act like there was nothing wrong when everything about Mom—about all of them—was wrong and had been, probably, since the day Max disappeared.

After a minute, there was a gap in her mom's crying and, in the silence, Avery had a weird feeling of wishing she'd never stopped talking to Ryan—one of the only people who had ever understood—or started things up with Sam, who was too nice for her, or too simple or something—or given up hoping that her brother was still alive.

Scooby-Doo, where are you?

"We'll find him, Mom." Avery stared at her worn flip-flops and wondered when the new ones she'd ordered would arrive. "I promise."

DAY ONE

Scarlett

"I need clothes," Scarlett said.

"And a toothbrush

and . . ."

Hairbrush.

Shoes.

Makeup?

Phone.

Purse.

Deodorant.

Wallet.

Lip balm.

Socks.

Underwear.

Bras.

Pajamas.

Swimsuit.

Tampons?

Driver's license?

What else?

"*. . . everything.*"

The woman—*her mother*—was on her fourth cigarette of the morning, the first three having been consumed while two detectives—one old, one young—asked Scarlett questions and got annoyed at her answers.

They asked about Max.

And whether any of the others had violent tendencies.

They explained about the accident.

Lucas's father.

Opus 6.

Hard to process.

Could she think of any reason why Lucas would want to harm his father?

No.

No, no, no.

How . . . *horrible.*

As they left, they told her she was to go immediately to an address they gave her, for a physical examination and an MRI. That she'd be informed of further appointments, like with a memory expert and possibly some others.

That time was of the essence if they were going to find Max and the person or people who had taken them.

After eleven years.

Now time was of the essence.

Scarlett was still in her mother's pajamas and wasn't sure which would be worse.

Putting on the clothes she'd come back in.	**OR**	Borrowing more from . . . her.

Her mother stubbed out her cigarette—"We should get going. I'll get dressed. We'll go shopping after"—and left the room.

ashtray.

the

from

rise

smoke

watched

Scarlett

The cat appeared, unsure at first, then hopped up onto the table in front of her. It had a collar and a name tag: Comet.

Scarlett lifted her hand to pet it but then stopped.

Looked at her hand.

Was she . . . allergic?

/

/

/

She got up and walked to her room, put back on the clothes she'd come home in.

The police had taken the map.

Would she be able to find the playground tonight?

Returning to the kitchen, she found her mother, also dressed, who grabbed a set of keys off a hook just inside the kitchen.

"We'll leave through the side door." Scarlett's mother reached for a baseball hat and a pair of sunglasses and held them out to Scarlett.

"No one's going to recognize me. I was five."

"People are going to want to know what you look like. Now. You're all going to be famous whether you want to be or not."

Scarlett took the hat and sunglasses and followed her mother to the car. When they pulled out of the carport and eased down the driveway, reporter types and cameramen ran for their vans like startled birds. Scarlett put the glasses on and slid down in her seat. Her mother tore out at the bottom of the driveway and then blew through a stop sign to get away from a van in pursuit but then had to hit the brake pedal too hard at a light.

The same red as . . .

"Did we ever go up in a hot air balloon when I was little?" Scarlett asked.

"Are you making *fun* of me?" her mother snapped.

"No!" Scarlett protested. "Did we?"

The sky so ridiculously blue.

"Of course not," her mother said. "I am not, you may have noticed, made of money."

"Okay, it was just a question. I thought we had." Something triggered a bunch of black birds to abandon a tree.

"You remember me, though?" her mother asked. "And stuff from before?"

"A pink flamingo in the yard." The side mirror said the birds were closer than they appeared.

"But nothing . . . bad?" Her mother checked her mirrors.

The van was gone. The birds, too.

"Not that I can think of."

"Well, that's good, then."

/ / / /

Scarlett didn't have the energy to even think what that might mean.

The MRI, at least, she was eager for.

This way they'd know there was no implant, no chip.

She would not, one day, be awakened by an alien device implanted in her heart.

She would not set about some evil scheme, maybe even involving killing the whole human race, including her own damaged mother.

She could prove it.

To her mother, and maybe just a little bit to herself.

This was how.

One little test at this totally ordinary-looking office-type building.

Easy as:

Following the nurse down a long hallway.

Changing into a pink surgical gown.

Lying very, very still as the machine whirred to life.

Listening to its sounds.

Looking for a tune.

Finding none.

When the humming stopped, Scarlett couldn't be sure how long she'd been in there, but it didn't matter.

It was over.

The doctor would speak with them shortly.

Scarlett returned to her mother, and then it seemed they were waiting a very long time and Scarlett decided to talk to try to pass the time.

"So," she said, "what have you been doing?"

Her mother *pffed* and looked at her funny. "For eleven years, you mean?"

"Yeah, I guess. What's your life like? Do you have a boyfriend? Hobbies? Do you travel? What?"

"Oh, sure, me and Hans go to the French Riviera every week."

Scarlett looked at her.

And blinked.

And waited.

"I've got a guy, yeah. Steve. Been together going on six years now."

Six was a lot.

Not as many as eleven but still . . .

"You don't live together?"

"No way, no how." Punctuated with four head shakes. "Had one of those. Had one move in and it turned out he was flat broke. Never making that mistake again. No, Steve's successful-like. He's a good guy. You'll meet him. He wants to take us out to dinner tonight."

Scarlett's gut contracted, released.

Contracted, released.

Like doing some ab workout without her permission.

"Tonight?"

"Well, he's dying to meet you. And, well, you know. He's been there for me. He's really been my rock these past few years. Him and the folks in the abduction group. And anyway, you got any better plans?"

As a matter of fact . . .

Abduction group?

How many hours until 8:00 p.m.?

How many hours until *him*?

"I'm just not sure we should go out to a restaurant right now. You know?"

"Oh, Steve knows a place. He knows the owner and they'll look after us, make sure the cameras stay away. And we'll go early. It's nice. On the water. A proper welcome-home dinner." Her mother nodded. "He's got some real good ideas for us, too."

"Ideas?"

"He can explain it better."

The nurse finally came to get them and led them to a room, where they waited a minute more.

Then a doctor came in.

The older detective from that morning was with him.

/ /

/

"What's going on?" her mother asked.

"Well," the doctor said, "there's something inside Scarlett. So I called Detective Chambers."

He clipped a film to a light board and switched it on.

Scarlett's insides—rib cage, esophagus, all—lit up in black and gray.

Brightest of all was a thumbnail-sized white oval in her gut.

She thought she might throw up.

Wanted to, even.

"*I can't even . . .*," her mother said slowly.

Scarlett stepped closer to the film.

Mesmerized by that glowing, misshapen moon.

The shine of it hurt her eyes.

Up.

Up.

Up.

Feet floating.

She turned to the detective when she said, "What *is* it?"

Lucas

At a low-rise building in a complex full of low-rise buildings, a smiling, youngish black man with a head covered in tight cornrows that led to ponytail dreads greeted Lucas. He wore a white lab coat over a T-shirt that had a drawing of a shark on it, and Lucas imagined that he'd just been surfing; he seemed balanced and invigorated-looking in a way that made Lucas feel a little bit dead inside.

"Doctor Todd Sashor." He shook Lucas's hand with both of his. "Cognitive-science specialist. Welcome home."

"Thanks." Lucas didn't want to release Sashor's warm hands. He was the first person who had seemed genuinely happy to see him.

"Let's get to work, shall we?"

Lucas nodded, let go reluctantly.

They went into the lobby—modern and clean—and up to the third floor, where Sashor pushed open a glass door that opened up on a large lab: glass cabinets on the walls and a few desks and filing cabinets and computers. He introduced two assistants—one male, one female—who then busied themselves around the room.

"I should confess I've never had to try to devise an intake process or test of this kind. So, we're winging it a bit. First we're going to test you on some basic brain functions and skills," Sashor said. "We want to try to figure out what kinds of things you've learned and know and remember. Then we'll sit and talk. Cool?"

Lucas nodded.

He took a math test (so easy), and then a more advanced math test (still easy), and then a test on world history (aced it), and one on general science (likewise). He filled in a blank map of the United States and much of the world. Then played checkers (he won) and chess (he lost) with the female assistant.

He was shown a series of pictures and asked to say the first word that came to mind. Same with a bunch of black ink blots.

He gave up on a trivia test with questions about pop culture when it was clear he didn't know any answers at all.

Likewise, a test about literature.

It bothered him he could not think of a favorite book.

He did not appear to be able to speak any other languages.

He was *generally* up to speed on current events—"At least as much as the average teenager, is my guess," Sashor said.

Then he finally sat down face-to-face with Sashor, and the questions began and blurred. *Do you remember anything about where you've been? Were there windows? What could you see? Do you know if the person who took you was male or female? Were you allowed to go out? How long were you in the van? Have you ever been made to do something against your will?*

Lucas almost laughed, shifted in his seat. "I'm pretty sure we wouldn't be here if I hadn't been taken against my will."

"Good point," Sashor said. "Have you ever been made to do something against your will . . . sexually?"

Lucas turned and looked out the window; across the street, a sign read Cheesecake Factory. "I really don't think so."

"Have you ever had *sex*?" Sashor asked with some hesitation, and Lucas wondered whether this line of questioning was maybe going off script but then remembered there really *was* no script.

He didn't mind.

He was curious, too.

"I'm not sure."

"Kissed a girl?"

"No idea."

"Have you ever kissed Kristen?"

"No idea."

"Scarlett? Sarah?"

"Don't know."

Sashor raised his eyebrows. "Have you ever been in love?"

A surprise: "Yes."

"With whom?"

"No idea."

Which was a lie?

"Then why'd you say yes?"

Lucas paused for a second, considering. "Just a feeling."

A feeling about Scarlett.

It felt like protecting her to not name names.

Moving on: "Do you remember anything from the day you were taken?"

"No."

"Anything suspicious in the days leading up to the event?"

"I have no idea."

"Do you remember things from before the abduction?"

SKIDDING SIRENS BLOOD

"Like kindergarten? Preschool?" Sashor asked.

CUBBIES. RED. SUPERMAN BACKPACK.

Lucas nodded. "I do. My mother died in a car accident. I was there. In the backseat. But I was fine."

Sashor nodded, then sat back in his leather chair. "What's the earliest memory that you can recall?"

Lucas looked back out the window, where a few meaty clouds had appeared. Dark gray and villainous. He closed his eyes and thought hard and had to push away:

CAROUSEL WHITE FIRE TEETH COTTON CANDY

This time, as he whirled, other images decorated his trips around.

BLUE BIKE. BLOODY KNEE.
SMALL BLACK DOG: WALKER.
BASEBALL MITT. BLEACHERS.
READY OR NOT, HERE I COME!

Lucas said, "I remember learning how to ride a bike, falling, hurting my knee badly. I remember playing hide-and-seek with my mom. That might be the only real memory I have of her before the accident. I remember the crash scene. I remember my preschool classroom, what it looked like. I remember a ball field, like going to watch my brother play? But earliest? I don't know. I remember our dog, Walker."

"Your dog walker?"

"No, the dog was named Walker. Because when you took him out it was like he was walking you instead of the other way around."

Sashor took a note, then looked up and said, "Do you remember a man carrying wrapping paper?"

"*A man carrying wrapping paper?*" Lucas repeated.

Sashor didn't make eye contact. "Yes, do you remember a man carrying wrapping paper?"

WRAPPING PAPER MAN CARRYING

"No." Lucas was tiring of not being able to offer up anything useful.

"What kind of wrapping paper was it?" Sashor asked, as if he hadn't heard.

CHRISTMAS WHITE BEARD
RED HAT

"Santa Claus."

"You remember the wrapping paper?" Surprise lit Sashor's eyes.

"I don't know. Do I? Or am I just picturing the first random wrapping paper I could think of?"

"Begs the question." Sashor took another note.

"Why are you asking me about wrapping paper?" Lucas tried to read the note but was too far away.

"Police asked me to."

"How are they ever going to catch who did this if we can't remember?"

"Memory doesn't always cooperate or align with our goals, but we might get lucky." Looking back at his paper. "Do you remember anything else at all about the first few days of kindergarten?"

"Kindergarten." Lucas sat for a minute with the idea of it. The whole notion of kindergarten. Did he remember . . . kindergarten?

CUBBIES. RED.

"Not really. Just the classroom. My backpack."

Sashor pushed a photo array toward Lucas. Max as a kid, then a series of sketches that aged him. "Have you ever seen this boy?"

"The FBI agents showed this to me," Lucas said. "And no, I don't remember him. At all. Before or after. And I have no idea if I kissed him, either. In case you were going to ask."

Sashor smiled, then took off his glasses and rubbed his eyes. For some reason, Lucas felt eager to please him. He also wanted a professional opinion. So he made this deal with himself:

He would talk about the carousel.

Not the tattoo.

Not until he found out tonight if the others had tattoos, too.

Not until he spent at least a little time trying to figure out what to make of it.

A camera shutter tattoo.

What did that even mean?

"I do remember one other thing really vividly," he said tentatively.

"What is it?"

"Riding a carousel. It was by the ocean. I get dizzy whenever I think about it."

It sounded even more ridiculous when spoken aloud than it had when it had just been in his head.

"How old were you?" Sashor seemed to pep up.

"I don't know. It feels recent. Like I was too old to be riding a carousel but I liked it anyway?"

"No such thing as too old to ride a carousel," Sashor said.

Lucas smiled. "Do you think it really happened?"

"Well, there were no drugs in your system, nothing that could cause hallucinations. So either it happened or it was put there as a decoy, a distraction."

"How would someone even do that?"

"False memories are actually pretty easy to create. Like if your brother told you that when you were kids you dropped your ice-cream cone and cried so hard that the woman in the shop gave you a new cone, you'd believe that it happened, even if you didn't remember it. And then you'd eventually tell the story as your own and even add details, like what flavor of ice cream it was and what the weather was like."

"Seriously?" Lucas couldn't think of his own favorite flavor.

"Seriously."

"So do you have a diagnosis?" Lucas asked. "Like a name for it? Apart from us all just generally being messed up."

Sashor explained *anterograde amnesia*, which is the loss of the ability to create new memories after an event, leading to a partial or complete inability to recall the recent past. And how it was possible to suffer from this condition while long-term memories from *before* the event remained intact, which was why he remembered his father, his brother, the house. This was also typically in contrast to *retrograde amnesia*, where most memories created *prior* to the event are lost, while new memories can still be created.

"I guess it's possible that someone or something triggered the first condition," Sashor said. "Because, presumably, during the time you were gone, you were able to make memories—and then, eleven years later, triggered the second condition. Leaving a long gap in between."

"But what would that trigger be?" Lucas wished he'd thought to take notes.

"The abduction itself could have been the first trigger? Your release, the next?"

Lucas had no theories. “How do I still know how to play chess and brush my teeth and all?”

“Neither of these conditions affects your *procedural memory*.”

“But how can I retain a memory of knowledge but not of experiences?” Lucas pointed at the map and his high-scoring world history test.

“Those kinds of processes are handled by different parts of the brain, as well. Working in tandem, sure, but separate physical locations,” Sashor said. “Honestly, unless they find the person responsible, I can’t imagine we’ll ever know what the purpose of the experiment was.”

“Experiment?”

“I’m a scientist, so that’s where my mind goes, yes.”

Lucas felt hopeful for the first time. “There can’t be that many experts in this field, right?”

“There are a *lot* of people around the globe trying to crack open one of the mysteries of memory and grab the spotlight. Probably half of them are unhinged or obsessed in some way.” Sashor seemed to pause to reconsider what he’d just said. “It’s also possible that you’re all very good liars. And that you remember everything and are putting one over on the rest of us.”

Lucas felt himself bristle. “Why would we do that?”

“To protect the identity of the person who took you?” Sashor said. “Because you’re suffering from Stockholm syndrome?”

“It’s nothing like that.” Lucas sat forward in his chair.

Sashor smiled sadly and stood. “But of course you’d say that.”

AVERY

Avery's mom was parked in front of the television, surrounded by crumpled tissues. "The Homecoming," as they were now calling it, was headline news with at least two networks promising "constant coverage."

Sarah and Adam were being interviewed by a daytime anchor with hard-looking hair. On the bottom of the screen, it said, **VICTIMS OF THE LEAVING DON'T REMEMBER WHERE THEY'VE BEEN.** Avery couldn't stop staring at them, actually crawled across the floor to sit crisscross-applesauce in front of the TV to see them better. They looked like aliens, like fake people, maybe because she'd never imagined she'd ever see them for real. It was like reading a book, then seeing the movie and not liking the casting. What did the others look like? Would they also seem beautiful and fake and all wrong and not at all what she'd pictured, if she'd even pictured them, and she wasn't sure she had, not in years, anyway.

The anchor dude was midquestion when Avery was able to focus her attention on what they were talking about. ". . . but you'll cooperate with the investigation?"

Sarah and Adam swapped a look, and Adam said, "We've spoken to the police and FBI, yes, but beyond that, we really feel like we've met our obligation, and we won't be submitting to physicals or mental evaluations. We're within our rights. We wish we *could* help, but we don't remember anything. And we really want to get back to normal."

The anchor said, "Another of the returned, Kristen Daley, told one of our reporters that she is going to try to be hypnotized to see if she can recall some lost memories. Are either of you interested in pursuing hypnosis?"

Adam said, "I wish my fellow victims well, and obviously we're all coping differently, but I prefer to keep my intentions moving forward private."

Sarah said, "Me, too."

"And surely you've heard about Lucas's father. How Lucas is considered a suspect in that investigation. Does that resonate with what you know about Lucas? Is he capable of violence like that?"

"I have no idea," Adam said. "We believe we were all together, but I can't speak to anyone's character. If he ever did anything bad or good in the past, I have no memory of either."

Avery wanted to reach through the TV screen and smack them both—the anchor, too. Why weren't they talking about Max?

Also, were they a couple? They seemed to be. That happened pretty fast. Or had they been together before coming back? And if they remembered *that*, why not other things, too?

What if they are all lying?

The topic of the constant coverage then turned its focus to Will's accident. Her dad had been the one to tell her just an hour or so ago, when he'd finally arrived home.

She still hadn't been able to bring herself to call Ryan.

Or cry.

That probably said something about her as a person, but she wasn't sure what.

She was, however, sure that her attempts to motivate her mom to get dressed or to take a shower or to eat or to *do anything* would not work. Dad was upstairs sleeping, claiming jet lag. The landline had been ringing off the hook all morning—nothing but news stations, if the first few calls were any indication—and so Avery had unplugged it.

Now, peeking out the front window, she saw two news vans, so she went upstairs to shower and get dressed, then went down and out the side door and up through her neighbor's yard, over a prickly hedge, and out onto the next block.

She blew past the fish market—with its sidewalk that smelled of bleached rot—and the psychic's storefront. Maybe Madame whatever-her-name-was was worth another visit? Now that she had things to ask that didn't have to do with when she'd lose her virginity? She went past the trailer park loaded up with RVs and half thought about hopping in one, driving away to someplace where no one had even heard of The Leaving, if there was even such a place.

She wasn't even sure what her destination was until she was already there, sweating from having walked so fast.

Opus 6.

A news van sat about a hundred feet from the base of the drive, but the guys in it didn't seem to see her. She ducked through the line of mangroves by the street and came out farther up the path to the house. A portion of the area was blocked off with police tape.

Were they really treating it as a crime?

Ryan would know more.

She hadn't been over to Opus 6 in a few years and, of course, it had expanded in new directions. She walked toward the round pool on the far end of the property, where she and Ryan had once gone for a dip when she was maybe eleven and still friends with him. She remembered treating the whole place like a playground. Climbing and jumping and chasing salamanders this way and that.

Somewhere along the way, Avery had lost sight of the meaning behind Opus 6. The *purpose* of it. It was meant to be a physical reminder to them all of what had been lost, or taken. She felt mortified now that she'd ever let that happen, ever decided it was time to move on; she hadn't even turned up at the tenth-anniversary vigil.

She heard a car and car doors and voices, and someone appeared at the far end of a winding path that led to a flat circle atop the main structure; for a second Avery thought it was her brother. She knew that Max had had brown hair. People had estimated he'd be around five feet ten inches by now.

Spotting her, he walked very slowly forward—like he was as suspicious of her as she was of him. "Can I help you?"

Of course it wouldn't be Max.

"Lucas?" She saw no recognition in his eyes.

"Do I know you?"

It was really him.

They were really back.

Flesh and blood.

Not from central casting.

She hadn't expected him to be so . . . *grown.*

Such a *guy.*

So . . . mesmerizing.

"You did," she said. "When we were little . . . You know. Before."

Before life got crazy, before the whole town turned search party, before everyone said dumb things about hugging your children closer at night, before closing beaches and dredging shorelines and ribbons on trees and candlelight vigils.

"I'm Avery."

He shoved his hands into his pockets. "I guess the polite thing would be to say it's nice to see you again."

"Where is he?" she blurted. "Why didn't he come back?"

"Who?" Lucas's eyes seemed blank for a second. "Oh. *Max?*"

"He's my brother." The air felt dense, weighted—like an invisible tarp was holding back a storm inches overhead.

Lucas looked tired and not at all like a murderer. Murderers couldn't possibly have such soft-looking hair, such sad eyes. Could they?

He said, "I have no idea."

"You were best friends."

"I'm sorry"—he started to walk away—"but I don't remember him."

"I don't understand." Avery stepped forward. "You couldn't forget a whole person. You must remember *something.* I remember *you.*" She raced around her mind for a specific memory. "Like remember they used to have a Halloween parade in the park over by the pier, and one year you were dressed as a sailor and Max was a pirate and you posed for a picture where he had his sword at your neck? Even I remember that and I was only four."

Avery had been dressed as Smurfette, her face a chalky blue that matched her eyes. That had been back when her hair was white blond—not light brown like now. Back when her mother got excited about holidays and used to make jack-o'-lantern cookies and wrap the front porch in spiderwebs.

"How do you know that you remember?" Lucas seemed annoyed now, his jaw tight; he had the same eyes as Ryan but leaner features; he was, for lack of a better word, prettier. "Maybe you think you remember it because you have that picture."

"I swear I remember it." She was not, however, sure.

"Swear all you want. It doesn't mean you do. I bet if you look at a picture of your kindergarten class, you won't remember all of them."

Avery felt herself getting annoyed, too—a tingling in her fingers and on the tip of her nose. "It's not *my* memory that's the problem."

He looked hurt but only for a millisecond. "All I remember is one ridiculous thing. I remember riding a carousel. So if Max had a thing for carousels, maybe that's a clue for you. Otherwise, sorry."

She and Max had ridden a carousel at Disney World once, the summer before The Leaving. There were pictures of that, too.

"You have to help me," she said then, desperate. "I need to find him."

"Listen—what did you say your name—"

"Avery."

"Right. Avery. I've kind of had an insane twenty-four hours and—"

"Everything okay?" Ryan was walking down the main path now, and Avery rushed to him, hugged him. "I'm so sorry." She should have called him the second she heard; she knew that now.

Ryan looked at Lucas and said, "Can you give us a minute?"

Lucas seemed relieved to have a reason to leave.

"You don't think he did it, do you?" Avery asked when Lucas had reached the house.

"I don't know what to think." Ryan rubbed his eyes. "Still no sign of Max?"

She shook her head, not finding words at first, then settling on, "I never thought any of them would come back. I figured they were dead or had new identities somewhere. I never imagined it would go like this."

"No one did," he said. "I mean, I'm happy he's back. At least I think I am. But it's just . . . It's so messed up. I actually had a thought today, that I'm *jealous* that he was the one who got taken and I was the one who was here."

"We don't know what they've been through," she said, now feeling bad about pretty much attacking Lucas. "What Max is *still* going through."

"Neither do they!" he nearly screamed. "And us, on the other hand, we've had to slog through *this* for years."

"I have to find Max," she said as she turned to go, almost to remind herself why she'd come. It had been a slog, yes. Depressed parents. Obsessed parents. Drunk parents. Absent parents. Anger. Grief. Miserable vigils and limbo. But to suggest they'd had it harder?

"It's not promising to be a story with a happy ending, Ave."

"I know," she said. "I just need to *know*. So we can all move on one way or another. Do you trust him?"

He looked off toward the house, then back at her. "I don't know. I can't think. I mean, this day. My *dad* . . ."

"Of course," she said. "Ryan, I'm so, so sorry."

She went to hug him again and he let her, and she tried really hard to have the moment just be about that—about him, his dad—but she couldn't do it. Couldn't hold it in. When she pulled out of the hug, she said, "What if they're lying?"

Confusion flashed across his features.

"What if they remember everything?" Her voice sounded sinister even to her. "What if they're *hiding something*?" Then, "I have to *do* something."

"You need to leave it to the police," Ryan said.

She stared at him for a second—he just didn't get it—then took off down the path. "Yeah, because that worked so well the first time."

At home, she went to the back door and then changed her mind.

Going around to the front of the house, she walked up to a news van and knocked on its side, then knocked on the other one, then stood on the front porch steps as newsies set aside their Starbucks and applied lipstick and fired up their cameras and microphones. The camera lights were bright even under full sun.

Go-time.

"I'm Max Godard's sister, Avery." Her voice cracked a bit, but she cleared her throat and went on. "And I want to say that we're really happy that Lucas and Kristen and Sarah and Adam and Scarlett are back home."

She could see in their eyes how excited they were, these people who'd been sitting around for hours, waiting for something—anything—to happen.

"But we miss Max as much today as we have since that first day and every day in between. And, well, I think they might know something. The others. I think they're hiding something." She took a breath and licked her lips, the last of her lip gloss gone—who even cared?—and thought for a second about Lucas, the bewildered look in his eyes, the curve of his shoulders. He was so . . . lovely . . . and yet.

"One of them remembers riding a carousel," she said slowly, clearly. "There must be more they remember. Things that could help us find Max. And our family fully expects answers, and justice. Thank you. That's all."

She turned to go inside as they shouted questions. "Who remembers the carousel?" "Which of them have you spoken to?"

The front door was, luckily, unlocked, so she walked in, then closed it behind her and leaned against it.

Oh god. What had she done?

No, it was good. Someone had to say it, so why not her?

She pushed to standing and went upstairs and changed into her swimsuit, then went out to the pool lanai and dove in. Surfacing, she pushed back into a float and looked up at the clouds—one of them the shape of a cow's head, another long and sharp-looking, like a knife.

Scarlett

"I *knew* they'd find something."

The smoke from her mother's cigarette seemed intent on blowing Scarlett's way instead of out her mother's open window.

"I just *knew* it."

Scarlett sat in the passenger seat with her hands resting on her belly. The smoke was surrounding . . .

. . . suffocating . . .

. . . like it was trying to strangle her from the

OUT
inside
OUT

The doctor had said they couldn't tell what it was.

That the shape was obviously wrong for it to be a coin, that the detail wasn't sharp enough.

That she'd have to keep an eye out for when it passed.

"Steve's never gonna believe it."

Of course he wouldn't.

Scarlett couldn't believe it, and it was inside *her.*

And all she could do was . . .

Tick

Tock

Tick

Tock . . .

. . . wait?

It seemed cruel.

Desperate to think about something—anything—else on their way to the outlets, desperate to get her mind off a foreign body working its way through her system, Scarlett said, "How'd you meet him? Steve?"

"Oh, he came into the bar one night. Then again the next night. And so on and so on . . ."

"What bar?"

"Thar she blows." Her mother pointed out Scarlett's window. They were on a small on-ramp to a bridge beside the Lamppost Hotel.

"It ain't . . ."

Isn't.

". . . the most glamorous job, but I've been there long enough I get to pick my own shifts and everybody pretty much leaves me alone. Haven't taken a drink myself since the day you went missing, but happy to hand 'em out."

"Really?"

"That night, the night before you were taken, I was three sheets to the wind when I was putting you to bed. And I was so H-O the next day when things got crazy—"

Aicho?

Oh.

H-O?

"*H-O?*"

"Hungover."

Like it should have been obvious.

"And I promised myself I'd be sober as a judge for whenever they found you. And they just never did, and I never could bring myself to take another drink. Just in case."

"So wait. You were *drunk* when I said that thing about going to the leaving?"

"Yes, ma'am. But I remember that clear as a bell." She looked at Scarlett and spoke slowly.

So slowly that Scarlett

could

see

her

mother's

tongue . . .

on the *l*'s in . . .

"*Clear as a bell.*"

Scarlett looked at The Lamppost Hotel's many, many windows and wondered whether anyone in there knew what was happening.

Whether guests with sunburns and big hats had the news on while they packed up their beach bags.

Whether the ticker at the bottom of the screen said:

GIRL REUNITED WITH ALIEN-OBSESSED RECOVERING-ALCOHOLIC MOTHER . . .

HAS NOTHING IN COMMON WITH HER . . . FULL STORY AT 8:00 P.M.

A song came on the radio that her mother turned up.

Something about wasting away again in Margaritaville.

It seemed to make her happy.

Scarlett wondered what that felt like.

Didn't know the song.

Any songs?

Her mother said, "Maybe after things calm down and all, we'll have a little party. You know, you, me, Steve, my friends. Bet your uncle Tom will drive down from Tampa."

Scarlett ran a search:

Uncle Tom. Uncle Tom. Uncle Tom. Uncle Tom.

/ / /

/

/ /

/

"What about my . . ."

Couldn't

Remember

Ever

Saying

The word:

Dad.

" . . . father?"

"Was never in the picture." Her mother pulled into the outlet parking lot. "So you wouldn't remember him at all."

"What about grandparents?" She'd seen a photo back at the house—a woman with curly black hair and a soft, round belly perched on top of a skinny pair of legs, and holding what must have been a toddler Scarlett—and she'd known it was her grandmother.

"With the good Lord." She made the sign of the cross. "Your grandfather in 2009 and your grandma the year after."

Scarlett couldn't focus.

When she'd disappeared, she'd been a girl with grandparents, and now all she had was this woman she couldn't bring herself to think of as Mom.

The word had felt so wrong,

so sour,

that one time.

"They took it hard. What happened to you. And then we had a falling-out because, well, we all had different ideas." She sighed. "Here today, gone Tamara."

"What does that mean?" They were out of the car and walking toward the stores.

"Oh, nothing. Just something Steve says."

The clothes were . . . too bright.

Too boxy.

Too . . . ?

Scarlett didn't like anything she tried on.

Most of it fit, technically.

But didn't fit her.

Made her look too . . . something.

Too other.

Too someone else.
Lines all wrong.
Colors all wrong.
Patterns that made no sense on her.
They bought most of what she tried on anyway.
Because, well . . . because.

Here today, gone . . .

Ah.

Her mother's *name* was Tamara.

"Can I call you that?" Scarlett dared as they walked toward the car. She'd worn a new dress out of the store and felt like an impostor. "Tamara?"

"No." Tamara unlocked the car. "You may not."

Lucas

A handful of people in FORENSICS shirts were taking photos and swabs near where Lucas's father had fallen.

Died.

Lucas watched from the kitchen window, where he'd been studying a map of Opus 6 that hung on the wall, and started counting stones, then gave up. He couldn't even begin to estimate how many there were, or how many hours it had taken his father—and by the looks of his brother's muscles, him, too—to cut and shape and place them all.

When Chambers turned up, Lucas stepped outside. "I wasn't sure I'd see you again."

"Well, they're letting me hang around for the time being." Chambers stood on the front steps facing out to Opus 6. "Professional courtesy because of my history with the case. I'll be acting as the liaison between you all and the FBI, generally facilitating things."

Lucas nodded. He was wearing a T-shirt Miranda had left in his room for him, and shorts and boxers borrowed from Ryan. The decal on the shirt had two purple fists meeting in front of a triangle and read WONDER TWIN POWERS ACTIVATE! He had no idea what it meant.

"So what can you tell me about the tattoo?" Chambers turned to him.

"Nothing."

Lucas had taken a photo of it with the phone Ryan gave him; he wanted to be able to study the image without craning his neck. The doctor who'd done his physical had glimpsed the top edge of it above Lucas's boxers in spite of his hopes to keep it secret.

"Think you did it yourself?" Chambers raised one eyebrow. "From the photo the doctor sent me, it looks kind of DIY."

"People do that?"

"Apparently."

"No idea." Lucas shook his head. "Anybody else have one?"

Chambers said, "Don't know yet."

They stood there, as if waiting for something to happen, like watching the wind. It was too nice a day for a murder investigation, and Lucas wished he could go surfing or ride a Jet Ski or anything but this.

Chambers probably felt that way, too.

"What did you mean the other day," Lucas said, "when you said The Leaving ruined your life?"

Chambers gave him a look. Like, *really?*

"What? I want to know."

"My sad tale?" Chambers pushed his shoulders back, stretching. "You can probably guess." He took a pack of gum from his pocket and slid a piece out.

"You were so focused on the case that you neglected your wife."

"*Ding ding ding.*" Offered the gum to Lucas, who declined. The detective put a piece into his mouth before he said, "*And* daughter. Don't forget the neglected daughter."

"And now they are . . . ?"

"Wife is remarried. Daughter is in college. 'Estranged,' I believe, is the word."

"And you?"

"I'm here with you, so what does that say?" Chambers shrugged. "And paying for college like it's some kind of penance."

"Did you know my father well?"

"As well as I knew any of them, I guess."

"Was he crazy?"

"Nah." Chambers shifted his gaze from Lucas to the middle-distance of Opus 6. "This all probably kept him sane."

The whole place was, on the one hand, extremely disturbing. Because what kind of crazed person would do *all that*? But there was something . . . calming about it, too.

"Are you going to charge me?"

"Waiting for the autopsy report," Chambers said. Then he turned and said, "You'll let me know if you think of anything? The tattoo?"

Lucas nodded and Chambers left. Lucas went inside and watched from the kitchen window until the forensic team also left, then he went back out to explore parts of the grounds he hadn't walked yet. The map of Opus 6 on the kitchen wall showed a large stone at the highest point, and Lucas imagined that was meant to be the final piece put into place—whether as a gravestone or something else. Now that top swirl of stones seemed to look particularly . . . empty.

He wondered whether the final stone was here somewhere, waiting.

Walking across a plain of stones down by a shaded area at the back of the lot, flattened and arranged just so, Lucas came to a bridge—one large, flat stone—over a passageway. Looking down before crossing, he felt a sort of vertigo—different from the carousel spins. Which maybe made sense, considering how his father had died, but was there something more to it?

Something wrong in his brain?

Something that would never heal?

Everything was too quiet.

He half missed the news vans.

Half wanted reporters to ask him questions that would maybe inspire answers.

He'd show them the tattoo, see if it led to anything. Since it was no longer a secret anyway.

Had it been forced on him? Or on *all* of them?

Had he done it himself?

Which was worse?

At the end of his tour—having given up on finding the centerpiece stone—he ducked through a long, deep tunnel, came out the other end, and saw something shining past a cluster of thirsty bushes. Pushing through some brush, he spotted a shabby, old RV with a ray of sun reflecting off the side-view mirror. It didn't appear at all road-ready.

Did someone live there?

He turned to head back toward the house to ask Ryan about it, whether it was even theirs, and to eat something before the playground meet-up, but his brother was right there.

Lucas nodded toward the RV. "What's that?"

"Come on." Ryan wagged a key in the air. "I'll show you."

AVERY

She texted Sam when she got out of the pool—

Can you come get me?

Crazy stuff happening

—then got dressed and waited on the front steps.

When he pulled up, she got in and said, "Just drive."

They ended up at Lakes Park—about twenty minutes inland. She and Sam had rented a bicycle for two on their first date here. Had even ridden the tiny train that ran around the grounds, through little villages made out of dollhouses and miniature oddities. They'd spent hours making out in the far corners of the parking lot, too, a few times since.

Not in a while, though.

They walked out to a picnic table on a bridge over the lake. A large white bird took off from a small island as Avery sat down.

Was Sam remembering, too? That first date? How fun everything had seemed at least for a little while?

Back before she started feeling like he was maybe not as cute as she'd originally thought. Or smart enough to be with her, either.

Being with him had started to turn her into this nasty, petty person.

"Everything okay?" He sat across from her.

"No, Sam, everything is not okay."

See?

"You know what I mean." He stared at her.

"What *do* you mean?" He was already annoying her. Being with the wrong person made you not right in the head.

"I *mean*, tell me what's going on."

"Well, I'll probably be on the news any minute now."

"What did you do?"

"I talked to one of them. Ryan's brother. He remembers a carousel. So I went on camera and said that if he can remember one thing, he can remember more. Right?"

"I don't know, Avery. I guess, yeah."

Sam was a *really good guy*. She reminded herself of that a lot, too. He was actually *too nice* for her.

He said, "I think maybe you should let the police handle it, you know?"

"I'm supposed to sit around and do nothing?" she said. "I'm sorry but if you don't understand why I have to find him, then maybe we shouldn't—"

"He's probably dead, Ave."

She felt like she'd been slapped. She must have looked like it, too. Who did he think he was? He knew nothing about anything. Nothing about what it felt like when your life was headline news.

"I'm sorry," he said, "but someone had to say it. Everyone is saying it."

"I'm not an idiot, Sam."

He shoved his hands into his shorts pockets; he was straddling the bench of the table, like he was ready to walk away at any moment.

"What else are people saying?" Avery asked. "Since everyone knows so much more about it than I do."

"I don't know. Just . . . stuff."

"What stuff?" She was losing patience.

"See, I don't even know if I can say it without you freaking out."

"Just say it."

"It's that maybe they're terrorists. Maybe they've been brainwashed into some kind of suicide mission or something." He seemed almost excited by the idea of it.

"Do you realize how ridiculous you sound?" she asked. Because hiding the truth about some possible wrongdoing—something involving Max—and becoming *terrorists* were completely different things.

Weren't they?

Sam shrugged. "I'm saying you shouldn't trust them."

"I never said I did! I went on camera to say that!"

"Are you *enjoying* all this?" Sam tilted his head. "The attention?"

Avery breathed hard. She was about to end it—because it was over—but if she cut Sam out of the picture, who did she have?

Was she enjoying it?

That would be messed up.

"I'm not enjoying it *at all.* I'm a *mess.*" She started crying and he reached across the table and took her hand. She said, "How could you even say that?

He said "I'm sorry" and got up and came around to her side and pulled her up and kissed her. She let him because she wanted to feel something a normal teenager should be feeling. Something giddy like lust or a crush. Or something sad but typical like heartbreak. A feeling that had pop songs written about it, so you could play them on repeat and deal and move on.

No such luck.

There was no sidestepping this, no way out but through.

"Who's saying all that terrorist stuff, anyway?" she asked then.

Even if that theory was nonsense, there *must* be people out there with information. People who'd seen them?

"It doesn't matter," Sam said.

"Well, do they have any ideas about what the supposed target will be?" How do you get information out of people?

"I don't know. Mall? School? Playground?"

She almost laughed. "You think someone would do all this? Go to *this length*? Eleven years in the planning. To blow up a playground?"

Money was how you got people to talk.

She'd break up with him after this whole thing was over.

In the meantime, she'd talk to her dad about posting a reward for information leading to Max.

A big one.

Scarlett

Steve hadn't let up all afternoon. He wanted dinner tonight.

If a 4:30 early-bird special qualified as "tonight."

"And there he is," Tamara said, as they entered the main dining room.

A salad bar stabbed full of long silver spoons ran down one side of the room. Windows facing the beach down the other.

Only one news van had followed them from the medical office to the outlets, then the phone store and home (so her mother could change) and here; it had been stopped from entering the restaurant parking lot by a burly valet.

"Well, aren't you a sight for sore eyes." Steve stood, came out from behind the table, embraced Tamara, then turned to Scarlett. "And you. It's a pleasure." He held out his hand to shake.

Scarlett took it, shook.

He was fit, compact, with a balding head and a small graying mustache, neatly trimmed. His eyes were borderline feminine—with thick lashes. He wore a necklace of twisted gold that peeked out at the neckline of a cream button-down shirt that was tucked into belted jeans.

"I have to say." Steve was shaking his head. "Let's just say I sure am happy to meet you." He looked at Tamara. "This woman is one tough cookie, right? She's been through a lot."

"Yes," Scarlett said. "She is. She has."

Haven't I, too?

Am I a tough cookie???

Do people like *tough cookies?*

The table was round and too big for them and Scarlett wished some of the others were here with her, wondered what they were all doing for dinner on this, their first day back.

Were there big family gatherings, full of hugs and happy tears?

Were Lucas and his brother surrounded by shocked, grieving relatives and casseroles?

And what about Max's family? Were they sitting at their table, hoping for the doorbell to ring, for it all to change to happy just like that?

She didn't belong here with these two people.

The view, at least, was lovely.

A long pier.

The water blue like ripe berries.

White clouds like chalk.

A burst of rainbow colors—someone parasailing by.

Just outside the restaurant, by a more casual outdoor seating area, a group of six girls and boys—close friends or cousins?—were laughing and running around in the sand.

Climbing up onto a big rock and then

jumping

off it.

Over and over again.

Climb. Jump. Climb. Jump. Climb. Jump.

"Do I have cousins?" she said.

Her mother looked at her like she'd just said something inappropriate. "No, your uncle Tom never married."

Scarlett nodded.

Another loss.

Then she said, "So you met at a bar?"

"Yes. A bartender who doesn't drink." He leaned over and kissed Tamara. "Speaking of which"—drinks were being delivered to the table by a waiter carrying a small, round black tray—"I ordered your old favorite. I figured she's back. We can celebrate. Right?"

Her mother raised her glass. "What a great idea!"

"Are you sure about that?" Scarlett asked.

"It's just one little treat," Steve said. "Right, Tammy? You know, after so many years."

Tammy.

Scarlett's skin felt prickly.

Was it a big deal?

Did it really matter?

She was becoming increasingly convinced, as the day wore on, that she wasn't going to be sticking around that long anyway. This just didn't feel like . . . home? Probably she'd spend a year in high school there, apply to college, then . . . leave.

Leave.

Leaving.

Would that word ever be normal again?

She pictured herself someplace cooler, someplace with autumn, and a proper winter, in an Adirondack chair, maybe staring at a lake.

Just . . .

. . . staring.

She said, "Well, I guess you've earned it."

She ordered a ginger ale. Then she turned her attention to the menu, not entirely sure what foods she even liked. Steve said, several times, that money was no object, that dinner was his treat, so that was good, at least. At the phone store, Tammy had done a lot of complaining about how expensive it was. Scarlett ordered shrimp cocktail and then a blackened grouper entrée and crossed her fingers that she wasn't harboring some fatal shellfish allergy.

Too quickly, her mother ordered another drink and said, "Steve here thinks you and me need to make some smart moves right about now."

"Yeah?" Scarlett slurped the last of her ginger ale loudly.

You and I, Tammy.

You and I.

"I see dollar signs." He sat back in his seat, folded his napkin, and put it on the table in front of him.

Now Scarlett saw them, too. They lit up behind her eyelids when she blinked.

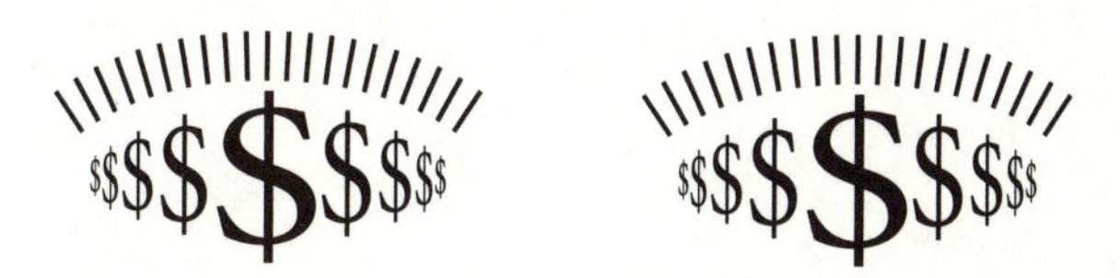

She held her eyes closed for a moment and saw spinning, like slot machines.

"Where are these dollars coming from?" she asked.

"Everyone wants to know your story." He leaned forward conspiratorially. "You can't see it, but there's not a table in here that hasn't talked about you. Pointed us out."

"Do you think I should go on TV?" They'd seen Sarah and Adam on one show briefly during their quick stop at the house. On the small screen, they had good clothes and haircuts and looked like strangers.

"Maybe, maybe not. If that's not your thing, there are other ways."

"Such as?"

"There are book deals, for starters."

The chatter in the room had become newly distracting, now that she knew some of it might be about her. She said, "I don't think I actually like to write."

"That's even better." He flagged a waiter over. "You sell your life rights and they'll hire someone to write the book for you, and then you just sit back and let the royalties roll in."

"Sorry," she said.

Life rights?

Right to life?

"Not interested."

He ordered another vodka on the rocks. "Someone's going to do it. I'm just saying . . . why not you?"

"Yeah, why not you?" *Tammy* said, and Scarlett wondered whether Adam and Sarah had already inked book deals. "You were always reading, reading, reading. Couldn't get you to stop reading. If you love books so much—"

"When I was five?"

"Yes," Tammy said.

"I knew how to read before kindergarten," Scarlett said, but it was a question for Tammy. Now that she was thinking of her as that—Tammy—she couldn't un-think it.

"Yes, ma'am." Tammy's foundation wasn't quite the right match for her skin.

"In this book of mine," Scarlett said, "is it aliens who did it?"

"You wouldn't have to say for sure." Tammy gave Steve a look and said, "As I've said, *no one* can say for sure. But I bet it'd sell like hotcakes if it was aliens."

"Maybe *you* should write a book!" Scarlett said.

"Maybe I will!" Tammy took a pull off her drink with a slim red cocktail straw, then looked out the window, like there was something really fascinating out there.

The silence felt tight around Scarlett's throat.

An invisible necktie of awkwardness and anger.

Squeezing

Steve said, "You do know how to tell a good story, Tammy. I remember those nights I'd just sit at the bar, when there was hardly anyone else there, and I'd be thinking, *Damn, she sure can talk.*"

Looking at the ocean, Scarlett tried to hatch an escape plan.

She should run to the end of the pier, jump off, and hope to be rescued by the crew of some boat bound for a faraway land.

Or she could just walk toward the shore and into the water until it buried her. Maybe hope for some dolphin or manatee or mermaid to deliver her to some fantastical underwater city? Or maybe just to . . . wherever she'd been before?

Steve was still talking. "Then I got to wondering what else you might be good at," he said, and Scarlett's mother said, "Oh, stop."

Yes.

Please.

Stop.

"Seriously, though. A book," Steve said. "Promise us you'll think about it?"

Lucas

Lucas half expected a flock of birds or bats to fly out of the RV, but it was eerily quiet.

Dead still.

He followed his brother into the dim compartment, swatting at thick spiderwebs. Ryan turned on a lamp that flooded the room with golden light. There were Post-its and articles on every wall and cabinet door; even the windows were mostly covered.

A large whiteboard blocked one window, with crazy notes scrawled in black marker.

Lucas saw his own name—the first box of six, in the top left corner—and read,

> ONE WEEK BEFORE IT HAPPENED, LUCAS SAID THEY WERE BEING FOLLOWED BY A MAN CARRYING WRAPPING PAPER.

He turned to Ryan. "What is this man-with-wrapping-paper thing all about?"

Ryan came to his side and stared at the whiteboard while he spoke. "We were walking home from my baseball game. And you kept stopping and turning around and then walking and stopping and turning around, and it was driving me *crazy* because I just wanted to get home and tell Dad about my two hits, and I finally asked you why you were stopping, and I guess I was mean-sounding and you said, 'No reason.' But then a few minutes later, you said, 'It's just that there's a man following us.'"

Ryan paused then, took a breath, shook his head.

"I told you that you were being ridiculous. And you said that he was carrying something that looked like wrapping paper, and I said something like, 'Oooh, the scary man is going to wrap us and take us to a party,' and that was the end of it . . . until a week later, when you disappeared.

"I told the police about it, and they interviewed some of the guys on the team, and people said they remembered seeing this guy with wrapping paper hanging around the ball field. But of course they never found the guy. There were a few attempts at police sketches, but none of them looked anything alike and they started to think that the guys didn't really remember seeing the guy, just wanted to be a part of something and be helpful.

"Anyway." Ryan looked like he'd aged two years telling the story. "If I hadn't been in such a hurry, maybe *I* would have seen the guy and everything would have been different."

"Maybe." Lucas felt his whole body un-tense now that he knew. "Maybe he was just a guy. With wrapping paper."

"Something *that looks like* wrapping paper is what you said."

"What *looks like* wrapping paper?" Lucas asked.

"*You're* the one who saw it." Ryan shrugged. His phone buzzed and he pulled it out. "I'm supposed to meet Miranda."

"What's the situation with you two, anyway?" Lucas lifted a pile of newspaper clippings, started to sift.

"The *situation*?"

"How'd you meet? How long have you been together? Is it serious? Does she live here?"

"What are we, girlfriends now?"

"All right, whatever. Don't tell me." Lucas headed toward the bedroom section to see what was there.

"Hold up," Ryan said. "Sorry. I'm just not much of a, you know, talker. About stuff like that."

Ryan sat down at the small kitchen table. Lucas came back and sat across from him. Their knees hit. The table was barely visible under piles of magazines and notes.

"She came into work one night about a month ago."

"You have a job?"

"Part-time valet at the Tiki Tower."

"That crazy-looking hotel?"

Ryan nodded. "I parked her car. We flirted. She was still at the bar with her friends when I got off, so we hung out and that was pretty much it. Dad was getting sick of her hanging around, I think. But she has roommates she can't stand, so we never go there."

Lucas tried to picture his brother wearing a lei, exchanging pleasantries with strangers. It was not an easy scene to imagine. "Shouldn't you be in college?"

"I am. Also part-time," Ryan said.

"Her, too?" It dawned on Lucas that he might actually have to go to . . . high school?

"She's taking a year off. She has this business that's actually doing okay. She sells these retro/vintage-type iron-on T-shirts on the Internet. Mr. Magoo and Betty Boop and all that stuff." He gestured to Lucas's shirt. "The Wonder Twins."

Lucas looked down. "Never heard of any of them."

Ryan shrugged and got up. "Anyway, I was thinking about seeing if she wanted to move in and start paying rent. Then hopefully you can start pulling your weight, too."

"How am I going to do that?" Lucas asked.

"I don't know. You can flip burgers, can't you? Mop floors? Whoever had you obviously taught you some basic skills. Or go on TV or something. Make some cash off your sad tale."

"Why are you so *mad* at me?" Lucas himself lit with anger, could almost hear the *swoosh* of it igniting. "Like one minute you're not, then the next second, bam. This *rage* of yours—directed *at me*—is just out of line."

Ryan started crying.

Full-body sob.

That was unexpected.

Lucas waited it out, didn't know what else to do.

Avery had looked like she was about to cry, too.

Then Ryan said, "I don't know, man. You're my brother and I want to believe you and be normal." Wiped his nose with his bare arm. "But how do I know? How do I know you didn't kill him? How do I know how to even act around you?"

"I'm as confused as you are." Lucas moved to a small sofa.

First her—Avery—not trusting him.

Now this.

"What do you want me to say, Ryan? That I'm sorry?" He looked up at his brother. "I'm sorry I came back?"

I'm sorry I don't remember your brother.

Ryan shook his head, the tears having gone as quickly as they'd come. "Everyone's like, 'What do they remember? Do they remember anything?' 'Oooh, it's so awful they don't remember anything.' Want to know what I remember?"

"I have a feeling you're going to tell me."

"I remember the day Billy Harrington spat in my face on the bus when I was in fourth grade. I remember Dad trying to read Harry

Potter to me, and he was so drunk that pretty much every word sounded like 'Dumbledore.' I remember counting to like a thousand or singing 'Ninety-Nine Bottles of Beer on the Wall' in my head to survive bus rides with bullies in middle school, and then using those same strategies to deal with Dad and Opus 6 and his having me work with him on it for hours. I remember this guy John Deniro, who was always *so mean* to me and then one day I was a jerk back and then he ended up getting hit by a car and I felt awful about it for years, even though he'd been this awful, *awful* person. I remember being made to eat food I didn't like, and night after night of going to bed early just to get away from Dad, even though I wasn't tired, and I'd just lie there wondering when my life was, you know, going to get better. When things were going to change. I remember sirens and blood and dead bodies being dragged out of the school after the shooting. My friend Liam was dead. Everybody crying and screaming. That's what I remember. I remember *being here.*"

Headspins:

BLOODY BACKPACK GUN CAROUSEL.

Lucas worked to still his mind, then tried to imagine his brother—younger, bored, miserable, picked on, grieving, everything—then half smiled. "Thought you weren't much of a talker."

Ryan gave him the finger, shook his head, sort of smiled, too.

"I didn't know," Lucas said. "I'm sorry you went through that."

"You were there, too. There was like an open house for families who were starting kindergarten the next year."

"I don't remember."

"Shocker." Another half smile.

"Did they at least catch the shooter?" Because justice helped. It had to, right?

"Killed himself. Dad said that it was a good thing because Dad would have done it if he hadn't."

Lucas sat quietly with that thought, rolled it around, trying it on for size, liking it.

Justice.

Or something else.

Revenge?

Yes, that.

Lucas said, "I want to kill whoever did this to me," and the spins started up again.

REINS. SADDLE.
FUN-HOUSE REFLECTIONS WRAPPED AROUND
GOLD POLES **STABBING** HORSES.

Ryan waved a hand dismissively. "You'll get over it."

"Why should I?" Lucas put his hands to his head, like he might somehow physically steady it.

"You want to go to jail?" Ryan said. "Right after you got back?"

"It'd be worth it."

"Well, if and when you find him—or her, or them—you let me know."

"So you can stop me?" Maybe he needed medication for this thing in his head? "No, thank you."

Ryan went down the hall to the sleeping area, and there was some slamming of cabinets and then he was back, carrying a wooden box.

He took a key off a hook on the inside of a kitchen cabinet—a pineapple keychain with a smiley face on it. Returning to the table, he opened the box, then spun it around and pushed it toward Lucas.

At the sight of the gun, Lucas stood, wanting to flee, wanting to tell Ryan to close the box, lock it, get rid of it.

But . . .

Then . . .

ONE RIGHT TWO LEFT HISS CLICK
SNAP UP DONE

Everything stilled.

Lucas took the pistol in his right hand—the magazine in his left—and loaded up.

Like he'd done it a thousand times before.

AVERY

Back at home around dinnertime, there were no signs of dinner. Mom was in bed, surrounded by still more tissues. The woman had become a movable flowering tissue tree, dropping fruit wherever she went.

"Have you eaten anything today?" Avery started collecting some of the tissues and put them in the small trash can in the master bath. "Where's Dad?"

"No appetite. Where else."

Avery breathed out hard. "I'll make you something." She muttered, "Guess I'll make myself something while I'm at it."

Her mother rolled onto her side, away from Avery. "Don't you want to know what's *wrong*?"

Avery wanted to scream.

"What's wrong, Mom?" Her arms stiffened at her side.

She held out a piece of paper to Avery. "This was in the mailbox."

Avery took it, mildly impressed that her mother had made it all the way to the pelican by the street.

It was a handwritten note on white paper:

I'M CLOSE. I'M TRYING TO GET AWAY LIKE THE OTHERS. HELP!
—MAX

Avery's hand started to shake.

Really happening.

Lowering the note, she said, "Did you call the police?"

Her mom yanked another tissue from a box. "They're useless."

Avery went downstairs and thought about calling Lucas, but that didn't make sense; she didn't even have his number, if he even had a phone. She hunted around and found the card the detective who'd come by yesterday—

No, not yesterday.

It had been that morning.

Today.

This is what tragedy did; it slowed time to a freaking crawl.

School would never start up again, not at this pace.

She'd never have another birthday, never celebrate another Christmas.

From that morning on—that *phone call* on—life was dog years.

The card was stuck to the fridge with a magnet from a random cousin's wedding. She dialed Mick Chambers. He picked up.

"It's Avery Godard."

She waited.

"How can I help you?"

It sounded like he had no idea who she was.

"I'm Max's sister."

"Of course."

"We got a note from him." The ink was black ballpoint; the writing all caps.

"A *note*?" Chambers said.

"Yes." Avery looked out the kitchen window, where a bee was bobbing near the rhododendrons. The setting sun was reflecting off the neighbor's window, like a ball of fire.

Some shuffling and then, "Okay, what does it say?"

"'I'm close. I'm trying to get away like the others. Help! Max.'"

"That's it?"

"That's it." It wasn't *her* fault there wasn't more!

"Who knows about this?" Sounding like an accusation.

"Just me and my mom. Maybe my dad, but I doubt it."

"Do me a favor," he said. "Don't mention it to anyone. Until I check it out. No more little on-camera stunts? And if I catch a whiff of any social media posting nonsense—" Chambers wasn't the most pleasant-seeming guy.

"It's a free country," Avery said. "What are you going to do, exactly? To check it out."

"I'll send someone over to pick it up. We'll get it to the lab. Dust it for prints or other trace evidence."

Avery said, "And you'll let me know? You'll call me?"

"I'll speak with your parents, yes."

"It would be better if you just called *me*."

He was quiet for a long second. "Everything okay at home?"

"Nothing's okay at home," she said.

"It's better if you call me," he said. "Give me a couple of days."

"Okay," she said. But she didn't want to hang up yet. "Do you think it's really from him?"

He breathed so loudly that Avery pictured his nostril hairs cowering in fear. "Truth?"

She stared at a flyer gripped by a magnet clip on the refrigerator. Dates and times for the auditions. Next Wednesday. A lifetime away. They had to post a reward before then. "Truth."

"It's probably a prank," he said, sounding almost nice. "A really sick, pathetic prank."

"What's *wrong* with people?" Her hands were still shaking when she ended the call.

Scarlett

She'd helped Tammy into the passenger seat and had gotten behind the wheel. She turned the key, put the car in Drive.

Had to look around a bit—horn, there.

Hazards, there.

Fluffy dice and stale air freshener there.

But *driving* felt familiar.

Someone had taught her to do this.

No encouraging mother or father in an empty mall parking lot.

No driver's ed class with friends.

Who *did* this?

What else did you teach me?

At home, she'd poured Tammy into bed and put a glass of water on her bedside table.

It was 7:00 p.m.

She went to her room to change her clothes.

Then changed them again.

And again.

Shorts didn't feel right.

At all.

Sundresses slightly better.

But florals, no.

Stripes?

Better.

She didn't want to seem ungrateful.

It was just . . .

. . . all . . .

. . . wrong . . .

Would have to go back . . .

But then what would she wear?

Would have to find better . . .

. . . other . . .

. . . stores.

Finally, she settled on the gray A-line skirt and black tank top.

Lying down on her bed, she searched for "oval metal objects" on her phone.

A locket maybe?

Religious medal?

She put the phone down.

Could not keep sleeping in this room.

Not with it like this.

All stuffed unicorns and Glinda.

She stood and stared at the cardboard witch for a minute and imagined a field of poppies,

a yellow brick road leading her to . . .

. . . where?

. . . then left.

She opted to drive and was early, even with all that, and had been sitting in the parking lot beside the playground for maybe fifteen minutes thinking about lockets and religious medals and flying monkeys when—

KNOCK-KNOCK.

Gasp.

Kristen.

Black cargo shorts.

White top with a black anchor on it.

Black bracelets on her left wrist.

Scarlett leaned over and opened the passenger-side door. "You scared me."

"Sorry."

Kristen exhaled cigarette smoke, then got into the car, bringing the smell with her. "You smoke?" Scarlett said.

Kristen shrugged. "Apparently."

/

/

Crickets.

/

/

Palm leaves brushing against each other in the breeze.

/

/

Just tell her!

/

/

Kristen said, "Do you think anybody else is going to show?"

"I think Lucas will." He had to; she needed to see him even if she wasn't sure exactly why. "It was his idea. But I don't know. Have you been watching the news?"

Kristen said, "They'll never show."

"I wasn't sure *you'd* be here." She'd heard about Kristen during that brief news clip, too. "Hypnosis?"

"Yeah, it was all Father's idea. And Mother's, too, of course!"

"Are they awful?"

"They got divorced, turns out. So I'm living in this totally weird house with my mother and now they have to figure out custody? I don't know. It's like they're offended that someone did this to them. It's all so . . . unsavory. My father thinks we were kept in some pervert's basement."

"And they want you to be hypnotized so you can remember *that*?"

"They want justice!" Kristen rolled her eyes. "They want answers! They want someone to blame! My father had this hypnosis chick's number ready, like he was waiting all this time."

"Maybe it'll work." It seemed like the right thing to say, even if Scarlett wasn't sure she believed it. "I'm surprised my mother hasn't suggested it yet. She thinks it was an alien abduction."

"No."

"Yes."

"Sorry."

"Thanks."

Kristen nodded toward the corner. "Why do you think we were dropped off *here*?"

"What do you mean?"

"I just . . . I don't know. It seems . . . cruel?"

"How so?" They'd been let go. That seemed *un*-cruel.

"It just feels like a taunt." Kristen played with one of her bracelets. "Here you go. Here's what you missed. Here's a lovely reminder of the piece of you that's gone forever."

Scarlett wished she could locate her own missing piece.

Was it puzzle-shaped and in her heart?

Or oval in her gut?

"Did you see the memory guy yet?" Kristen asked. "Get poked and prodded yet?"

"Just MRI today. The rest tomorrow." She should tell her, but something was stopping her; she didn't want to be the only one. "You're all done?" she asked, fishing.

"Yeah, what a waste of time." Kristen shook her head. "Like, what did they think they'd find? The memory guy was at least interesting."

"How so?"

"He's cool. Kind of hot, actually." She slipped off her sandals and put her bare feet up on the dash; a blister was forming near her left pinkie toe. "We were talking about memories as units. Like how when you have a memory it had a beginning and an end. So what triggers those beginning and end points, like who's the editor in your brain? Why do you remember one minute and not the minutes before it?"

"Does he have any theories? About what happened to us?"

"He doesn't know, except maybe it was some kind of experiment. Which is a better theory than aliens or perverts, though I suppose it could be two out of three. I can't breathe." Kristen slid her feet back down to the floor, slipped her sandals back on, opened the door and got out and closed it, and headed for the playground gate.

Scarlett got out, and then felt a tweak of pain in her gut.

Imagined it.

Surely.

Unless . . . ?

Was it possible?

That whatever it was . . .

Had hidden sharp edges

. . . and could rip her right open?

Had to ***push push push***

the thought away.

Followed Kristen to the swings.

Who else could she trust if not the others?

Started to form the sentence in her head.

There's something inside—

"I remembered something about you right after the session," Kristen said. "About *us.* Just a feeling, and I had it again as I walked toward your car."

/

/ /

"What?"

/

/

/

Kristen sat on a swing, twisting its chains. “I remembered that we don’t really like each other.”

The stabbing feeling again.

This time for real.

Lucas

He was on foot, heading for the playground, wondering who would show up, half hoping it would be only him and Scarlett.

What would he even tell her?

Or them?

Did they know how to load guns, too?

If he hadn't come across a gun, he wouldn't have even known.

Maybe he should have brought it?

Tested them?

No.

Why had he felt so still, so calm, with that gun in his hand?

Why had he . . .

. . . liked it?

Would they remember the carousel, too?

GOLDEN SADDLES. PEANUTS. WHITE FIRE.

Or a man carrying something that looked like wrapping paper?

SANTA. BEARD.

Would they have tattoos?

CLICK CLICK.

And if so, the same as his or different?

It was finally starting to cool off, and the sun had shifted from blue to gray as evening sank in.

Maybe his brother was right not to trust him.

Maybe Avery was, too.

Why did he know how to load a gun?

Kristen and Scarlett were sitting beside each other on swings, not swinging.

"Hey." He approached.

"Hey." Scarlett stood; Kristen pushed off gently on her swing, setting herself in motion.

"I'm so sorry." Scarlett walked toward him and then stopped as if encountering an invisible force field. "About your father."

He nodded, wishing she'd come all the way to him. "Thanks."

Kristen said, "Yeah, sorry about all that," sounding like she was already over it.

"It's hard to even know how to feel about it." He spoke to Scarlett as if Kristen weren't there. "On the one hand I barely knew him."

"You can't really be a suspect," Scarlett said. "They have to realize it was an accident. Right?"

"They will." He had to believe it, himself. Then, "How are things with you guys?"

He couldn't ignore Kristen the whole time.

"I'm okay," Scarlett said. Her black tank top showed off her figure in a way he found distracting.

SKIN. VALLEY. BONES. LIPS.

A memory?

A fantasy?

She said, "My mother is a crazy person who thinks aliens took us."

He'd seen a note about that in the RV and had hoped it wasn't actually true. At least not anymore, not now.

"My parents, who are amicably divorced, vote for pervert with a basement prison," Kristen said. "Mother is pretty much treating me like a foreign exchange student from some war-torn, godforsaken country, which feels right, in a way?"

"That's a lot to have to deal with," Lucas said.

"I'll manage," Kristen said.

"That explains why your address didn't sound familiar," he said.

"Exactly."

"You guys don't remember Max, do you?" Lucas asked.

Scarlett shook her head; Kristen, too.

"And do either of you know anything about a man carrying wrapping paper? Being followed? Anything like that?"

"No, why?" Scarlett said.

"I said I was being followed the week before. I told my brother about it. I thought maybe if you'd been followed but hadn't told anyone . . . I don't know. I remember stuff from before . . .

WALKER. SUPERMAN. CUBBIES. READY OR NOT.

. . . so I thought you might."

Scarlett said, "I told my mother we were going 'to the leaving.'"

Lucas nodded. "Do you remember saying it?"

"I don't." She seemed irritated. "Why would I say that?"

"I don't know," he said. "Yet."

He pictured that scene—a young girl telling her mother she was going on a trip, to the leaving, while they were tucked in bed and reading books.

Kids say crazy things, silly things, weird things.

She probably hadn't thought anything of it until . . . after.

"You are getting sleepy." Kristen's voice was an octave deeper. "You are getting very sleepy. When I snap my fingers, you will remember."

Lucas didn't like the pattern of freckles on her nose.

"Just trying to lighten the mood."

"We'll get there." Lucas turned back to Scarlett. "We'll figure it out. We have to." He could practically feel the cool metal of the gun in his hands when he said, "Someone has to pay. For doing this to us."

"Can either of you think of what kind of clothes I used to wear?" Scarlett asked.

He looked at her, that tank top.

SOFT. WARM. KISS.

Blinked.

"Really?" Kristen pushed off on her swing harder and started to pump her legs. She was going too high. "That's your concern right now? Fashion?"

Scarlett looked down at her clothes. "I just don't feel like . . . well . . . me."

Lucas knew what she meant—she somehow didn't *look* like her—but there were more important things to be thinking about. He was about to say something—about guns, or weapons in general—to feel out Scarlett and Kristen, but then Kristen said, "Look who decided to grace us with her presence."

Sarah seemed smaller somehow; she had expensive-looking clothes on.

"Hey," Lucas said.

"Hey," she said.

"Now we just have to wait for Adam," he said.

"He's not coming." Sarah shook her head. "I shouldn't even be here. I just. I just wanted to see you all."

"I guess we're lucky you had some time between interviews," Kristen said.

"Adam's parents pushed for that. I think it'll die down. I don't know. One of you obviously talked, too. Max's sister was on the news right before I left and said something about a carousel?"

HOW CAN YOU FORGET A PERSON?
STONES OF OPUS 6 REFLECTED IN AVERY'S EYES.

Why would she *do* that? How could he have been so dumb?

Don't trust people who don't trust you.

"That was me," Lucas said.

Scarlett sounded genuinely confused. "When did you talk to *Max's sister*?"

"She came to the house. Looking for help. It just slipped. Do any of you remember a carousel by the beach?"

They all shook their heads.

He waited for the dizziness to come back, but it didn't.

Scarlett said, "I remember riding in a hot air balloon."

Kristen said, "Horseback riding in a meadow."

Sarah said, "Playing with a puppy."

"What about Adam?" Lucas asked.

"A roller coaster ride," Sarah said. "He thinks they're just hallucinations we had. But I don't know. I feel like I can picture this gray house. An old-looking gray house. Adam says I shouldn't say anything to anybody. I wanted to know if any of you remember that? Like charcoal gray?"

Lucas didn't. Neither did the others.

Kristen said, "I'm meeting with a hypnotist again in the morning. Maybe I'll remember."

"Did you remember anything *today*?" Lucas asked, and for a second, it seemed like Kristen and Scarlett shared a secret look, and then Kristen seemed to break it off.

She said, "They're not telling me what I said yet. They want to preserve the integrity of what I recall when I'm under for at least a few sessions."

Lucas looked at Scarlett, who was staring at the ground.

Were they hiding something from him?

"I won't hold my breath," he said.

"It's worked for people before," Kristen snapped. "There were a bunch of kids who were kidnapped on a school bus in California years ago. They managed to escape, and the bus driver remembered a license plate under hypnosis and they caught the kidnappers, so . . ."

"I have to go." Sarah started to walk away.

"But you just got here!" Lucas protested.

She turned. "I snuck out. I don't want to get caught. I shouldn't have come."

"Don't you want to find who did this?" Lucas ignited again, but this time low heat. He said, "We all need to work together," but wasn't honestly convinced Sarah would be any help at all.

"I don't know what I want." Sarah starting walking in circles like the night before, and now talking in circles, too. "I want to go back. I want to move on. I want to know why it was us and not some other kids, and I don't want to know anything at all!"

So many questions.

So many ways in.

Why us?

Why then?

Why now?

Why here and not any other town?

"At least give me your phone number," Scarlett said, "in case anything urgent comes up." She and Sarah exchanged information via text and Sarah walked out of the playground. They watched her go until they couldn't anymore, then listened until distance silenced the slip-slap of her sandals.

"Let's *all* exchange numbers," Lucas said. "So we can be in better touch."

And as they did that, headlights fell on them.

A local news van pulling up right at the gate to the playground.

"How did they find us?" Lucas said as he finished typing the word—"Scar"—into his phone.

"That's my cue to go home." Kristen stopped her swing and stood. "We don't know anything more than we did yesterday anyway."

Lucas actually wanted her to leave. She put him on edge in a way he couldn't explain.

If he were alone with Scarlett, he thought he might tell her about the gun—the tattoo.

"Maybe Sarah and Adam have the right idea," he said. A news crew of two were now standing by a curly slide.

A woman called out, "We just want to talk."

What else would they want?

"What do you mean?" Scarlett asked Lucas.

Lucas had the urge to take a photo of her, framed as she was by the chains of the swing, her face lit softly from the van's headlights. "I've been avoiding them," he said. "But why? We don't have anything to hide."

Nothing that anyone needed to know about, anyway.

"I just mean maybe they can help," he said.

"How?" Scarlett asked.

"Follow my lead." He walked toward the slide, stopped, and said, "Whenever you're ready." The cameraman hoisted his machine.

The reporter held out a microphone.

Lights burned on.

Lucas could almost see into the camera—lens after lens in there reflecting and capturing.

"Why are you all meeting in secret?" the reporter asked.

"I wouldn't say it's a *secret.*" Lucas stood up straighter, pushed his hair out of his eyes. "We're in a public place. We arranged to meet when we were dropped off here because we had no idea what was going on. We wanted to check in on each other. To make sure we were all okay."

"Who remembers the carousel that Avery Godard is talking about? Why aren't Sarah and Adam here? Has there been a falling-out?"

"I'm the one who remembers the carousel," Lucas said. The light was near blinding.

"And I remember riding a horse in a meadow," Kristen said.

When the microphone was presented to Scarlett, she said, "I remember riding in a hot air balloon."

"So *maybe*," Lucas said, "the person who owns the horse or the hot air balloon or runs the carousel will remember us?"

"What about Adam and Sarah?" the reporter pressed. "Do they have memories, too?"

Lucas said, "They've shown that they're quite capable of speaking for themselves. Anyway, there hasn't been a falling-out. We've all just had a lot to deal with, obviously. That's all we remember. We really hope they're able to find out what happened to Max."

Would Avery see this report? He hoped so.

Hoped that maybe she'd believe him now.

He turned to look at Scarlett and Kristen, then back to the camera and said, "That's all we have to say right now. Thanks for your time."

The reporter smiled with large white teeth—"Awesome"—took out her phone, and started to walk away. "I've got the new lead on The Leaving," she said. "We're heading in." Then the cameraman opened the van's back door, put the camera in, and closed it. They both got in—their door slams loud like gunshots. Lucas realized he didn't even know what station they represented, but it was already too late; they were gone.

"And now we wait," Lucas said.

"I can drive you home if you want," Scarlett said to both of them.

In her car, stopped at a light beside an RV camping site, Lucas thought about getting out. Grabbing her hand and just abandoning the car right there. They'd hop in an RV and just drive and drive until they found a place where no one knew them.

But then . . .

Max.

Avery.

Wherever he went, this need to know what had happened would dog him. It had its teeth sunk into his flesh now and would need to be dealt with . . . extracted . . . properly.

The light changed and Lucas said, "It's up here on the right."

Opus 6 appeared like a jack-o'-lantern, sections of it glowing golden with solar-powered lights. It seemed to have eyes, and a mouth out of which a winding tongue of lava pulsed weakly down toward where the car pulled up.

"What on earth—" Kristen said.

"This is Opus 6?" Scarlett asked.

Of course.

They hadn't ever been there.

Scarlett got out of the car at the base of the driveway and left it running, her door open. She took large, confident strides up the main path, casting her own shadows on the glow, and in a minute she was standing at the top plateau—where the final stone was supposed to go. She spun around, taking a full rotation, making Lucas think of sacrificial virgins on altars and ceremonial dances. She said, "This is amazing," like a prayer. "I saw it mentioned in some old clippings I looked through . . . but wasn't really sure what it was."

Kristen wasn't even interested enough to get out of the car. She'd lit a cigarette that glowed the same color as the solar lights.

She was far enough away not to hear.

The wind blew Scarlett's hair into her face and she pushed it away.

Lucas said, "Do you have the feeling that you and I were . . . together?"

He had no better way to phrase it.

Then, for a long moment, he stared at her, waiting.

She said, "I think so, yes."

DAY TWO

AVERY

There would be no break in spring break—no sleeping in, no time-wasting.

She had set an alarm and was waiting for her dad when he came down into the kitchen. She'd heard him on the stairs and had abandoned the maze on the back of the cereal box to pour coffee for him. Black, two sugars.

"You're up early," he said when he entered the room, a tie draped around his neck.

"We need to offer a reward for information leading to Max being found." She delivered his mug to him. "A big one."

"I'm not really sure—"

"Dad." She perched on a stool by the center island. "It looks bad, you not really doing anything. There is someone out there who did this and who maybe has Max, and right now they think they are going to get away with it. But someone out there *knows* something—they have to—and money talks. I mean, if the note's real, and he's really out there? We have to act. Now."

Her dad took a long sip of coffee, then put the mug down and adjusted his watch. "How much are we talking?"

"I don't know," she said. "Ten grand? Twenty? Twenty-five?"

"That's a *lot*, Avery."

"You can't put a price tag on Max, can you?"

"That's not fair." Another sip and a minute of silence. "And the note probably isn't real. You get that, right?"

She nodded. "Still."

"I'll think about it." He put the mug down but didn't let go of it.

She said, "While you're thinking, time is being wasted."

"If I do this, you need to not go on the news again."

"Deal." This was almost too easy.

"It is weird, though, isn't it?" he said.

"What's weird?"

"The carousel, the hot air balloon, horseback riding." He let go of his coffee to sort through a stack of mail.

"Hot air balloon?"

"It's on this morning's news." He opened a bill. "They each have one unique memory."

"I hadn't seen." She turned the TV on. They were doing the weather, but it would cycle back soon; if not, she could look for the story on her phone. "So you'll do it?"

He tossed the bill back onto the pile. "I'll do it. I just need to, you know, figure out how one even goes about doing that, talk to my lawyer, speak with the police, the FBI. And you realize it's going to bring out some crazy people."

She went and kissed him on the cheek. "Thanks, Dad. You'll see. It's the right thing to do. The right message to send."

He went to finish getting ready for work, and she just sat at the kitchen island and waited for the segment to air again, which it did. She watched as Lucas and Scarlett and Kristen stood together in a playground—looked like the one over by the Publix—and stated their memories one by one.

Sam would have more theories, for sure, but Avery could now think of nothing other than Scarlett. She remembered looking up to her as a kid, remembered chasing her around the playground, playing games about fairies, and hunting for treasure.

Now she was back, alive, gorgeous, and she was standing next to Lucas. She was standing so *very close* to Lucas that it annoyed Avery, and then she was annoyed that it annoyed her. She needed to find Max—or his body, *Sam!*—and move on. She did not need to be daydreaming about Lucas or any of them. She did not need to be replaying her conversation with him at Opus 6, rewriting it so that it ended with her in his arms. So that it ended with an embrace, a kiss.

This was why she'd distanced herself from Ryan in the first place. So that she could go forward, pass Go. Lucas would be a backward move.

She could not stop thinking about him.

Finally, she heard the sound of the garage door opening, and the car pulling out, and the door closing, and the car going away down the street. The coast clear, she went into the garage and rooted around for the bolt cutters. Her dad had bought them during a brief period a few years back when her mom had taken up biking around the neighborhood. Mom kept forgetting the combination for her lock, so she kept calling, needing to be picked up at random places. Or she'd end up walking home, then sending Dad out to retrieve the bike.

Thank god that was all over with.

The bike was collecting dust and spiderwebs over by the subzero freezer.

Cutters in hand, Avery headed out on foot, taking a back way through the Youngs' yard—so as to avoid walking past the strip-mall security cameras with the clippers in hand—and down the bike path that ran along the bay.

She slowed and watched a guy who was paddleboarding by. His dog was on the board with him—a tiny burst of gray-and-white fluff, just sitting by the guy's feet as he paddled past.

People could really be ridiculous.

She didn't feel like talking to Ryan.

She didn't feel like asking for permission.

If she had, she wouldn't have bothered bringing the cutters.

She needed to get into the RV, didn't know why she hadn't thought of it yesterday. So when she finally got to the back end of Opus 6, she bypassed the house and approached it. Would the old video-game console she and Ryan had hooked up out there when they were like ten (her) and thirteen (him) still be there? Would their secret candy-bar stash in the oven have been eaten by mice? Would she hear the echoes of their younger selves talking, all those years ago, about their messed-up parents and how it was okay because in a few years, they'd be able to leave town?

The lock was open, just dangling there as her foot crunched a branch.

"Who's there?" came a voice.

"Ryan?"

The door creaked open and Lucas popped his head out. "No."

No.

No.

No.

"I came to apologize," she said. Would he see it in her eyes? That she'd had . . . thoughts . . . about him?

He scratched his neck.

"I shouldn't have mentioned the carousel." Saying it made it feel true.

"Come in." He swatted the air. "It's too buggy out here."

Climbing up the entry steps, she followed him in, ducking around cobwebs lit white by sun rays peeking from behind curtains. The walls were just as she remembered them—covered with corkboards layered thick with newspaper clippings and police reports, and whiteboards covered in wild writing.

"You've been here before?" he asked.

"Not in a long time." She looked around to see what, if anything, might have changed. "But yeah, me and Ryan used to hang out here sometimes."

"I haven't found anything that makes sense to me."

He saw the tool in her hand.

"So you *didn't* come to apologize." He seemed confused about it, like he was a new person and hadn't read his instruction manual yet.

"But I do want to apologize"—she gently put the cutters down—"now that I'm here."

He waved an arm. "What are you hoping to find?"

She had been *hoping* that something would just stand out. "I thought I'd know when I found it?"

He nodded and she felt something weird between them, some kind of bond forming out of unpredictable atoms. And yet, when she thought about mentioning the note from Max—the most recent break in the case, if it was one—or the reward, she couldn't bring herself to.

What if they're all lying?

"Well, have a look around, I guess," he said, and Avery turned toward a whiteboard:

AUGUST 9TH. IS DATE SIGNIFICANT?

WHY THEM?

WHY THAT DAY?

All of which were good questions, but they'd all been asking those questions for a long time and still had no answers. What she was looking for was something new or at least something that *felt* new, now that they were all back except for Max.

Lucas was flipping through a binder of clippings of some kind.

She went to the whiteboard that was divided into six boxes. Each box had a name in it, and Avery's eyes landed on the box for "Scarlett." She'd been over this board many times before—so many times that she could almost recite by heart the bullets under the photo of five-year-old Scarlett that was taped to it.

- SAID SHE WAS GOING "TO THE LEAVING"
- PRIOR CONTACT WITH ABDUCTOR THAT SHE MIGHT RECALL?
- MOTHER, TAMARA, SUSPECTS ALIEN ABDUCTION
- WHERE IS HER FATHER? [FBI CLEARED HIM. LIVES IN JERSEY. NEW FAMILY.]

Next to that was the box about Lucas; she knew these bullets well, too.

- ACCORDING TO RYAN, ONE WEEK BEFORE IT HAPPENED, LUCAS SAID THEY WERE BEING FOLLOWED BY A MAN CARRYING WRAPPING PAPER. THEY WERE COMING HOME FROM THE BALL GAME.

"Do you remember being followed?" she braved. "The week before?"

"No." Lucas came to her side and stood there quietly for a second, then said, "Who knows if it was anything anyway, I guess?"

Lucas stood very close to her now—so close that she could smell his sweat, see his pores, imagine what his skin would feel like.

Sam wouldn't like any of this, wouldn't like how much she liked it.

She didn't care.

It wasn't going to be like that.

She couldn't let it be.

She read her brother's bullets:

- *MOTHER, JILLIAN, DEPRESSED.*
- *FATHER, PAUL, TRAVELS FOR WORK. MOSTLY TO SEATTLE. WORKS FOR A TECH COMPANY.*
- *SISTER, AVERY. ONE YEAR YOUNGER.*

She didn't like seeing her name, still there in Will's notes after all this time, didn't like that he'd kept caring long after she'd stopped.

"What was he like?" Lucas said. "Max. Do you even remember?"

Avery turned to him. "Yes and no. I just remember everything being happier, you know? Everybody just . . . normal?"

He nodded. "We used to all be friends?"

"Me and Max and you and Ryan, yeah."

She remembered a fort they'd built out of sheets. Flashlights under there on a rainy day, shadow animals.

"What about Scarlett?" he asked. "Were we friends, too?"

Oh please no.

". . . and the others?"

No no no.

Because why would he ask about Scarlett first? Why would he separate her from "the others"?

They'd been standing *so close* in that playground.

Hadn't they?

Were they . . . *involved*?

She said, "We knew Scarlett. I remember being sad about her being gone, but I'm not sure about the others. Why?"

Why else?

"Just wondering." He looked away. "I remember certain things from before . . . like my dog and my brother . . . but I don't remember any of the others in any specific way, really. You said Max and I were best friends?"

"Yeah. You were at our house *a lot.* I remember being annoyed about it. Because you were boys and you didn't want me around."

"What did we do? Me and Max?"

She felt like she was digging deep and hitting stone. Then felt a strange panic about how much she had forgotten, just in the course of a normal life. People who were gone only lived on in your memory if you had memories. Why hadn't she held on tighter?

To Max.

To everything.

She said, "You made forts and tents. You played with LEGOs and action figures. All that stuff is still there if you can believe it. His room. My mother turned it into a shrine."

"I don't think they saved anything of mine." He nodded up toward the house.

"Sorry," she said. "Your father. I guess he wasn't the most sentimental guy. Not in the traditional way."

"Did you know him well?" he asked.

Did she? Not really. What had she been doing all this time?

"Only really through your brother. Sorry."

"It's okay. Seeing all this research, and Opus 6. It's better than old toys, right? And it shows that he . . ."

"Loved you," she said, and her face pulsed hot.

He nodded and turned away from her and sifted through some clippings. She faced the whiteboards, overwhelmed with useless facts.

"Did you really mean what you said?" He had moved over to a small desk and was riffling through the papers there. "That you think we're hiding something?"

Avery looked at him, felt him transforming before her eyes—from an alien fake person into a real-life boy. Someone not to fear or distrust. Someone, maybe, to . . . pity? Or love?

"I'm *really sorry* I said that," she said, pretty sure that she meant it.

"Why the change of heart? Why trust me now?"

Why.

Why.

Why?

She wanted a good reason.

She said, "I guess if you really *were* hiding something, you'd come back with a better alibi—not this crazy story about not being able to remember anything."

He nodded.

She nodded.

Some kind of agreement.

They both went back to looking around.

But she couldn't stop herself, couldn't hold her tongue. Needed to know whether he was with Scarlett without actually asking . . .

She said, "It seems like Adam and Sarah are a couple. Which would be really weird, right?" Her face felt hot. "Like if they somehow remembered that?"

"Yes," he said flatly. "That would be weird."

And the way he said it, she just *knew.*

She'd had a calendar once—one she'd made by hand with a ruler and pen. It was a countdown to the approximate day she'd be able to go away to college. She wondered where it was now. Wondered whether anything—anyone—could get her to stay.

"My father is going to post a reward," she said. "For information leading to finding Max."

Lucas said, "That's great."

"He thinks it's just going to bring the crazy people out, but I said he has to do it anyway."

Talking was a good distraction from feeling her heart being broken without warning. A balloon that had a tear in it before it had even had a chance to fill up and float.

"Sometimes crazy people know what they're talking about." Lucas was looking through another stack of papers, oblivious to the fact that everything he said or did now mattered in a new way she didn't even understand.

"You think?" Maybe she was the crazy person here. Allowing herself to even feel . . . what . . . *attracted* to him? Like she was falling, and in a way that she'd never fallen for Sam.

"Sometimes, right?"

"I don't know." She flipped through some papers, too, and now couldn't get Sam out of her mind. "*Some* crazy people think that those memories of yours are clues to some target you're all going to blow up when you awaken from your brainwashed trance."

He got very still, and she half wondered whether he couldn't say for sure or not if it was true.

"You're serious?" He sounded so innocent, almost hurt. He was that new human again. His skin not toughened in the right places.

She nodded and he shook his head, like he was disappointed in whoever was saying that—or in her—then went back to sifting.

He had his back to her so she was able to take in the whole of him. The way his shirt stretched a touch too tightly across his shoulders, the way his jeans fit just right, the way he stood—feet pointed straight ahead, perfectly aligned with his shoulders. Like a castle guard.

Beyond his sneakers, back against the wall behind the desk, an old book lay near a large clump of dust. "There's something back there."

She went over and bent down and couldn't reach, so she had to get on her bare knees—rug burn—and stretch far enough that she pulled a muscle in her arm. Nerve endings in her neck woke up, annoyed.

It was an old paperback—like from the 1960s or '70s was her best guess.

It was the kind of thing she'd find on the bookshelves in the guest room where she slept when they went to see her grandparents—small, dusty, pulpy.

When she stood and read the description, he was so close that she could hear his breathing, feel his elbow against hers, bone on bone.

IN A FUTURISTIC SOCIETY, SCIENTISTS INSPIRED BY FREUD, WHO SAID THAT THERE'S NO SUCH THING AS A HAPPY CHILDHOOD, HAVE SET OUT TO ELIMINATE CHILDHOOD COMPLETELY. BEGINNING WITH SIX TEST SUBJECTS, THEY HAVE PERFECTED AN ELABORATE MEMORY-WIPING TECHNOLOGY.

NOW THE COUNTDOWN IS ON, TO THE DAY WHEN ALL CHILDREN WILL BE SENT AWAY FOR A PERIOD OF TIME THAT WILL COME TO BE KNOWN AS THE LEAVING.

"I don't understand," Lucas said.

Avery felt a singular chill run through their bodies.

Scarlett

Scarlett knew the answers to all the history questions, filled in a map of the world without blinking, and was a virtual math whiz. She imagined the others had all come back with the same skill set and liked the idea that they could all sail through high school as seniors next year, get into good colleges, and just forget about The Leaving—

/ /

/

/

/

Forget about The Leaving?

The thought made her happy anyway.

She had more memories from before The Leaving than she'd realized—only thought of them because Sashor had asked.

Like so:

Remembered drawing a picture book in preschool, about a girl named Jane who had a pet dolphin.

Remembered dressing up as a mermaid for one Halloween.

Remembered falling off a high pool ladder at her mother's friend's house—blood cutting a river down her leg.

When Sashor seemed to be done with his questions, she asked, "Do you think it's possible we'll start to remember? Like in a year or even ten?" Because she didn't want to find herself, a decade from now, in that Adirondack chair, surrounded by fluffy, raked piles of red and yellow leaves, suddenly remembering the horrors of her lost childhood. That would ruin the scene entirely.

"I'm honestly not sure," Sashor said. "There was a famous case of something called *transient global amnesia.* A man who just turned up at a Burger King one day and had no idea how he'd gotten there or who he was. He had a handful of vague memories about his life, but no one ever came forward to ID him.

"That is *really depressing.*" She wondered whether Tammy would have come to claim her at Burger King if she'd had to. "Is that what you think we have?"

She watched Sashor.

Counted his blinks.

One.

Two.

Three.

"No"—his eyes wide open and unblinking now—"I mention it only as an example of how complex and unpredictable these kinds of retrieval disorders can be."

"Retrieval disorder," she repeated, thinking that was a good term to describe the situation with the object inside her, too.

There was still no, well, *movement.*

Sashor said, "It's possible the memories are still there and that your brain just can't access them."

"Eleven years' worth of memories?"

Tried really hard then.

To retrieve.

Like with a long arm.

/ /

/

/

"Well, you have to remember that the average sixteen-year-old only has a limited number of memories of the last eleven years of their life as well."

Now she felt her own blink. "How many?"

376

4,567

1,111

6,984

786

7,493

3,049

65,097

11

300,009,099

8,765

9,089,888

100,000,000,006,000,000,000

85,968

85,969

"No way to know for sure, but think about it this way. The majority of people walking around probably have no exact memory of their eighth birthday or tenth birthday or of their ninth Christmas or any of that."

Normal people don't remember everything.

Normal people forget.

Do normal people ever have just one memory that is so . . .

very . . .

unrelenting/unavoidable/unfathomable?

"The hot air balloon and carousel and all," she said. "Do you think those things even happened?"

She'd spent her time in the waiting room searching for hot air balloon companies and carousels in the area on her phone.

Horse stables, too.

It was useless.

So far, Lucas's plea to the world to help them had turned up nothing, and she had zero expectation that it would.

"As I told Lucas and Kristen," Sashor said, "it's a lot easier to implant a fake memory than it is to erase a real one—though it's true that people are having success in treating trauma victims with post-traumatic stress by just recasting the trauma—like if they witnessed a car accident or something awful. But the reverse is much easier. So it's possible that the hot air balloon memory was implanted in you, though to what end? It would be one thing if you remembered that your captor was a man, say, with a scar on his forehead. Because if that were a fake fact, an implanted memory, it would throw the police off the trail. A hot air balloon? What's the point?"

/

/

/

He went on to say that the problem now was that "source errors" could creep into their minds. That, at least in terms of helping to locate Max, Scarlett and the others were becoming less reliable with each passing second.

"You'll think you're recovering your own memory," he explained, "when it's actually something you pulled out of a news report or movie or article."

/ /

Great.

She asked, "Do you think hypnosis could really help?"

Then tried to imagine it.

You are getting sleepy.

Very

very

sleepy. zzzzzzzzzz

Was that how it really worked?

“I have my doubts,” Sashor said. “The person Kristen is working with has been at the center of an ongoing controversy for years now. She’s been involved in a few prominent abuse trials, and there’s concern about false recovered memories.”

“She said she remembers not liking me,” Scarlett said. “How does that work? Like memories of emotions?”

It was a nice, roundabout way of asking about her longing for Lucas.

She’d answered “yes” to the question about being in love.

She couldn’t recall a single incident of kissing, but had visceral memory of what it would feel like.

Had felt like.

With him.

Last night, at Opus 6, it was all coming together.

So many rocks and winding, looping paths.

She liked it there.

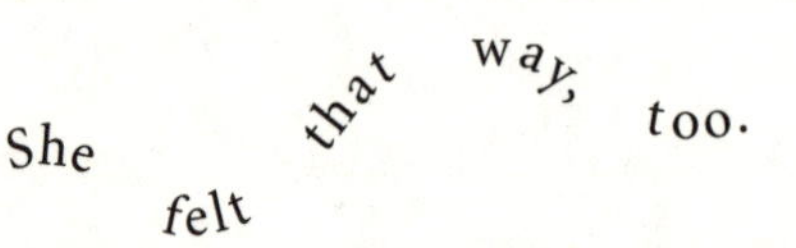

Maybe when they got together later—just the two of them, like they’d planned—they’d *know.*

Know what, though?

Something.

Anything.

Sashor said, "That aspect of memory is still one of the most mysterious."

"Do you think it's weird that I'm not sure I *want* to remember where we were?" she asked then.

He shrugged. "What *do* you want?"

She considered saying "To be with Lucas" or "To be with Lucas again."

What she said instead was another truth. "I want Tammy—that's my mother—to accept that aliens weren't involved."

He laughed.

"No," she said. "For real."

"Oh." He cleared his throat. "Well, that's unfortunate."

Scarlett liked this guy.

"I did a study once of people who claimed they were abducted by aliens," he said, surprising her. "I wanted to try to see if they were prone to false memories in other facets of life."

"What did you find out?"

"That people who think they were abducted by aliens *really* want to believe they were abducted by aliens." He smiled and picked up a tiny horseshoe from a game on his desk, tossed it at a small sand box, missed the pole. "And that they get mad at you if you suggest that maybe they experienced an episode of sleep paralysis and it was scary and now this is how their brain has constructed a script around it. It gives their life meaning."

"That sounds like her, all right. She keeps saying how we were chosen. For this special thing."

"Well, you were," he said, and he wrote down the word "chosen," underlined it. "But probably not by aliens. Just don't tell her I said that."

"So I'm pretty much doomed," she said.

"You'll be okay," he said. "You're strong. All of you. And you seem like, I don't know, good kids. So whoever raised you seems to have done a decent job, if you discount the fact that it wasn't his or her or their right to do it in the first place. Either that, or you all formed a support system for each other."

"Can I try?" She nodded at the game, and he pushed it toward her.

"Actually I have one more question for you," he said. "It's really just for my own research purposes."

She took the tiny horseshoe in her hand and aimed. "What's that?" she asked.

"I know you were only five, but do you remember anything that was happening *in the world* before you disappeared?"

"Such as?"

"Anything. Like a presidential election or space shuttle launch. I'm interested in when a shift occurs and memory starts to include not just small personal memories but has more context in the world."

Scarlett's kneejerk feeling was to just say no, but she took a minute.

The world?

The news?

Her mother's clippings came to mind.

"Oh, like that school shooting?" she said, adjusting her grip on the toy.

"You remember hearing about that?" Sashor sat up straighter.

Well . . .

"No," she said. "I saw it mentioned in some articles about The Leaving." She tossed and her horseshoe clinked around the pole. "I imagine that would be the kind of thing my mother would have gone out of her way to make sure I didn't hear about, right? Since I was going to be going to the school."

"Probably, yeah," he said. "Makes sense." He held up another tiny horseshoe. "My turn."

Lucas

Ryan wasn't home for Lucas to ask questions about the book, so he started reading it.

The Leaving, by Daniel Orlean—copyright 1968—was a slim 150 pages.

The author bio said only that Orlean lived in Florida and this was his first novel.

In it, Frank Mamet has decided that he doesn't want his son, Joseph, to go away to the newly enforced government Leaving period. "They think they can raise my kids better than I can?" he says at one point. "They're wrong. Because sure, children should be protected from society's evils—but by *their parents*—and they simply can't be raised without an awareness of the realities of the world around them. A whole generation oblivious to the truth of the human condition is a recipe for the collapse of society."

On the eve of Joseph's Leaving, Frank takes Joseph on the run. And while they're being chased down by Leaving police, he tries to teach Joseph what life was like before the new government was formed and The Leaving started—telling him stories prompted by a small collection of old family photos. All the while, they are searching for a mysterious man who supposedly grants exceptions to families who are willing to go to work for a burgeoning shadow government.

His wife *wants* her children to go away like all the other kids. She wants them to be protected from the horrors of childhood; she is newly diagnosed with cancer and wants her children to not witness her decline and death. She wants them to *leave* and come back like the others have, with memories of having had a happy young life.

Frank has taken their son against her wishes.

Eventually Frank finds a community of people who are off the grid, living the old-fashioned way. Raising families together in an underground city cut off from society. He very much wants to stay, but he has left behind a dying wife and a daughter. So he leaves his son there and goes out to try to bring them back.

Turns out, his wife has died and his daughter is being cared for by a very pro-Leaving neighbor. He has to kill the woman—a childless widow—to claim his daughter and bring her with him. Alas, forces align against them and they are caught. He's sent to prison. His daughter is sent to The Leaving. His only hope is that his son will one day rise up and fight back. His son, the keeper of those family photos, the keeper of all that is real about life and loss, may one day become a hero.

By the time he was done reading, Lucas was starving. The pickings were slim, so he grabbed a slice of cold pizza and wondered whether he knew how to cook. If he didn't, it was time to learn.

What was taking Scarlett so long?

Why hadn't she texted yet?

The keeper of photos.

The camera tattoo.

He went back to his room and lay down on the sagging mattress, watching dust dance.

His brain sought connections but found none.

Then, soon, noises.

Ryan.

Miranda.

The TV.

The news:

"*Meanwhile, the victims of The Leaving are starting to be met with increasing skepticism about their story that they don't remember anything about the past eleven years, or about Max Godard, whose fate remains unknown.*"

Lucas got up and joined them just in time to see the clip of Avery playing again:

"*They must know something.*"

He shouldn't have rushed her out of the RV like that.

Shouldn't have told her that, no, she could not come talk to Ryan with him.

They'd exchanged phone numbers before she left, and he'd promised her updates, but she was a distraction.

"Have you ever seen this book?" Lucas held it out to Ryan. Miranda went to his side to also look.

"No." Ryan took it from him and thumbed the pages, and the air suddenly smelled old, borderline vomit-y. Then he turned to the cover, to study the illustration of small children in pods beneath the title: *The Leaving.* "Was it out there?"

"Out where?" Miranda asked.

"Yes." Lucas ignored her. "You've really never seen it?"

"No." Ryan turned it over.

Miranda stood at his shoulder also reading the back cover. "That is messed up," she said, almost too quickly.

"There've been a few books," Ryan said.

"This was written in 1968."

"Wait, wait, wait," Ryan said. "This is ringing a bell now. Dad was writing to some author's son or something. It was a few years ago. I'd stopped paying attention and he'd stopped telling me what he was doing anyway."

"Where's his computer?"

"Bedroom."

They went down the hall together, and Miranda followed. Ryan powered up the laptop on the desk in the corner, and they waited.

Lucas hadn't been in there yet, hadn't seen how his father had been living—in a small brown room that barely fit the queen bed and desk. Lucas was sure there had once been curtains with flowers on them, perfume bottles on a silver tray reflecting sunlight. But she was long gone and all that was, too.

Miranda had the book now. "If you don't mind my saying it, this is a stretch."

Lucas said, "Scarlett told her mother she was *going to the leaving.*"

"All right, all right," Miranda said. "So you think it's the author? Or his son?"

"Maybe," Lucas said. "I don't know."

But it had to mean something.

When the monitor lit, Ryan clicked to an e-mail bookmark, and the mail loaded. Lucas went to sit at the desk.

There was a lot of recent spam and more than thirty-five thousand e-mails in the account, so Lucas searched for the name Orlean and found a correspondence with the author's son, Paul, from several years ago.

Thank you for your letter, Paul had written. *I handle all my father's correspondence now that he has gotten on in years.*

"I'll read through this," Lucas said. "I'll tell you what I find."

Ryan nodded—"Of course"—and took Miranda's hand, and they left.

I would say that my father's novel became a cult classic in the truest sense of the word. It's not that it was cherished by a small group of people; it's that it became doctrine for a smaller group of fringe elements. People who really thought the country was going to hell and that the government could do something about it. He has a few boxes of fan mail, which makes it look like he has a lot of fans, but they're mostly repeat customers. People who called him a visionary. He was, for a time, a well-respected scientist, but his reputation suffered after he wrote the novel. (Mind you, the print run was minuscule.) People thought he started to let the more "out there" ideas he put forth in the novel creep into his research and that he'd lost his way. Maybe he had. Anyone who saw any value in his scientific work, which focused on erasing memories, mostly saw applications for PTSD, but he started to move away from that line of research.

Which is a long way of saying that yes, it's possible the situation you are describing has something to do with his work, though I can't for the life of me see a direct connection—unless perhaps . . . a fan?

His father had written back,

Can you send me the letters? Or the names and addresses of his biggest fans? Did you ever speak to the police after my son and the others disappeared? Didn't you see a connection?

That e-mail was never replied to.

How had his father even found the book?

Lucas's own Google search turned up almost no hits, and none of the coverage Lucas had seen of The Leaving had mentioned it at all.

Had his father gone to the police with it?

Lucas opened a new window, and his fingers went to work. He knew how to type, and quickly. He composed his e-mail without a single wrong keystroke:

It is with regret that I write to inform you that my father, Will, with whom you had corresponded on this matter, has died. I'm his son—returned after eleven years with no memory of that time—as you may see if you follow the news at all. I was hoping we could meet? I am interested in this line of research my father was pursuing with regard to your father's book and fan base as potential inspiration for this crime.

He hit Send, then found a barely-there Wikipedia page about Daniel Orlean.

Noted again that he lived in Florida.

Then mapped directions to Tarpon Springs.

A day trip.

Easy.

Clicking away from the window, he noticed the screen saver for the first time. It was a photo of him, Ryan, and their mom and dad. On the beach. Smiling. His mother with heavy black sunglasses on. He wanted very much to see her eyes through them but couldn't, so he closed his eyes and tried to picture them there but drew a blank.

His phone buzzed.

I'm home, Scarlett had written.

On my way, he wrote back.

The computer dinged.

The e-mail had bounced as undeliverable.

AVERY

They were hanging out on the lanai eating popcorn and making a list of suspects who might have written the note as a prank.

"Morgan Bestler?" Emma said.

"She loves me!" Avery said.

"Never mind!" Emma laughed.

"What? She doesn't like me?"

"I don't know. Maybe?"

Chambers had sworn her to secrecy and she'd sworn Sam and Emma. It wouldn't be her fault if they blabbed. And to her credit, she didn't say a word about the old book. Lucas's secret she felt she had to keep, if only to keep his trust now that she had it.

If she even did?

At the very least, she had his phone number. That was something.

"I'm thinking Maggie Corrigan." Avery couldn't decide if she wanted to bother swimming or not. "She's just evil for evil's sake sometimes, you know? And she had a crush on Sam around the time we started going out."

"Don't drag me into this," Sam said. He got up. "I'm going in."

He took his shirt off and Avery felt a pang of regret with the feeling of knowing she had to end it. He was cute, just not . . . right. He dove in and she made a wish that when he resurfaced, she'd see his face and think, *Of course I want to be with him. Why wouldn't I?* But when he came up and wiped his lids before opening his eyes and flicked his hair off his forehead, she felt nothing.

"What if it's really him?" Emma said. "What if it's really Max and he's just scared?"

"I highly doubt he'd write a note and put it in your mailbox," Sam said. "How would he even know the address? It's not like he'd remember? Would he?"

"No," Emma said. "Probably not."

"And if he can show up here to drop a note off, why not ring the doorbell? It makes no sense."

"I'm telling you," Avery said. "It's Maggie Corrigan. It has to be."

Emma said, "She's definitely at the top of the list."

"Oh, man." Avery lay back in her lounger and put her sunglasses back on. Rita was inside vacuuming and Avery found the sound comforting. "I need to plot my revenge."

Sam said, "I want no part of whatever evil scheme you dream up." He grabbed his stuff, kissed Avery on the lips quickly, and said, "I've got to go."

"All right," Emma said when he'd left. "I'm dying. I'm going in."

She got up and adjusted her polka-dot suit and dove in and then swam underwater the length of the pool. When she surfaced at the far end, she pushed off and backstroked back to Avery.

"Do you think they'll go to school?" she asked, putting her forearms on the pool edge and resting her chin on her hands.

"Who?"

"The ones who are back."

"I guess so," Avery said. "What else would they do?"

"It's weird to think about," Emma said. "That one guy is hot."

"Lucas?" Avery's gut tightened.

"No. The other guy."

"Oh, right. Yeah. Good."

"Good?" Emma pushed up out of the pool and grabbed her towel. "Why good?"

"You have to promise you won't tell Sam. Or anyone."

Emma crossed her heart and rolled her eyes. She shook her hair in Avery's direction, getting her wet.

"I went to see Lucas yesterday. We spent some time in the old RV his dad has—had?—that I told you about. We were friends when we were kids and stuff. It's just weird to see him now and, well—"

"You're *crushing* on this guy?"

"I wouldn't call it a *crush*." Avery suddenly felt older and wiser than Emma. "We have something, is all. Some kind of bond."

"I thought you didn't trust him," Emma said. "I thought for sure I saw you on the news saying something like that."

"I do now. At least I think I do. The way he looks at me—"

"In my world, we call that a crush."

"Since when do you watch the news?" Avery asked.

"Only since it involves my best friend!" Emma sat down and got settled again with a magazine. "Do you think any of them have had sex? And like forgotten?"

"That would be such a waste," Avery said. "I mean, to finally decide to do that and get it out of the way and then not know?"

"Seriously," Emma said.

And Avery sat wondering about Lucas. And Scarlett. But she mostly tried to push the idea of it out of her mind. They were only a year older than her, and tons of kids waited longer than that. She grabbed Emma's magazine and said, "All right, lady. Let's hear this audition song of yours."

"Now? Here?"

"All the world's a stage, my dear."

Emma pulled her tank dress on over her swimsuit and stood by the pool steps and sang "When I Grow Up" from *Matilda the Musical,* which everyone had wanted to be the school play, but it wasn't allowed for some annoying rights reason. Emma was pretty much nailing it, and Avery was suddenly very grateful for her sunglasses because it was a weirdly sad song about how things will be better when you're grown up and, frankly, she wasn't so sure. She felt herself bloating with emotion and willed it back down.

Cheers erupted from a distance when Emma was done. Avery got up and joined her looking out toward the bay, where a small motorboat was passing. A bunch of older guys holding beers whooped and clapped.

"Can we come over?" one of them screamed.

"Oh my god," Emma said.

Avery cupped her hands by her mouth and shouted back, "Losers!"

Emma pinched her arm. "Why do you have to be like that?"

"Because I am," Avery said.

A pirate tour boat was next to pass—larger, farther out in the water. It was painted black and flew a skull-and-crossbones flag. Avery had never been on a pirate boat and thought that if she'd had a brother *longer,* she would have.

Someone with a too-loud microphone said, "Land ho, mateys!"

"You're going to break up with Sam, aren't you?" Emma said.

Avery said, "Afraid so."

They went back to magazines, and Avery got her phone out and went to Amazon and eBay, and there appeared to be no copies of *The Leaving* for sale . . . anywhere.

Or, wait, one, but it was in Wisconsin and cost thirty-five dollars and how long would it even take to receive it? And where the hell were her flip-flops? And why did he have to grab the book like that? Why hadn't he asked her to go up to the house to talk to Ryan with him? *She'd* been the one to find it.

How could a book that sounded inspired by The Leaving have been written before The Leaving?

She ordered the copy in Wisconsin—even sprang for expedited shipping. She'd figure out the connection, and she'd go to Lucas with it and he'd realize how amazing she was. Together they'd figure out where Max was. The thought of it made her heart tangle and flip like tumbleweed. She imagined it rolling down the street and plunging softly into the canal where manatees sometimes came to stay warm.

Scarlett

Brushing her hair, Scarlett felt the weight of it dragging her down and suddenly very badly wanted a haircut.

Who had been cutting her hair all these years?

Maybe it wasn't actually the clothes that were wrong?

Maybe it was the hair?

She hunted for scissors and then went into the bathroom. Using a comb, she wet her hair a little, then she pulled half a head full over her left shoulder and chopped off four inches in jagged cuts.

XSnip.

X

Snip.X

XXXXXXXXXXX

XSnip.

XXXXXXXX

X

XClumps . . .

Falling and feathering to the floor.

When she went to do the other side, she realized, of course, that she couldn't, so she went to find her mother and presented the scissors. "I need help."

Looking horrified, Tammy said, "What on earth . . . ?" then stopped herself with a disappointed huff. "Come. Sit."

They'd had an argument.

Scarlett had declined an invitation to go meet some of Tammy's friends tonight at the Abduction Group gathering. Since then, their interactions had been limited to short exchanges every time Scarlett came out of the bathroom.

Anything?

No.

Anything?

No.

So this was progress.

Tammy put her scissors down and ran her hands through Scarlett's hair, fluffing it up some. "Best I can do," she said.

"Thanks."

She turned and grabbed a magazine and a glass of lemonade she'd already poured and said, "I'll be out back. Back to the grind tomorrow so better get some sun."

Yes.

Better do that.

Now Scarlett waited on the front steps, studying the front yard for ghosts of her childhood self. She tried to conjure an apparition of herself blowing bubbles or skipping rope, but couldn't.

What had ever happened to that pink flamingo, anyway? She'd have to ask Tammy later.

Lucas appeared on a bike and came to an awkward, almost-crash stop out front on the sand. He leaned the bike against a palm tree and walked with purpose toward her. She half thought he was going to grab her and kiss her, from the look of intensity on his face, and she felt her whole body perk up at the idea of it.

A tingling in her lips.

And other places.

All over.

He held out a book to her. "I found this in my dad's stuff."

She took it from him and read the title, and he said, "It was written before we were taken," and felt like she was back on that cliff of her life.

This time, her existence was . . .

. . . an

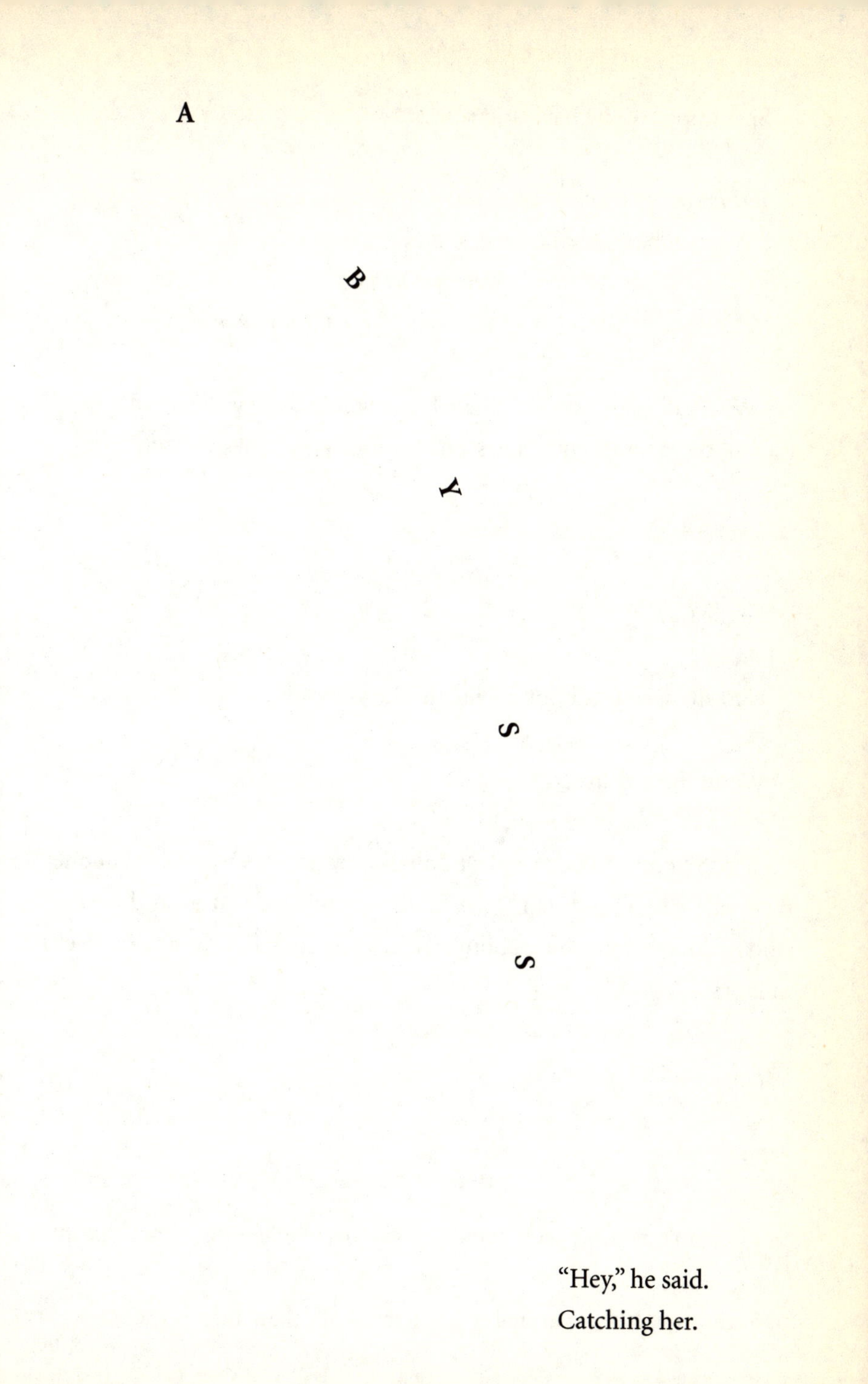

"Hey," he said.
Catching her.

She flipped to the back and read.

Futuristic . . .

Eliminate childhood . . .

Memory-wiping . . .

Countdown . . .

"Where did he get this?" She felt her whole body wake up in a new way, all those lights going back on at once. "What does it mean?"

I'm going on a trip.

To the leaving.

Had she seen this book—*read* this book?

When she was five?

"I don't know," Lucas said. "I don't know how he even heard about it or where he found it. There's hardly anything about it on the web. And of course everything about *us* comes up first. But the author lives in Florida."

/ /

/ /

/

"We can't possibly have been in pods this whole time," Scarlett said.

Pods on Earth was arguably a worse theory than alien pods.

"Not *literally*, no," Lucas said. "I don't think so. It's really only the concept that's the same. They start with six kids as test subjects before the whole thing goes wide."

"And they don't remember anything when they come back?" Scarlett asked.

"No, they remember. But they remember an awesome childhood. An entirely fake childhood. And there are sort of hints that these new types of kids—ones who've been to The Leaving—when they come back, they just can't cope with reality, even though they seem like they have it all together. So the book is about how if you sanitize childhood, society will implode. Oh and the kids all know they're going; they know before that it's happening."

/ /

"Like I did."

/

/

She wanted to call for Tammy, but wasn't allowed to call her Tammy. She had completely mastered avoidance of the direct address.

"Come with me."

She went out to the backyard where Tammy was sitting on a folding chair with her feet in an inflatable kiddie pool shaped like a fish. "Have you ever seen this?" Scarlett held the book out.

"No," Tammy said. "Why?" She spied Lucas and sat upright.

Took her sunglasses off.

"It's really you," she said.

"It's really me," he said.

Tammy stood and went to hug him. "I still can't believe it," she said. "That you're back. That Will's gone."

Lucas seemed receptive to the hug, and Scarlett hated to ruin the moment but . . .

"Have you ever seen this?" She held the book out again, more firmly.

Really wanting an explanation.

Needing something to

shift

and make sense.

She said, "It's a book about a society where kids are sent away for their childhoods."

"There were a bunch of books written about it." Tammy finally let go of Lucas.

Scarlett felt her breathing change and deepen. Had she been jealous? Of the hug? Of contact? She said, "This was written *before* it happened."

"My father had it," Lucas said.

"In that old RV?" Tammy returned to her chair and pulled her sunglasses back down. "Did he talk to the police about it?"

"I don't know," Lucas said.

Scarlett looked at Lucas pointedly. "Let's go in and do that."

Back in the house, she stood at the kitchen aisle. "Where in Florida does he live? Were you able to find *his address*?"

"No, but I found the town. Tarpon Springs. We could go there, maybe. Ask around? My dad was e-mailing with his son a few years ago, but the e-mail I sent bounced."

"So we stop people in the street?" She had no idea what their next steps should be but for some reason felt that it shouldn't be calling the police. "What would we even ask him?"

"I don't know. Where he got the idea? If he has any theories about us?" A look of fear and excitement on his face all at once. "For all we know, it's *him*."

"Do you *want* to talk to Chambers?" she asked, making it clear in her tone that she didn't.

"What are you two plotting?" Tammy was there; she'd brought the scent of her sunscreen—coconut and chemicals—with her.

"Nothing," Scarlett said.

Tammy went to the fridge and refilled her lemonade. "Liar."

Scarlett said, "We were thinking of trying to talk to the author."

"You don't think Will did that already? Or Chambers?"

Scarlett started piecing things together. "Chambers would have shown it to you if he knew about it. He would have asked you about it, since I was the one who said I was going to the leaving. He would have asked *us* about it yesterday."

Tammy twisted her mouth to one side. "Suppose you're right."

Scarlett felt something inside her turn sour when she said, "It looks like in the book this is an advanced society that is aware of and in communication with intelligent life-forms on other planets."

Tammy's eyes turned beady.

Rightfully so.

Scarlett said, "I'll go with you tonight, if you let me do this."

Tammy picked up her lemonade and turned toward the hall. "You want to find someone like that. A writer. You go and you ask around in the bars." From down the hall she called out, "The dive-ier the better."

Scarlett turned to Lucas and almost laughed.

He raised his eyebrows and smiled. "It's actually a really good idea. What's tonight?"

"Long story," she said. "Should we invite Kristen?"

Lucas seemed to stiffen when he said, "If you feel like you have to."

Scarlett was shaking her head. "Not really."

Had to trust this.

Trust him.

With everything.

Had to start now.

She said, “She told me she thinks she remembers not liking me.”

“I’ve been feeling like I’m not sure I like her,” he said. “So just us?”

She nodded. “Just us.”

The words felt familiar.

Just us.

Just them.

Against . . . the world?

What?

She said, “I have something inside me, Lucas. Something I swallowed but of course I don’t remember doing it. It’s metal and oval. Turned up on the MRI.”

He touched her arm softly. “Are you going to be okay?”

“Yes.” She nodded.

“Are you in pain?” he asked.

“No.”

Had he even *thought* about kissing her?

“So you’re just . . . waiting?”

She nodded again.

“I have a tattoo,” he said. “It’s like a camera shutter.”

Click.

Say cheese.

Tried to picture what that would even look like, in ink.

/ /

/

/ /

/

"Where?"

He pointed.

Where he pointed.

Intimate.

All of this too intimate.

Showed her a picture on his phone.

Made her

stomach

flip.

"We're going to figure this out," he said. "So we'll go in the morning?"

"Yes."

They lingered there a moment, and then he said, "Can you take me somewhere now, actually? I don't have a car and—"

"Of course." Thinking anywhere. "Where?"

He said, "I want to buy a camera."

Lucas

He left her reading in the car and went into a large electronics store. They hadn't been able to find a proper camera shop close enough, so this would have to do.

He'd wanted her to come in with him.

He could tell her all about the book, already had.

But no, she wanted to read it herself, couldn't wait. Because what if only she could make the connection?

The news was on a wall of televisions inside, and they were talking about The Leaving. Apparently nothing else was happening in the world, or at least in Florida.

"*. . . explain the distrust?*" the anchor was saying.

A man in a suit was saying,

"*The whole community down here was a part of this thing, you know? You'd be hard-pressed to find someone who wasn't deeply impacted by this when it happened.*"

Lucas stopped for a moment, watched.

"People came from miles away to help with the search; there were vigils and there was a whole ribbon campaign if you recall, with people tying ribbons on trees and mailboxes."

All too strange.

"Even years later, the turnout at those anniversary vigils at Opus 6 was huge. This was not a personal tragedy. So there are a lot of people who feel very emotional about this, and to have them come back . . . but not all of them. It leaves a sour taste."

Lucas turned away from TVs to find cameras.

"People want the happy ending, they want answers, they want, mostly, someone to blame. And if we can't blame the person responsible, there's a tendency, yes, to blame the victim."

There was a good-size selection—a long row of cameras loosely wired to the display shelf—but Lucas couldn't spend a fortune, so he narrowed the choices quickly. Ryan had given him some cash to keep him going while they waited for their father's estate to be settled, at which point Ryan guessed they'd have enough to live on for a year or so if they were lucky.

Lucas began handling the cameras in his price range to see how they felt. He liked the styling of some and not others and didn't like snap and shoots, felt drawn to more elaborate machines with manual lenses. He held up a SONY he liked the feel of and peered through the viewfinder, one eye closed.

"I see we have a shutterbug." A saleswoman leaned on the display with a bony elbow.

"Excuse me?" He lowered the camera.

"Most people these days just hold it up and look at the screen."

"Oh," he said, scrolling through some controls to see how intuitive or not the setup seemed. "Yeah. I guess so."

"Do I know you?" She tilted her head; her name tag said her name was Meg, and she looked maybe forty, forty-five? "You're real familiar-like."

Her voice had shifted in a way he didn't like; the wall of TVs still blared that there were no new developments in the case of his life. He said, "I think I'm going to take this one."

She unlocked a cabinet beneath the display and slid out a SONY box.

He followed her to the register and she rang up the camera while studying him curiously. All at once the TVs switched to a baseball game. He handed over a wad of bills.

"I just figured it out." She held out his change. "I *do* know you."

"No offense"—he took his change, folding the bills around the coins and shoving them in his front pocket—"but you don't *know* me."

Her lips curled with offense.

"Maybe you *recognize* me," he said. "But don't for a second think you *know* me."

He grabbed the camera bag and turned to go.

"No one believes your story," she called out after him.

The automatic door slid open and he stepped out, heart hammering at his ribs.

Camera crews had the car surrounded.

He had to fight his way through them to get to the passenger-side door.

Inside, Scarlett was in tears.

"What do you think it is?" a reporter shouted. "Why do you think you would swallow something?"

Then another, louder: "Why aren't you doing more to help find Max?"

"Start the car," Lucas said.

She nodded but didn't move.

"Start the car," he repeated.

This time, she turned the ignition with a shaky hand and put the car in reverse and inched back; the reporters pulled away and scattered and banged on the car some, but she just kept going, slow and steady, and in a moment they were free.

"I like your haircut," he said at a stop sign, and her hand went to her neck.

She said, "Thanks."

AVERY

It was a ridiculous thing to be jealous of. Scarlett, with some mysterious object inside her, at the center of the drama. Avery was on the outskirts and didn't like it out here. She needed to be closer to the action, closer to information. Because her mother was going downhill fast. She spent her days pacing and her nights fighting panic attacks. She'd wake up thinking she heard a knock on the door, then cry uncontrollably when it ended up not being anyone at all. Avery actually found herself wishing for a Mannequin Mom. She'd pose her by the pool with an umbrella drink and leave her there until all this was over.

"What do you think it is?" Emma asked.

They were on the beach; Emma had insisted. The hotel they were parked near was having a Hula-Hoop contest.

"I honestly have no idea." Avery was watching one contestant in particular; thinking maybe if *Scarlett* did some Hula-Hooping the object would get unhinged and come out faster. She'd thought about calling Lucas maybe three hundred times today already.

"I can't imagine what she feels like," Emma said. "The whole world waiting for her . . ."

". . . to take a dump," Avery said.

"Exactly."

Avery shook her head. "I can't really imagine what any of them feels like."

"What do you mean?"

"I just mean the whole thing is messed up. Imagine if you didn't remember the last eleven years."

Emma sat quietly, tilted her head. "Nope. Can't imagine."

Avery laughed. Emma was maybe not the deepest person in the world.

"What?" Emma asked.

"Nothing." Couldn't even explain.

"No, what?"

"You're a good friend, is all." Avery nodded. "Talking about this with me endlessly."

"You're a good friend, too."

"Not lately."

"No?"

Emma was the kind of friend who would give her a kidney if she needed it. Avery wasn't sure she'd give anybody a kidney—let alone Emma.

"I'm keeping secrets from you," Avery said. "Do good friends do that?"

There was no tracking information available on the book. There was no way to track the feelings she was having for Lucas now.

"Maybe I'm keeping some from you, too." Emma shrugged.

"You know who wrote the note?"

"No, of course not. Not that."

Her mother had started checking the mailbox like crazy, too.

"What am I going to do about my mom?" Had the woman even gone beyond the mailbox since this all started again?

"This may make me sound awful," Emma said, "but that's really your dad's problem."

"But he's not dealing."

"Then I don't know. I guess you're just there for her in whatever way you can be, without also losing your mind?"

"I feel like that's my whole life story. If I ever write my biography, that'll be the title. *I Was There*."

There at the bus stop.

There at the police station.

There on the news.

And on his birthday.

And on Christmas.

When they pretended it wasn't really Christmas.

And on the anniversary.

And then his next birthday.

The next anniversary.

And on and on, and in and out of breakdowns and misery for years.

Emma said, "You need a subtitle."

"*I Was There*," Avery said, "*The Story of the Girl Left Behind*."

"Not bad." Emma nodded. "Not bad at all."

Avery stretched out her legs, brushed some sand off one foot with the other. "Do you remember last week?"

"What about it?" Emma giggled, not understanding.

"Last week, my biggest concern in life was buying new flip-flops and getting ready for auditions and planning the many ways in which I could do nothing this week."

"Yeah." Emma sighed. "I liked last week."

A few dolphins were swimming past. People who'd apparently never seen dolphins were making a fuss. "Is it wrong that I don't really have any hope that they'll find him alive?"

"I don't think so," Emma said. "It would be wrong if you didn't *want* them to find him alive."

Avery sat with that thought.

Imagined a teenage brother in the house.

Imagined him damaged, annoying.

Because what if it went that way?

What if his coming home had the potential to actually make things *worse*?

Emma said, "Now is when you're supposed to say '*Of course* I want them to.'"

"Right," Avery said. "Of course."

Scarlett

Walking up a lit pathway to an adobe-style house, Scarlett hoped that aliens might *actually* come and snatch her and spare her this experience.

Trish and Ted lived on a golf course, basically, in a community with clones of houses and fake lakes with fountains, and a pool and clubhouse where people probably played bingo or had a trivia night, maybe a book club. The couple had, they claimed, been abducted together. Which made sense. It was hard to believe that someone who hadn't been abducted would stay married to someone who thought they had.

Six people were gathered in the living room, where cheese cubes in a variety of yellow-orange hues sat on a round glass platter. The couches were floral, stiff. The AC was on too high and Scarlett goose-bumped instantly.

Tammy greeted some of the people with small waves, and one man got up to hug her. Then she presented Scarlett with a bit of fanfare. "This"—she clasped her hands together, like to thank God or *someone* up there—"is my daughter."

"Welcome to our home," Ted said, and Trish, by his side, took Scarlett's right hand in her two hands and squeezed.

Something about the look in her eyes—
so deep and meaningful in intent—
made Scarlett go

/ /

/ /

and say, "I'm not sure I really belong here."

Trish smiled. "Everyone feels that way the first time."

Scarlett was about to explain that she *really* didn't belong.

But it was too late.

Trish took her by the elbow and guided her to a seat by the cheese cubes.

Chatter kicked up as Scarlett busied herself with a too-soft, essentially flavorless piece of possibly cheddar, and soon her mother's voice rose about the others: "She doesn't remember. I thought maybe if she heard your stories . . ."

One by one, they went around the room and shared.

Lost hours.

Lost days.

No memories of how they got to the kitchen floor, let alone naked.

Being levitated on light beams.

Small creatures with big eyes.

Glowing hearts.

Spacecraft large enough to shadow entire city blocks.

Each of them seemed to tell their story as if reciting, like they'd told it a million times before.

Scarlett wondered whether she'd have her script down by the time she reached adulthood, whenever that was.

I was one of the six victims of The Leaving.

Yes, we were gone for eleven years.

No, we don't remember.

No, they never figured it out.

Would she, too, eventually become bored by her own narrative?

If she did end up writing a book, would it be one she even wanted to read?

The room got quiet. She felt the soft pressure of their gazes, like feathers.

"Could you point me toward the restroom?"

Trish stood and pointed. "Just this way."

In the powder room, she checked the time on her phone and saw she had a message from Sarah.

Listened.

"*It's me, Sarah. I think I'm remembering more things. I remembered someone else there with us. But not Max. Another girl, I think. But I don't know. It's like I can only see her as a police sketch in my head or something.*"

Then voices through the line, then Sarah saying, "*I gotta go.*"

Hanging up.

Putting her phone back into her purse, Scarlett examined herself in the mirror—another outfit that felt wrong on every level—and fixed her hair.

Another girl?

/

/ /

/

/

Was Sarah becoming unhinged?

I'm going on a trip.

To the leaving.

Going on a trip.

Tomorrow.

Or was it Scarlett who was losing purchase on reality?

Nothing about the novel had felt familiar at all.

But she'd said it.

I'm going on a trip.

To the leaving.

She felt the urge to go to the bathroom, but not here.

She shut it down.

And realized she could.

So maybe had.

But it wouldn't last.

Couldn't.

"Anything?" Tammy said when she returned to the living room.

"No."

"What are you *waiting* for?" she snapped.

Their feather gazes felt heavier this time around, dead birds on her lap.

Scarlett cast an apologetic look at Tammy. "I really don't think we were abducted."

Ted said, "Maybe the hot air balloon is a trick of the mind. Maybe it was a craft of another kind."

"I didn't remember at first, either," Trish said. "Give it time."

"Tell us something." Ted leaned forward. "Was there something special about Max? Why do you think they would keep him?"

"I don't remember Max," Scarlett said. "Everybody knows that by now, don't they? I mean, it's all over the news, right?"

The walls all seemed to inch just a tiny bit closer.

"Some of us have had good experiences with hypnosis," another woman said. "I saw that one of the others has consulted a hypnotist."

Yes, the room was definitely shrinking.

Scarlett needed space to breathe.

She said, "Do any of you know of any group abductions? Like when six people were taken?"

This sparked a lively conversation that Scarlett didn't pay attention to, except to occasionally nod. Mostly, she was watching the walls—which were back where they'd started—and Tammy, who seemed at ease here. So maybe she and her mother were and always would be aliens; maybe the only goal that made sense was peaceful cohabitation on their shared planet until Scarlett was old enough to leave.

Maybe most teenagers felt that way.

"So what did you think?" Tammy asked as they walked to the car after the meeting wound down.

All Scarlett could think to say was, "They seemed nice."

Maybe some of them had been part of Sashor's study.

"Why were we chosen?" Scarlett asked when they got into the car. "Why do you think we, specifically, were chosen?"

"Because I was a terrible mother." Tammy started the car and lit a cigarette. "Because I didn't deserve you. Because I was screwed up and I was going to screw you up, too."

Scarlett opened her window. "A lot of people are bad parents, if you even are."

"Not *as* bad as me." Her mother sniffled and ashed out her window.

"Well, I'm sure you were doing the best you could. And anyway, you changed. You're better now." From the driveway, through the living room bay window, the people inside looked so normal. Scarlett willed her mother to put the car into Drive.

"Am I?" Exhaling smoke through her nose. "Or is it just that I mostly stopped having to be a parent so I couldn't be a bad one? You're here and I'm still your mother, but you don't need me the way you did when you were little." More ash out the window; the cigarette seemed like it wasn't getting any shorter. "I swear, there were days, like when you were throwing some kind of tantrum, like about getting dressed, and I'd just say to myself, *You just have to make it one more hour with her and then she'll go to preschool and you can have a drink.* And I'd have a drink after I dropped you off. At nine in the morning. I used to tell the others moms I walked to pick-up to get the exercise, but it was because I'd be too drunk to drive by noon."

/ / /

"That's why we were chosen. To teach me a lesson."

"Did you learn it? What was the lesson?"

"Bad people don't deserve to have children."

"But they gave me back to you," Scarlett said, trying not to breathe in smoke. "And also, it's not like I was the only one taken."

"The others were no prizes, either," Tammy said. "And yes, I've been given a second chance and I sure as hell won't blow it. But you're practically grown anyway. I could hardly mess you up now."

/ /

"No," Scarlett said. "Somebody else already did that."

/ /

"That's the thing," her mother said. "You don't actually *seem* that screwed up."

She finally started to drive.

At home, the urgency was impossible to ignore.

Something glinting.

Chopsticks.

Tupperware.

Rubber gloves.

Soap.

Paper towels.

Hand sanitizer.

More soap.

More paper towels.

So gross.

Not a locket.

Not a religious medal.

A stretched penny.

"Manatee Viewing Center: Anchor Beach."

"I Love You."

/ / / /

/ /

Just . . .

She washed it again.

Could not wash it enough.

Then put it in a clear disposable glove she took from a box under the sink and tucked it into her skirt pocket.

"Anything?" her mom asked.

Scarlett walked toward her room. "Nope," she called down the hall. "Good night!"

I love you.

I love who?

Who loves me?

She looked up "Anchor Beach" on her phone.

A power plant.

Where manatees go to stay warm in the runoff.

Smokestacks on the water.

White steam mimicking clouds.

A long stretch of beach.

Piers of wonky wooden planks.

She'd been there?

I'm going on a trip.

I love you.

I'm leaving.

DAY THREE

Lucas

Lucas snapped a picture of Miranda when she came out of Ryan's room. He'd been awake since too early, too eager for the day to start, and was on the couch teaching himself how to use his new camera.

"Not this again." She shuffled toward the bathroom.

"Excuse me?" He studied the photo on the screen, liked the lighting but not the framing. He looked up—"Not *what* again?"—and found her blinking at him.

She tilted her head. "I had a boyfriend once. Took pictures of me all the time without asking me if he could. It was annoying."

"Oh," he said. "Sorry."

"Why are *you* up so early?" she said.

"We're going to try to find that author today."

"Yeah?" She scratched her head. "Did you talk to the police about all that?"

"Not yet," he said. "We want to see if there's anything to it first."

She turned to go into the bathroom. "Well, good luck with that."

Scarlett would be there any minute, so Lucas started to pack up a bag. Just his camera. The book. Some cash. He considered going out to the RV and getting the gun and bringing that, too. He could hand it to Scarlett, as a test to see if Scarlett also knew—

CLICK HISS.

Maybe they all did.

And if they did, why?

Had they been *trained*?

She texted that she was there and he went out and it was already too hot and he was overdressed in jeans and a T-shirt.

"Hey," he said, getting into the car.

She wore a gray tank-top dress and had black sandals on, and he had the feeling that each time he saw her she was somehow a little bit more herself. Her knees were knobby and pale by the steering wheel. She handed him a clear pouch of some kind.

"This is it," she said. "This is what I swallowed. I mapped it and it's not that far from Tarpon Springs. We have to go there. Today."

Lucas took the penny out and studied it.

I love you.

Flipped it over; it glinted.

Manatee Viewing Center: Anchor Beach

"Do you remember it?" he asked. "This place?"

"I don't. But I must have been there, right?" She shook her head. "Because why would I swallow something like that? It seems, I don't know . . ."

He completed the thought: "Desperate."

"Yes."

"Which is closer?" he asked. "Tarpon Springs or Anchor Beach?"

"Tarpon Springs." She nodded. "We'll be there in time for lunch."

They suffered through beach traffic, then followed signs for Tampa, Sarasota, Orlando, and something about leaving town—something about the promise of other places—seemed to lift a weight the size of a large stone off Lucas's chest.

He wished he'd told Scarlett everything when he'd told her about the tattoo.

Wished he'd told her about the gun.

Wished he'd told her about . . .

AVERY. THE RV. STANDING SO CLOSE. ON HER KNEES. ELBOWS TOUCHING. ELECTRIC.

No, maybe not that.

How had she learned how to drive?

Had he?

There was no point in asking; she wouldn't know.

Her mother's car's rearview mirror was loaded up with junk. A string of shiny green shamrocks caught the light of the sun. A pair of fuzzy dice entwined with them. An air freshener shaped like an orange, with two green leaves, couldn't do much to fight the smell of cigarettes.

They'd kept the windows down as long as they could, but when they hit the main highway, they had to close up.

She turned the radio on and scanned the stations and listened to a handful of songs for a few seconds each. "I don't know any of these songs," she said. "You?"

"No," he said.

"Do you think we just never listened to music? Or did we somehow just forget that, too?"

"I don't know."

"And why do I know how to drive? It seems like if we could drive we could . . . leave. Or escape."

"Maybe we didn't want to escape," he said. "Maybe we thought wherever we were was where we were supposed to be."

"We must have."

"Who have you told?" he said. "About Anchor Beach?"

"No one," she said. "I thought we should go there first. I don't trust anyone. Except you. Is that weird?"

He shook his head. "Not to me."

"Who have *you* told?" she asked. "About the book. About Orlean."

"Just my brother," he said. "His girlfriend."

A sign for the Ringling Brothers Circus Museum conjured the image of a large statue of an elephant; Lucas imagined figures made out of wood or plastic perched on trapeze bars overhead. He hoped there'd be a big tent, a photo opportunity where you could put your face into a ringmaster's body, with a super tall hat atop it. Or maybe a midway, with funhouse mirrors, where he and Scarlett could stand side by side and be small and tall and warped like he felt inside now that he'd lied to her about Avery.

His guilt ticked up with the car's odometer, increasing with each mile of the long drive.

And yet he kept his mouth shut.

Finally, the exit for Tarpon Springs came up and they drove down a long four-lane road lined with fast-food restaurants and motels with hourly and day rates posted on big white boards with black letters.

At a light, Scarlett turned to him and they shared a look that meant things he couldn't articulate but mostly that they were a team. He was becoming increasingly sure that they had been in love.

And still were?

Could be again?

Had he given her the penny?

Been there with her?

HIS HANDS. HER HAIR. HER MOUTH. HER NECK.
MEMORY? FANTASY? SOURCE ERROR?

Once?

More than once?

But first this.

Daniel Orlean.

"Where do we start?" Scarlett had just parked in a municipal lot and they were heading for the main street through town.

At the top of it, an old boat sat in a canal with a display out front about the town's history as a sponge-fishing hub. Lucas stepped up to an antique scuba suit on display and felt like he knew what the bends felt like; he'd been plunged deep into The Leaving and was now coming up out of it and into the light too quickly, without guidance. A thick rope net full of yellowed sea sponges made him wonder what his brain looked like, with holes in it that hadn't turned up on his MRI. Holes where memories should have been.

Scarlett pointed down the road. The sign on a corner building said "McHale's" beside a shamrock. Unlit neon signs in the window promised Miller High Life and Rolling Rock. Three empty kegs formed a line by the side door.

"Looks pretty dive-y to me." Lucas said.

No one there knew Orlean.

No one at the next place, either.

They were on their fourth bar, and Lucas was thinking it was just about time to either give up or change strategies altogether when the bartender met eyes with him. "Sure! I remember Danny."

AVERY

She'd forgotten entirely about Sam's cousin's wedding. So when Sam had called that morning and asked her if she'd come with him to pick up his suit "for later," she'd panicked and choked and couldn't think of an excuse. So here they were, in Men's Wearhouse. If she'd ever been to a more depressing place, she couldn't remember it.

Rows and rows of suits. All lined up like soldiers in some sleeping army that might at any moment come to life and attack—maybe hit her over the head with a briefcase or strangle her with neckties.

Black troops here.

Gray troops there.

Occasional AWOL brown or cream. Sam disappeared into a dressing room to try on his newly tailored suit, so she sat in a leather armchair and called Emma. There was a lot of background noise on the other end.

"Where *are* you?" Avery asked.

"The mall in Bonita Springs. Oh my god, I just saw Courtney. She told me if you don't audition, she'll probably get the lead and I want to kill her."

Emma said, "Yeah, just hold on a minute." But not to Avery.

"Who are you with?"

"Just my mom and brother," she said. "My brother who is *driving me crazy.*" Then after a second, "I'm so sorry. I didn't mean it. I didn't mean—"

"Don't be ridiculous," Avery said. "Tell him I said to buzz off." The urge to cry snuck up on her and she tried to dodge it. "And listen up. You're a *way* better singer than Courtney. Just make sure you *project.* You'll be onstage. Not in your shower."

"You can't bail on this." Emma sounded far away. "I only wanted to do it because you were doing it and it's like the only remotely fun thing to do between now and summer vacation."

Avery stood and started walking among the suit troops. "It just doesn't feel like a priority right now? Things are so crazy."

"Well, it's good that there's the reward now, right? It'll be good to have answers and it seems like you'll have them soon."

The reward had been announced that morning; a tip line had gone live.

"And then what?" She stopped in front of a wall of ties. Men were so weird. The idea of Sam in a suit . . . something about it bothered her.

"What do you mean?"

"I mean, what then? When there's not this big thing hanging over the three of us anymore."

"You'll get back to normal."

"But we never really were normal."

"Well, then you'll become normal."

Avery closed her eyes and tried to picture normal.

Her and Lucas, girlfriend and boyfriend, kissing at the lockers between classes.

Going to prom together.

Huddling in bleachers on cooler fall afternoons, watching football.

Making out in her room while trying to get homework done.

Going to movies.

Bowling.

The beach.

Her mother decorating for Halloween again, maybe even baking.

"Avery?" It was Sam standing beside her.

"I gotta go," she said into her phone. "Call you later."

"He needs like twenty minutes to fix a problem with the pants," Sam said. "Let's get lunch."

The IHOP was frigid and everyone was old and/or overweight. Their booth table held tented placards that announced SIGNATURE SPRING PANCAKES!—loaded up with whipped cream and more—and some new menu item, HAND-CRAFTED GRIDDLE MELTS!

A slow death between two slices of bread.

Everything looked and sounded and probably tasted fake.

They ordered and Avery looked out the window at the suit store, and imagined a platoon crossing the highway—Left! Right! Left! Right!—sending cars into tailspins and armed with enough ammunition to turn the IHOP into the international house of pain and take it down to the ground.

He dropped her back at home to get ready and drove off before she even hit the mailbox because now they were running late.

The pelican's mouth was open.

She looked in.

Another note:

WHATEVER YOU DO, DO NOT TRUST THEM!

—MAX

Up the street Mrs. Gulden's yippy dogs were having a conniption.

Scarlett

On their way out of the bar, down a long flight of stairs, Scarlett skipped the bottom step

landing hard on her right foot
on the ground level.

A moment later Lucas did, too.

/ /
/ /

/

"Why did you just do that?" she asked.

The entry foyer smelled like old beer and cigarettes. The smell had crept into her hair, her pores, her nostrils—would probably stay with her all day.

"I don't know," he said. "Why did *you* just do that?"

She shrugged.

Realized she'd done it before.

The steps from Tammy's back deck down to the patio in the yard. Had he done it that day, too, and they just hadn't noticed?

She said, "Habit?"

/ / /

Then thinking out loud: "Maybe we were somewhere where that mattered? Where the bottom step was . . ." She looked at the stairs there in the hall . . .

"Squeaky?" he offered.

She pushed the door to the street open.

Rogue drops were falling from clouds the color of steel.

He reached out and took her hand and squeezed it and she squeezed back, ran a thumb along his thumb.

Which also felt like a habit.

They held hands the whole way to the car.

They had a new destination.

Because the bartender had shouted across the room. "Hey, Jimmy!"

And Jimmy, with a Guinness at a table in the corner, had said, "Yes, sir!"

"Whatever happened to Danny? You know, the one whose son died?"

"Same as happens to everybody."

Scarlett had braced for bad news. He was dead, too. The *Wikipedia* page was out of date.

But then Jimmy had said, "Whispering Pines, I think?"

"There you go." The bartender had knocked on the bar two times with his knuckles.

"Whispering Pines?" Scarlett had repeated.

"Nursing home up the road."

Relief had mixed with . . . something else.

"How did his son die?" Lucas had asked.

"Brain tumor." The bartender had put his hands on his hips. "Was dead a year after they found it." Some head shaking. "Just one of those things."

"He ever talk about his work?" Lucas had presented the book. "This book?"

The bartender had looked at it. "He wrote this?" A shrug. "Never mentioned it." Then he'd looked at *them*. "Hey, wait . . . you're . . ."

Scarlett didn't want to let go of Lucas's hand when they got to Tammy's car, but he let go for her. She unlocked the car and got in.

She didn't like the idea of trees being able to whisper.

Because what would they say?

I see you.

I see everything.

I remember everything.

I remember you.

"Lucas?" She had her hand on the key but couldn't turn it. "I'm scared."

That was the something else.

Fear.

"It's just a nursing home." He smiled. "Anyone tries to mess with us, we can so totally outrun them."

"I don't mean that," she said.

What *did* she mean?

/
//

Hot air balloons.

Swallowed clues.

Old staircases.

Old books.

An unreturned boy.

She didn't like any of it.

Didn't like where any of it was heading.

"My mother said the aliens took me because she was a bad parent."

"You can't possibly believe—"

"No," she interrupted. "Of course not. But we were chosen. Right? By someone? Why us?"

"I don't know. Maybe that was part of it. That we were all in these messed-up families? I just don't know."

"So why give us back now?" she asked. "Why is it over?"

"Because we were an experiment like in the book?" he said. "Test subjects? And all experiments have to come to an end, so there can be conclusions to draw."

"What's the conclusion?" She started the car. "What did they prove?"

"That's what we're trying to find out, Scar."

/

/ /

"You're the only one who calls me that."

Then more drops landed and burst on the windshield.

Then slicing rain kicked in, tiny knives attacking the car.

/

/ /

/

/

/ / / / /

/ //

//

/ / / / / / / / /

//

/ / / / / / /

/

/

And in her mind's eye she saw them together.

Running.

Panting.

Warm.

Wet.

Lucas

Waiting out the downpour, he showed her some of the pictures he'd taken—of Opus 6, of Miranda and Ryan, of nothing at all.

"Wait." She reached out for the camera, stared at the display. "I remember your brother, I think. From when we were little. I think he was with me when I chipped a tooth once."

"Yeah? Was I there, too?"

"I don't remember. And that's his girlfriend?"

Lucas nodded. Then he leaned back as far as he could toward his door and snapped a photo of Scarlett: her face pale and angular, the raindrops streaking the windows and blurring the world behind her into a fuzzy kaleidoscope of grays and red and blue. The brown of her eyes like wet dirt in spring, almost black.

"Can I see?" she said.

He leaned toward her, their shoulders touching over the console.

"I like it," she said. "So do you think you used to do this? Take pictures? That that's what the tattoo has to do with?"

He lifted the camera, looked through the finder. "I held it like this in the store and the salesperson noticed it and said only people who are like real photographers do that?" He lowered the camera. "So maybe."

Then he said, "It just feels easy. It feels comfortable. To hold the camera."

Same way it had to hold the gun.

He had to tell her.

Had to trust her.

Had to trust her to trust him.

He said, "I know how to load a gun."

"What?" she said. "How did you even figure that out?"

"My father has—had—one and when Ryan showed it to me, I just . . ."

CLICK HISS UP AND
CALM.

"I just picked it up and loaded it. Without even thinking about it."

She turned away from him and stared at or out the windshield, where rivers and streams were cutting their way down. He thought he saw her hand move to the door handle, thought that maybe if it weren't pouring she might open the door and run.

"Why would I know how to do that?" he asked, trying to lure her back, trying to make her his ally in this.

"I don't know," she said, and it got quiet.

He hadn't actually realized how loud the rain had been until it stopped.

"Do you think we were trying to escape?" she asked. "Plotting it?"

"It seems like with the penny, and my tattoo, it's like we knew what was happening, like we knew we were forgetting or were going to forget?"

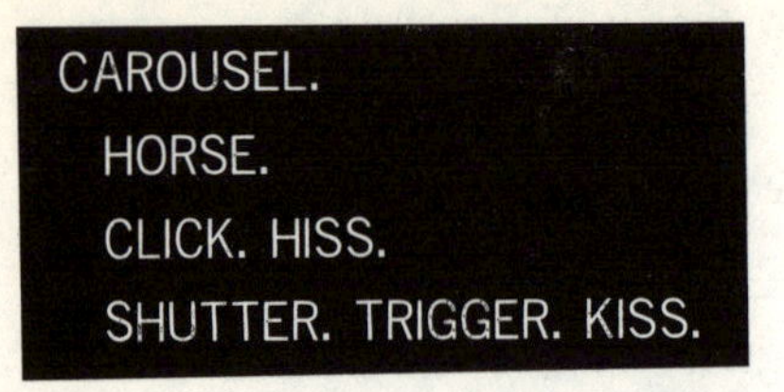

He said, "Maybe we were trying to find ways to remember."

She took the penny in her hands again, and the sun ripped a seam through the clouds. She started the car.

AVERY

"Any problems at school?" Chambers sounded bored, like this was some run-of-the-mill traffic stop. "Anyone who might be messing with you?"

He and her father were looking at her.

"Me?" Avery was surprised to have the conversation turn to her so quickly. She thought she and Emma and Sam had mostly been kidding around.

"Yes, we know kids can be particularly, well, cruel," Chambers said. "I wonder if there's someone with some grudge against you."

"I'm like one of the most popular people in school," Avery said.

"I'm serious," Chambers said.

"So am I." Avery pushed her shoulders back. "Everybody loves me."

"Don't take this the wrong way—but you're smart, pretty, you have a boyfriend, this house. Seriously, look at you."

She was fully dressed for the wedding now. Makeup. Hair blown out. Nails done. Heels. A tight purple dress that she wished Lucas could see her in.

"No way everyone loves you."

"So you'll go to the school?" her father asked. "Investigate?"

"No," Chambers said. "We don't have time for that. You're going to assume it's a prank, because it is, and you're going to ignore it. When we wrap this whole thing up, whoever it is will stop."

"That's it?" Avery protested.

"That's it."

"But—"

Chambers stopped her with a hand held in front of her. "Do you want me to focus on finding Max or focus on finding some girl with a beef with you who's laughing about this with her friends?"

"Max," Avery said. "Of course."

"Of course," her father said.

"Good." Chambers headed for the door.

"Anything from the tip line yet?" Avery asked.

"It's not even been a full day," Chambers said. "We have to be patient."

"I do have one question for *you*," Chambers said to her father, and they stepped outside and closed the door but not all the way and she moved to try to listen.

"The school shooting," Chambers said softly, sounding almost confused. "Was Max there that day?"

"With my wife, yes. At an open house." Her father also sounded confused. "Why do you ask?"

"It's probably nothing," Chambers said. "I'll be in touch."

Dad poked his head in the door. "Sam's here."

She checked herself in the mirror, blinked away sad eyes, and grabbed her clutch.

"Just have fun tonight, okay?" Dad said, kissing her on the forehead at the threshold. And the way he looked at her made her think about this father-daughter dance they'd gone to when she'd been a Girl Scout, how she'd worn a dress from when she'd been a flower girl in her aunt's wedding, how she'd had a wrist corsage of glitter-spattered carnations. He still smelled of the same aftershave—the scent of trees she'd never seen and that grew only in rugged mountain terrains.

She almost tripped on the steps on her way out to the car.

Damn heels.

Scarlett

It didn't seem like the worst place to go to die.

Palms and blooming shrubs. Pathways winding down to a park on the waterfront with benches and still more palm trees and a few small fountains—a kneeling stone woman pouring water onto stone flowers from a jug, a small petrified birdbath replete with immobilized birds.

Scarlett imagined herself old, in an Adirondack chair, listening to the fountains' trickles, then wondered about where this Adirondack chair obsession of hers had come from.

She had parked the car facing the Gulf.

The whole of it was shiny and gray, like dolphin skin.

"What's our plan?" she asked as they approached the double glass doors of the main building.

"We're friends of the family," Lucas said.

"No, really." She stopped walking.

He stopped, too. "Yes, really." He tilted his head toward the door in encouragement, totally confident.

But then . . .

What if they'd been kept *here*?

The whole place seemed suddenly shadowed in gloom.

Like some light filter had fallen over it.

Every window might have been a room where they'd been locked.

Every person there might have been an accomplice.

They shouldn't have come.

"Scar," he said, "it's just a nursing home. We're just going to try to talk to an old writer."

"But what if . . ."

/

/

/

". . . it's really him?"

"Then we'll deal with that." He nodded.

"What if it's him and we don't know it?"

"Then we'll deal with *that*."

She couldn't move her feet for a moment.

But knew she . . .

. . . had to.

Inside, the air smelled like lavender bleach, and the floor was so bouncy that she actually looked down to see what she was standing on. It was just carpet but it was padded beyond reason.

No one would ever break a hip here.

A large floral arrangement on the front desk partially explained the scent but also obscured the view of the woman sitting there, so Scarlett and Lucas stepped to the side of it, and Scarlett met the eyes of a middle-aged nurse with short bleached-blond hair. She wore navy-blue scrubs and looked up at them like they were nothing out of the ordinary.

Relief.

Disappointment.

Had Scarlett wanted someone to recognize them?

Wanted alarms to sound?

Gates to drop?

Maybe.

Maybe if it would end the

/

/
/

clicking in her head.

"We're here to visit Daniel Orlean," Lucas said.

The nurse looked at him, then at Scarlett, then back at him.

"We're friends of the family," he said. "Old friends of his son's."

"Oh, just awful," the nurse said, hand to heart. "What happened to him. Just awful."

"Yes," Lucas said. "Truly."

"So you're familiar with Danny's condition, then?" The nurse pushed a sign-in sheet on a clipboard forward, and Scarlett decided to make herself useful. She searched her brain for made-up names and signed them in as Matt Jones and Anne Shepherd.

"Of course," Lucas said.

"You been here before, right?" she said.

"First time," Lucas said.

"Oh." She seemed unconvinced.

Scarlett set the clipboard down and nodded solemnly.

"Well, he'll be happy to see you. Most of his visitors are from the lab."

She came around from behind the desk. "He's usually in the courtyard around this time of day. I'll show you."

Scarlett followed the nurse down a long hallway—Lucas at her side.

Past a dining room with high ceilings and heavy curtains on huge windows.

Split-pea soup weighted the air.

Then out a set of double glass doors that opened automatically as they approached.

Outside, old people with walkers inched like zombies across the concrete patio.

A few trellises held creeping vines, and some large pots presented tall, leafy plumes.

The nurse headed for a man seated on a bench on the far side of the courtyard and said, "Daniel! You have visitors!"

"You don't say!" He squinted up at them.

So very old.

The skin on his face like shriveled fruit.

His white hair, lifeless and dry.

His eyes, bright but . . . vacant.

Like a baby's.

"Friends of your family. I'm sure they'll reintroduce themselves." The nurse turned and presented them, and Lucas held out a hand to shake. Daniel shook it back.

"I'll leave you to it." The nurse walked away.

"Well, go on," Daniel said. "Pull over a chair." He turned to Scarlett. "You, my dear, can sit right next to me."

Scarlett, realizing something about herself.

She didn't like old people.

Did anyone?

But—

It was just a book.

He was just an old man.

He couldn't have been the one to do this.

Lucas pulled a wooden chair, stained a redwood hue, closer and sat in front of Daniel.

"Now I feel like I would've remembered a good-looking couple like you. Tell me how I know you?"

"Well, I'm Anne and this is Mark," she said, being sure to catch Lucas's eye.

Lucas took the paperback out of his bag and held it out. "We're fans, you see."

He presented the book to Daniel, who took it, curiously.

This all felt very wrong—him so interested, them so deceitful—but there wasn't much to be done about it.

"What's this?" Daniel asked.

She was shouting into that abyss now.

Hands cupped to her mouth:

"Nooooooooooooooooo!"

The sound of it echoing back to her.

"It's a novel," she said, hearing an edge of annoyance. "You wrote it."

"I did?" Now he reached into his front shirt pocket for glasses, put them on, and looked at the book with new interest.

"You did." Hands turned to fists in her lap.

His lips moved as he read the description. "Sounds hinky," he said. "Is it any good?"

"It is!" Lucas said.

"Did it make me rich?" Daniel smiled.

"I don't think so." Lucas laughed and gave her a pleading look.

His condition:

Alzheimer's.

Of course.

Scarlett softened her voice when she said, "We were hoping you'd be able to tell us about the book. You know, where you got the idea from, that kind of thing."

Daniel looked out toward the water, like he was trying very hard to spot an answer—a memory—on the horizon.

Then after a long moment, during which Scarlett followed his gaze, maybe hoping she could find it for him—

or at least find a memory of her own—

he turned back to them, reset.

"Well, I like to read. Thanks very much for the recommendation." He smiled. "Tell me how I know you again? You're from the lab?"

It was hard to not be disappointed.
crushed.

"No," Scarlett said. "What are the folks at the lab like?"

Maybe the lab was where they'd been.

Maybe the lab was a clue.

"Oh, they're fine. They're, you know, trying to help me remember." Daniel looked sad then, like he had actually remembered something. Maybe just how much he'd forgotten.

Then he shrugged and said, "I figure if I forgot stuff it's because I didn't need to remember it. That's what I think. I remember the important stuff."

"What's the important stuff?" Scarlett asked.

"You mean you don't know?" he asked in a whisper.

/
/
/
/

Scarlett shook her head.

Really wanting to know.

Manatees.

I love you.

Not Lucas to her.

Luke.

Luke and Scar.

Needing to know.

Like, wanted to take him by the shoulders and shake him.

What is the important stuff?

Daniel said only, "Well, you're young. But when it happens, you'll know it." He turned to her, and the wind puffed his hair up, then let it fall again. "There will be stuff you can't forget no matter if you tried."

Still screaming into the abyss:

"Will you read that book?" Lucas asked. "And we'll come back in a few days to talk about it. Maybe you can write down any thoughts you have about it?"

"You must mean this for the book club." He went to give it back. "I'm not in the—"

"Please," Scarlett said. "Read it? For me?"

He thumbed the pages. "I'll give it a whirl."

On the way out, she set out to find a restroom, peeking around doorways on a long hall.

A woman in one of the rooms saw her in the doorway and said "Oh, hello! Would you like to see my drawings?"

She wore a red blouse and pearls and ivory slacks and looked like maybe she was a visiting artist who did art therapy with patients.

Behind her hung a painting of a girl in a brown field, crawling up a hill toward an old house and a barn.

The girl's positioning seemed . . . off.

Had she just been hobbled?

"Dear?" the woman said.

"I'd like to," Scarlett said. "I just need to run to the restroom."

There, she threw some water on her face.

Things you can't forget no matter if you tried.

Things you can't forget no matter if you tried.

Like how you should skip that last step.

And go back to Anchor Beach?

She returned to that doorway.

The woman looked up. "Oh, hello? Would you like to see my drawings?"

Scarlett was about to say "I just was here," but . . .

. . . no.

Not a visiting artist.

A patient.

Regretting getting involved now, Scarlett felt she had no choice. "I'd love to."

The drawings were swirls and color-blocks drawn in colored pencil.

They were happy and ordered.

Some like peacock's feathers.

Others, like maps.

"I like them," Scarlett said.

"Thanks." The woman picked up an orange pencil, turned to a work in progress.

"I'm sorry, but I have to go," Scarlett said. "My friend is waiting."

"Bye, then!" the woman said brightly.

Scarlett stopped at the nurse's desk.

She had to know.

"The woman with the artwork in that room there," she said. "Does she have Alzheimer's, too?"

"Oh, that's Goldie." The nurse was shifting file folders. "Rare case of viral encephalitis. She's lost the ability to form short-term memories. Or long. That's why they call her Goldie."

"Goldie?" Scarlett waited.

The nurse was putting a file into a cabinet, which she slid closed with a *thunk.* Looking up, she said, "Because she has the memory of a goldfish?"

/

/ / /

/

"That's awful," Scarlett snapped. "They should call her by her *name.*"

Lucas was waiting by the elevator, but there were a few people in wheelchairs waiting, too.

Scarlett headed for the wide stairs to the lobby—

Had to get out

Had to get out now—

That EXIT sign there.

and Lucas followed and then caught up to her. "What's wrong?"

Scarlett pushed—

EMERGENCY DOOR

Too late.

Sirens sounded.

She stepped out into the sun, wanting to run.

Without memory you were a goldfish.

Swimming in circles.

Without memories you were . . .

/ / /

. . . no one.

Lucas

They drove. Mostly quiet.

Just:

"Maybe we should see if Chambers will check out the memory lab? Maybe there's a connection there?"

And, "You think he'll remember anything?"

And, "I doubt he'll even remember he promised to read it."

And, "You okay?"

And, "Yeah, I think so."

And, "Goldie."

And, "I know."

It hadn't been a dead end, exactly.

Maybe he'd read the book, maybe he'd give them something.

But it didn't seem . . . likely.

Something eventually had to look familiar.

Something had to trigger a memory.

Crack this ice.

Had he ever seen that building?

Driven or been driven down this road?

Had he ever been to a bowling alley like that one or a hibachi house like that one?

When the road turned desolate—clear-cut fields and some plagued-looking stretches of woods where emaciated trees leaned on each other for support—Lucas tried to let his mind go blank.

To stop working so hard.

HORSE. HISS. CLICK. SADDLE.
GOLD POLES. COTTON CANDY.

The image still always there, to fill the void.

He closed his eyes.

Pushed it away.

Put this in its place.

KISS. BEACH.
LOVE. PENNY.

If you remember the important things, you should remember . . .

LOVE.

But it didn't stick.

Images faded too fast.

Floated on the surface for a moment before a pebble rippled them away.

"There it is," Scarlett said.

His pulse started to tick up when he opened his eyes, saw four smokestacks. The one car on the road in front of them seemed to be going too slow intentionally.

Then a sign for the Manatee Viewing Area appeared and she said, "I feel sick."

"There," he said, pointing to the next sign.

She turned into a parking lot and pulled into a spot one down from the only other car there.

Again she got out with the engine still running, left her car door swung open, and seemed to sleepwalk to the gate.

He killed the engine, got out, and closed both doors before joining her. An arch featuring the silhouettes of two manatees marked the entrance. Beyond the gates, steam burst out of four tall chimneys like dragon breath.

Scarlett had been tugging at the chains on the gate—the clanging of wind chimes made of shackles—but now gave up, let the padlock fall mute.

"The manatees only really come in winter," she said. "I should have thought of that."

"We would have come anyway."

"Manatees never forget," she said.

Lucas turned to her, raised his eyebrows.

"When I was looking this all up last night, I read that about manatees. How their closest relative is the elephant and how they can remember miles and miles of coastlines, places to find warm water. Places like this. Why don't I remember it?" She sounded like she was about to cry.

"Hey," he said. "It's okay." He stepped toward her, face-to-face, put his hands on her upper arms, a half embrace.

Afraid to give in to this.

Afraid to scare her off.

"We could try to hop the gate," he said, releasing her and turning back to the park. "See if we can find the penny machine."

She pointed at a few security cameras up high on posts.

"Could do it anyway." He shrugged. Just inside the gate, the sign on the gift shop where the penny-stretching machine probably was hung crooked on its mount.

"Not now," she said. "Come on."

They walked down a long path and followed a wooden walkway along the water and found themselves on the beach, where three piers stretched out into the water. The pier Scarlett chose to walk was impossibly narrow—so she led—and finally they stood at the end, an onshore wind pressing hard against them, like it wanted them to go back to wherever they came from.

"Do you think you gave me that penny?" she asked. "That we were here together?"

He liked the idea of it, that they were getting closer to answers, and to each other, too. "It's the only thing that makes sense."

"It seems important," she said. "That we remember. Like there might be some clues in that story? In us?"

He nodded, took her hand, and held it up to study it.

To look for a birthmark or some clue that he'd maybe held it before.

She had the remains of bloodred polish on two of five nails.

She squeezed his hand, released it, and turned.

This—being here with her—felt like some kind of reset button or rebirth.

He liked knowing at least one thing about himself for sure.

He loved her.

Or had . . .

When they circled back to the car, they were holding hands, and he couldn't recall the moment they'd done that, reached out and held on.

They passed a small security booth near the manatee center gate.

The guard poked his head out his window and smiled. "Haven't seen *you two* in a while."

Scarlett let go.

AVERY

The bride was beyond annoying.

It was like she seriously thought the whole world revolved around her and Ballroom B of the Hotel Bonavista on Sanibel Island. She was like some Disney princess who hadn't gotten the memo about how women were supposed to have brains and lives of their own and not just be little eye-candy damsels in distress who lived for true love's kiss—the wedding of their dreams. Every time the woman turned her head, it was like she was posing for a picture with an Instagram setting that filtered out humility. Avery was half tempted to write "You're not all that!" on the big canvas guests had been encouraged to sign during the cocktail hour.

Now the couple was gearing up for their first dance and Avery wasn't sure she could stand to watch, thought maybe she could go hide in the photo booth in the corner where guests were expected to put on funny hats and glasses and pose.

They'd taken dance classes.

They'd picked that played-out John Legend song.

There was no escape.

She had to watch the whole dance.

Then the song ended and people clapped and the bride preened and the DJ asked other couples to join them on the dance floor.

Sam took his seat.

Avery wasn't sure if she was irritated or relieved.

Then it started:

"How long have you and Sam been going out?"

"Sam says you're involved in the school play?"

"Isn't she just a gorgeous bride?"

Avery excused herself from the table—Sam's cousins all—and went outside onto a balcony that overlooked the pool deck where the cocktail hour had been. Men in white jackets were still clearing plates and glasses and empty bottles. An older guy was smoking a cigarette a little ways down, and she found herself toying with the idea of asking for a smoke. She'd tell the guy who she was, how they were hoping for some solid tip *any* minute now.

"Hey." It was Sam. "You feel like dancing?"

She could hear the bass line of some old funk song and said, "Not so much, no."

She didn't feel like telling him about the new note and how full of himself Chambers was, and she *couldn't* tell him about why she was really in such a bad mood and constantly checking her phone. She wanted to hear from Lucas, wanted to know what he'd found out, but didn't want to have to call him.

"Photo booth?" Sam said.

It was the last thing she wanted to do, really. But she couldn't exactly stand out there by herself all night. She said, "Sure."

When she saw that the photo booth company was called Making Memories, she almost turned away. But Sam already had hats and boas and Minecraft sunglasses picked out, so they threw on their accessories and ducked through the black curtain.

They had four exposures coming.

First one: regular ole smiles and Minecraft.

Second one: tongues out, her two fingers behind Sam's head, boas.

Third one: eyebrows raised, hands up like looking confused, hats.

And for the fourth one, Sam pulled her toward him and kissed her hard and she didn't like it.

Back out in the ballroom, they took off their props and waited by the photo delivery slot. Sam reached for them first.

"They came out good," he said.

Avery took them and didn't recognize herself at all.

"You guys!" the bride said as she blew past them in a waft of champagne and mini crab cakes. "You are just *too cute*." She hugged Sam. "This is absolutely the best day of my life."

Avery fake-beamed and wished for a different kind of prop option—a mask that might hide who she was—until the bride moved on. Her cheeks hurt when she released the smile.

Scarlett

For a second, she thought it had to be a cruel joke.

Haven't seen you in a while.

Like in eleven years, *ha-ha.*

But the guy looked calm.

Happy to see them, even.

And now Scarlett didn't feel as alone on that cliff as before.

Someone else had been there.

Seen her.

Borne witness to . . .

"You *know* us?" she asked.

"How do you know us?" Lucas said.

"From here. You used to come here." Confusion seeping into the guard's features. "But not in a while now. Like a couple of months, maybe?"

"How did we get here?" Scarlett asked. "Which direction did we come from? Was anyone else ever with us?"

"I don't know." His confusion seemed to morph into suspicion now. "It's not like I was watching you. I saw you, is all. You seemed like a cute couple. I figured when you stopped showing up you'd split up or something."

"We were a couple?" Scarlett asked.

He nodded. "Well, you were holding hands. Kissing. But I had a theory about you."

"What kind of theory?" Lucas asked.

"You were always in a hurry. Always looking over your shoulders. I figured one of you was getting some on the side."

/

/ /

/

Getting some.

/ /

On the side?

Oh.

Awkward.

Scarlett found a flawed seam on her skirt, followed it to where it ended.

Took a breath, then looked up. "Do you remember anything about what I was wearing?"

Maybe black jeans and T-shirts had been all they had?

Lucas said, "Scarlett, I don't think he's going—"

"I actually do," the guard said. "You had this jacket that was hard to forget. Old-fashioned-looking. Like vintage, you know? Or more like homemade. It was like a quilt, if that makes any sense?"

"Yes," Scarlett said, her fingers feeling funny, her foot tapping. "That makes perfect sense."

"You wore it all the time. Even when it was like a gazillion degrees."

Why would she do that?

"Were we ever with anyone else?" Lucas asked.

"Not that I can think of," the man said slowly; then his eyes sparked. "Hey, wait a second . . . You're those kids."

Scarlett turned to Lucas.

Shared a look:

Concern, yes.

Panic, no.

"Yes," Lucas admitted. "Are you sure you didn't just . . . see us on the news? You're sure you saw us here before?"

"I'm sure." The guard nodded. "I yelled at you once. For carving your initials into the pier."

"Where?" Scarlett asked. "Which one?"

"Middle one. Down the end on the right somewhere."

She took off . . .

Not quite running . . .

But . . .

Lucas was saying, "Thanks for your time" and "Can I get your name and number in case the police want to follow up?"

But she was halfway gone, back down toward the beach.

And when she got to the end of the pier, she felt happy for a moment—even fearless—just standing there, with the air full of seagulls and salty mist.

This was the place they'd found to be together.

This was where they must have plotted their lives together, their escape.

She'd swallowed the penny to bring them back here.

It had worked!

They were going to figure it out.

They were going to get it all back.

Then she found their initials, in a heart—but stabbed over and over so that they were almost entirely obscured.

And everything churned.

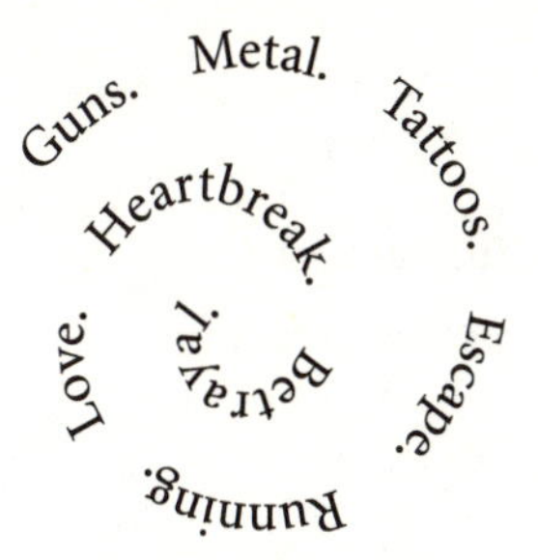

Lucas arrived, breathing hard from walking so fast.

She nodded at the initials, ran her fingers over the splintered wood. "Why do you think they're crossed out?"

"Could have been anybody who did that," he said. "For no reason at all."

"But what if it was one of us?" She half feared this happiness, this moment of rediscovering something real, was going to be lost too soon.

Or was false.

Or was . . .

Was . . . what?

"We have a long drive," she said. "And we have to tell Chambers. Everything, I guess."

"But what if there are other people here"—he turned—"people who saw us?"

"Look around," she said. "There's no one here."

She suddenly didn't want to be there, either.

Didn't want to be there alone.

With him.

/

/

Running.

Panting.

Wet.

/
/

She said, "We can always come back."

"I want some quick pictures." He took his camera out.

How would they ever figure out what his tattoo meant?

So what if he liked to take pictures?

How could that possibly be a clue?

They decided he would drive this time. So that she could call Chambers, tell him about the penny, the guard, everything.

Just not yet.

Because as soon as they were on a main road again, stopped at a light, Lucas reached out and took her hand again.

And she held on and it felt strange and right.

And he kept looking over at her, and she at him, and after a while it started to feel like he shouldn't be driving, not when they were both so distracted.

And finally she said, "Pull off somewhere."

And at first it seemed like there was no possible good place to stop, but then she saw an old motel with a large parking lot in front and said, "There!" and he pulled into the unpaved lot, kicking up a cloud of dirt.

The GulfShores Motel was abandoned—stickered with orange signs about violations of who even knew what kind. Drapes blew through broken windows. An ice machine sat silently alongside a pillaged snack machine.

It didn't matter.

They weren't going in.

He parked in a far corner of the lot and turned off the engine.

She waited.

But only for a moment.

Then leaned toward him and

—so fast—

he pulled her into his arms and kissed her and she kissed him back and . . .

Attacked.

X'd out

/

/ / /
/

And the kiss was freeing.

And claustrophobic.

And familiar.

And there was this unease that pricked at her heart.

And just kept

pricking

and *picking*

and *pecking* away.

"We were in love," she said when she pulled away.

He nodded.

But . . .

And he went at her again.

And . . .

This time, less tentative.

This time, all in.

Her hands in his hair, their bodies finding their way to each other over consoles and stick shifts.

His chest against hers, his hands finding the skin on her lower back, his mouth moving to her neck and ear and back again.

This wasn't the first time.

But all that was lost and might never be recovered.

But she'd chosen him once.

They'd chosen each other.

That said something about who she was, who he was.

That in spite of all they'd forgotten, this had come through.

This hadn't entirely been erased.

She had to trust that.

The penny.

Had to see it through.

She could almost feel the weight of a light jacket—her handmade jacket?—on her shoulders.

Could feel her fingers, pushing fabric through a machine.

She could feel him,

wanting her,

taking it off.

Lucas

Driving seemed to steady him. Pushed away the

SPINNING HORSES KISSING BEACH
CLICK HISS SW + LD HEARTS

The swallowed penny had worked. So what of the tattoo?

Why, if he'd done it himself, had he gone to all that trouble only to make his clue so vague? So unclear? So that if the plan to escape hadn't worked, the tattoo would have seemed . . . what . . . benign? Meaningless?

They drove in silence.

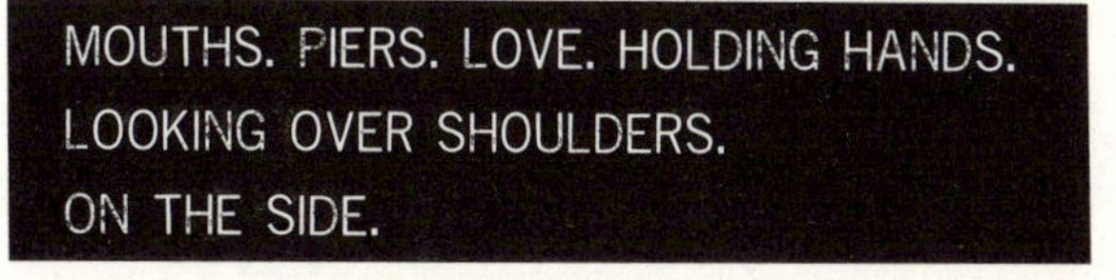

So much to process. He was afraid to speak, really.

Then finally, as they approached town, she got her phone out and called Chambers. She told him about the penny. About Anchor Beach. About the guard there. How he remembered them, and her jacket. How their initials were carved into the pier.

"Tell him about the book," Lucas said.

She nodded and explained it all. It already felt like so long ago—Orlean with his unruly hair and sad eyes. The bar, the rainstorm.

"Oh, and one more thing," she said after they'd agreed that Lucas would meet with Chambers to speak more about *The Leaving* in the morning.

For a second Lucas couldn't think what she'd left out.

"We've both been skipping the bottom step of staircases," she said. "Like out of habit? That has to be a clue, too, right?"

Lucas pulled up to Opus 6 and turned off the engine.

Scarlett said, "I don't think I can make that promise," and ended the call abruptly.

"What was that about?" Lucas gathered his camera and bag.

"He wanted me to promise we wouldn't go off on our own again, wouldn't try to investigate." She got out to come around to the driver's side. He stood and wondered, should he kiss her again? And he studied her eyes, her body for clues. But now it seemed like somehow—here—that was all gone.

All a dream.

That photo.

EYES LIKE SOIL. FUZZY DICE. RAIN.

It was real.

They were real.

It had happened.

But . . .

"Chambers said he'd go there, interview the guard," she said, getting into the car. "And I guess let me know what he says after you talk to him?"

"Of course," Lucas said.

She closed her door and drove away, and he stood so very still and watched and his eyes followed the stones at his feet, just picked a path and stone by stone it led to up to that empty plateau.

He made a promise to himself to do something about that, then went up to the house, where lights were on and Ryan said, "How'd it go?"

Miranda was there.

Miranda was always there.

This time standing at an ironing board in the middle of the living room, ironing a decal onto a shirt.

"Someone recognized us." Lucas went to the couch and sat aside a tall stack of neatly folded T-shirts. "Like from before. He told us where we'd carved our initials into a pier."

"That's incredible," Ryan said. "So what now?"

"Wait." Miranda's iron hissed. "Where was this?"

"Anchor Beach?" Lucas said.

"That's where the author of the old book lives?" Ryan asked.

"No." Lucas said. "About an hour away."

"So how did you end up *there*?" Miranda held the shirt up, examined her work, set it aside. The room smelled of melting plastic.

"It's a long story," he said. The penny was Scarlett's to talk about.

"So," Ryan repeated. "What now?"

"We told the police. We'll talk more. They're going down there to check it out."

"So they'll search for Max?" Ryan asked.

Like that, a rush of guilt.

A surge of shame.

Hadn't even had a thought about Max. Or

AVERY. DEFIANT. ELBOWS TOUCHING.

HOW COULD YOU JUST FORGET A WHOLE PERSON?

Had been so caught up in

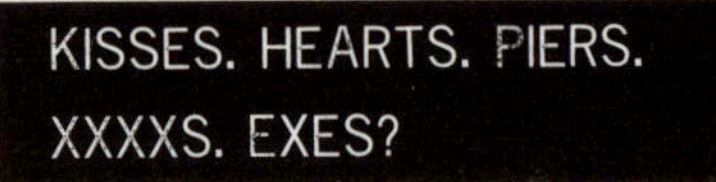

And now, wanted to be the one to tell her.

About all this.

So she was maybe . . . what . . . ready?

"Hey, where do they live?" he asked, and had the feeling of hiding something. "Max's parents, I mean."

AVERY

She recognized him walking in the dark, a castle guard doing his rounds, as Sam drove up the block to drop her at home. She didn't say anything, hoped Sam hadn't even seen him, and bent to slide her heels back onto her blistered feet. How much worse would they hurt right now if she *had* decided to dance?

"I'll talk to you tomorrow." Sam leaned over and they kissed, but barely.

"Sounds good," she said, feeling something fake in her voice.

Then she got out and walked up the front path and the front steps and put her key in the door and opened it and turned and waved. Sam seemed intent on watching her actually go inside, so she went in, annoyed about it, as quietly as she could and then watched through the peephole as he drove off, and then she stepped back out.

The street was crickets-quiet.

He was probably still four houses down.

Why was he out? Lurking?

Her ears were ringing from hours of boogie-woogie nonsense.

Electric slides and last-dance-last-dance-tonights.

Finally, his footfalls broke through and then he was standing in front of her house, but not seeing her, maybe looking for a house number.

"What are you doing here?" she asked in a loud whisper.

"Avery?" he whispered back.

She stepped forward so he could see her and realized her wish was coming true.

Her in her purple dress.

Him here to see it.

"Yes," she said, going down to meet him. Still feeling small next to him, even in heels.

He looked at her hard. "I almost didn't recognize you."

"Is that supposed to be a compliment?" she said.

"No"—he seemed embarrassed, flustered—

Good.

"I mean, yes."

"What are you doing here?"

"I went to talk to the author of *The Leaving* today. I wanted to tell you about it. And we went to a place where someone recognized us. So we told the police and maybe they'll find Max there. I don't know. It's all still unfolding. I just. I wanted you to know."

"Who's 'we'?" she said, knowing what the answer was going to be but wanting to hear it anyway. "Who's 'us'?"

"Oh," he said. "Me and Scarlett."

She nodded. "Did she read it? Did she know why she said that about going on a trip? What's it even about?"

"It's pretty out there—people living in an underground city to avoid sending their kids away, that kind of thing."

"Anyone left behind? Killed? Anything that could be a parallel to Max not coming home?"

He shook his head. "No, sorry."

"So what did the author say?

"He has Alzheimer's."

"Tell me you're joking."

Sometimes life was too much.

"No," he said. "I'm not."

She shook her head and thought again about the calendar with the countdown to getting out of Florida. Why would anyone in their right mind want to spend the prime years of their life there? Florida wasn't the Sunshine State. It was the prune juice state. The Depends state. It was where you went to go to Disney and visit your grandparents, sure, but it was no place to actually *live*—not if you had a healthy pulse. Maybe whoever had done this knew that. That Florida was no place to raise kids. They should've moved away after the shooting. Then maybe that would have been that.

"The police were asking my dad about Max and the school shooting today," she said. "Whether he was there. What do you think that's about?"

"I don't know," he said. "*Was* he there?"

"Yeah. An open house thing. "

"I was there, too," Lucas said.

"I know," she said. "Ryan and I used to . . . talk."

He nodded. "Why would they be asking about that now?"

She honestly didn't know. Had they all been there? Why would that matter? Everyone had been there.

"Do you remember it?" she asked.

"No."

"It's just as well," she said.

They stood there on the front path for a minute and she really just wanted to go inside, take her shoes off, and have everything be different.

"What's with the camera?" she asked, noticing the strap across his chest that led to a small case.

"Oh." He pulled it forward. "I have a tattoo of a camera shutter and I seem to know my way around cameras."

"And?"

"And I don't know. Maybe it's a clue that maybe connects to Scarlett's clue? We don't know yet."

"Are you *with* her?" she asked. "Scarlett?"

"We're trying to figure that out but yeah"—he seemed totally fine with telling her—"I think so, yeah."

She had to turn away to hide a burning behind her eyes.

Scarlett

Scarlett sat outside, windows down in the darkness, listening to the surf and trying to make sense of the day, for a good long while.

Then, finally, she went inside, tapped on Tammy's door, found her in bed with her laptop.

"Did you pass the alien probe yet?" Tammy asked.

"Why do you want it to be aliens?" Scarlett plopped down at the foot of the bed.

Feeling so completely drained.

She'd tell her about the penny.

Just . . .

later.

Tammy looked at her over her reading glasses. "I don't *want* it to—"

"It's the *least likely* explanation," Scarlett cut in. "So just answer the question."

Her mother's whole body tensed.

Then she breathed out loudly through her nose.

Her voice was a few tones deeper, almost possessed-sounding, when she said, "Because I do not want to believe that *another human being* could have done this to you."

For a second, looking at the anguish on her mother's face under the golden glow of the bedside lamp, Scarlett could almost remember the deep *hmmmmmmmmmmmmm* of a spaceship.

Could almost remember a creature . . .

Its eyes in a V.

That w a l k e d
on light.

She could almost remember

* * * * * * * * * *

toward . . .

up

. . . floating weightlessly

Scarlett's gaze found some crooked stitching on a throw pillow on the armchair in the corner. "Do you have a sewing machine?"

Her mother was blowing her nose. "Sure, but I haven't used it in years. I was starting to teach you, you know. We were making little purses and stuff. Hemming curtains."

"Can you show me?"

DAY FOUR

Lucas

Chambers stood outside the precinct, holding a cup of coffee top-to-bottom between his thumb and middle finger. "I've got good news," he said. "The coroner has ruled your father's death an accident."

Relief, of course, but also:

"I'm not sure I like your definition of good news."

"I should clarify. There's no *evidence* to support any theory that there was wrongdoing, *nor* is there evidence to vindicate you." He shifted his coffee to the other hand, took the lid off, blew on it. "But you won't be charged."

"Well, I guess I should be grateful, then."

"Your brother said your father wished to be cremated, so that's being arranged, and we'll have the ashes delivered."

Lucas nodded.

No family, no funeral.

It was easy that way.

"So." Chambers put the lid back on. "Tell me about the book."

"It's from the sixties. It's about a society that sends their kids away for their childhood. My father e-mailed with the author's son a few years ago and I tried to contact him, but he's dead. Brain cancer. Their e-mails mentioned that his father had a cult following. I don't know. Maybe there's a connection? Obviously, the Alzheimer's makes it impossible to get any information out of him."

Chambers sipped his coffee, winced. Took the lid off again.

Lucas said, "His research sounds relevant. It never came up before?"

"No." Blew on it again. "But, Lucas. You have to just let me do my job, okay."

"I wish you would!" Lucas wanted to knock the coffee out of his hand. "Did you even Google the words 'the leaving' back then?"

"Don't be a smartass. Of course. The book didn't pop! They're not exactly uncommon words."

"Unreal," Lucas said.

Chambers just shook his head and looked away, letting it go. "Come inside so I can take notes."

So Lucas followed him in and told him again about Orlean—and no, he didn't have the book, because he'd given it to Orlean—and went over the whole story of the nursing home and Scarlett's penny and the security guard.

When they were done, Lucas said, "Why were you asking about Max and the school shooting?"

Chambers seemed to be considering, like deciding on a chess move. His phone rang and he took the call. "Yeah?"

Then, "Okay. Be right there."

"I have to go," he said to Lucas. "Something's come up."

"Something to do with us?"

"When I can tell you," Chambers said, "I will."

"So that's a yes."

Chambers let out a loud breath. "That's a yes."

"Why were you asking Max's parents about the shooting?" Lucas repeated. "I was there, you know."

"I know."

"How do you know?"

"I asked your brother."

"Why?"

Chambers tilted his head, annoyed. "What did I just say about letting me do my job?"

AVERY

Again with the landline.

Just ringing and ringing.

Why did they even still have the thing?

She got up from where she was sitting at the kitchen island and picked up: "Hello."

"Avery?"

"Yes."

"It's Detective Chambers." The dishwasher dinged that it was finished.

"Hi."

"I need to speak to your father, please."

"He's not here." She opened the dishwasher door, and hot air pushed out into the room.

"I've tried his cell ten times," Chambers said. "I've left messages. Do you know where he is? Can you reach him?"

"I can try his cell, too. Or call his assistant."

"What's that number?"

She had to go get her phone and look it up to give it to him.

"Okay, thanks."

"No, wait, you can't expect—"

He hung up.

"You have GOT to be kidding me!" Avery screamed.

She called her father's cell, but it went straight to voice mail.

She texted him: **CALL CHAMBERS! THEN CALL HOME!**

He was no better than her mother, really: She was upstairs, in the bedroom, in bed, watching TV. He was hiding under his own pillow at work. Her phone rang.

"Sorry," he said. "Meetings."

"What's going on?" she said.

"It's—they got a tip that sounds reliable. But—"

"A tip about what?"

He breathed loudly. "The location of a body."

"*Max's body*?" She nearly screamed it. Then regretted her mother might have heard.

"They don't know, Avery. A body. That's all. *Do not mention* this to your mother yet. Understood?"

Avery said, "Understood."

"And let's not jump to conclusions, okay? Let's just sit tight. I'll come home as soon as I can."

Sam came and got her when she texted him the news—*I will not call Lucas. I will not text Lucas*—and they went to the Love Boat for ice cream because she couldn't think of anything else to do and neither could he.

As usual, he ordered a flavor she didn't even want to try.

Pistachio.

Who did that?

Who didn't at least try to coordinate?

They'd had to wait a long time to get served—the kid in front of them had a peanut allergy and the mom had asked them to use a clean scoop and open a new gallon of whatever flavor the kid wanted—and by the time they got outside, there were no tables worth sitting at. Only two seats at a table where someone had spilled what looked like a combination of chocolate-chip-mint and blue-raspberry sorbet. They'd melted together into a green and purple swirl that she half wanted to take a photo of. She could study it later and decide whether it looked hideous, like a close-up of some aggressive cancer cell, or beautiful, like something the aurora borealis might whip up in the sky. So they headed for the car.

"Have there been any more notes?" Sam asked, and it took her a second to figure out what he was referring to. "Because they can't really be from Max if . . . Well, you know."

"There was another one yesterday," she said.

"Why didn't you tell me?"

She shrugged and took a swipe at her coconut almond fudge with a hard tongue.

"Well, hopefully this will put an end to all that."

"You mean *if* it's Max's body," she said.

"Can't I say *anything* right?" He shook his head.

"I don't know, can you?"

He shifted his green cone to his left hand, then reached over and took her hand. "I know this is unbelievably stressful for you. I can't even imagine."

"No, you can't."

"That's what I just said!" he shouted.

"I'm sorry," she said, even though she really wasn't; she just didn't want a scene in the parking lot at the Love Boat. "I'm just so on edge."

"Come on," he said. "I told Emma we'd come get her."

Avery stopped walking. "Why'd you do that?"

"Uh," he said. "Because she's our friend? Because I thought you'd want to see her?"

"I didn't know you guys, you know, texted."

"Sometimes," he said. "Is that a problem?"

"No," she said. "Should it be?"

"Why *would* it be?"

He got into the car and she got in, too, and he started to drive toward Emma's. After a few long blocks, her ice cream had reached that point of no return, where it was melting faster than she could reasonably lick it, and she opened her window and tossed what was left of it out. It hit the car with a thud as Sam took a sharp turn.

"What the hell, Ave?"

"I didn't want the rest of it." Her hands were sticky, and the only napkin she had left was sticky, too.

He shook his head. "We could have found a trash can."

She leaned out to look in her side mirror, saw a racer's stripe of ice cream. "There's a car wash up on the right. My treat."

They stopped at a light that had to be in the running for the longest red in the world, and then he pulled into the car wash. She handed him a ten to slide into the machine at the entrance and then he pulled up to the doorway, put the car in neutral, and they were off.

First came the rainstorm.

And she knew she wasn't making it up, the tension between her and Lucas. The way that he looked at her, the way the air felt around them. You couldn't make that up.

Then the blue-and-purple foam soap. She wanted to take a picture of that, too, compare it to that ice-cream swirl.

Then the dullflapping of those oversize brushes—the car basically being pummeled clean by some palsied rubber octopus.

She could remember all this, seen from the backseat when she was little.

A feeling of car sickness and fear and wonder.

He felt something for her.

Something more.

She knew it.

Then more rain.

Then huge fans to blow it all dry.

A gale.

Avery picked a droplet of water on the windshield and watched as it held on for dear life—so much longer than the droplets around it that she actually started rooting for that little guy and then it finally surrendered and went *poof* in the now blinding daylight.

She slid her sunglasses back down over her eyes.

Sam reached over and squeezed her knee as he pulled away. "You okay?"

She nodded and looked out her clean window, saw everything in sharp focus. "I think we should break up."

Scarlett

Her hands on fabric,

her foot on the pedal,

her eyes focused on the line of stitches.

She made a skirt first, to get her fingers used to working the machine again. It was the only thing she'd done since coming home that felt right.

Her mother had had some old fabric lying around, so she'd used that.

She didn't love it.

It didn't matter.

There'd be time.

She'd shop.

She'd make dresses.

She'd make simple tops.

She knew how to do all that and had a moment of gratitude for . . . whoever.

This, at least, was a small gift.

Some small consolation prize.

Maybe the others had secret skills, too. Things that could bring them even a small bit of . . . joy?

Sarah had seen things in her mind like sketches.

Scarlett went and got her phone and called her.

It rang.

And rang.

And rang.

Then voice mail—the robot kind, prerecorded.

"Sarah. It's Scarlett. Listen. I want you to try to do something. I want you to try to draw what you see—the house, the girl. You said you see them like sketches, so just pick up a pencil and see what comes out. I just realized I know how to sew and, I don't know. Maybe you can draw. Call me? Okay?"

She went back to the machine with the last piece of fabric she had on hand, thinking just to practice more, to maybe make a small purse.

She ran the machine and lost herself in the rhythm, the hum, the *click-clicking* of the needle.

When she stopped, she hadn't even sewn along a seam.

She'd made a series of lines with right angles.

Nothing but three rectangles.

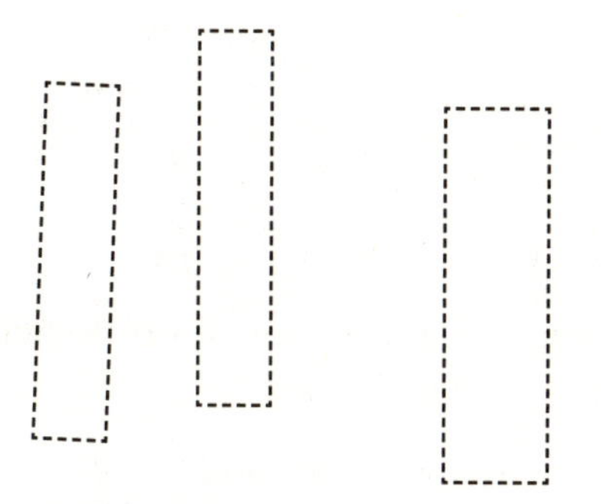

Such a waste of fabric.

She'd have to find a seam ripper and pick them out.

She heard Tammy's phone ring, heard her pick up and then, a moment later, say, "Yes, thanks. Of course I'll tell her."

Tammy came into the room and stood there, looking . . .

/ / / / / / /

. . . and Scarlett said, "What?"

"They found a body."

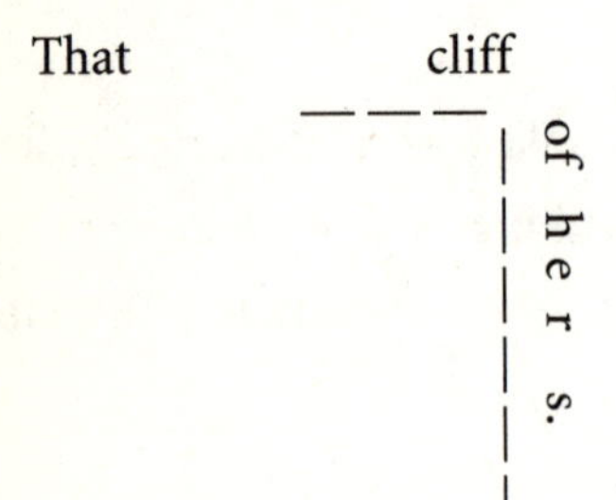

"In the Everglades."

Flattening.

"Max?"

. . . And becoming solid ground worth standing on.

"He ain't saying"—*isn't!*—"but who else would it be?"

. . . And the bottom

dropping out.

Lucas

Lucas was on the computer, reading about the shooting. Because maybe doing so would help him remember that day? It was before they were taken. So in theory, he should be able to remember. The way he should be able to remember maybe taking his first steps, the sound of his mother's voice. So far, though, nothing.

His phone buzzed a text. It seemed too fast for there to be an ID. Chambers had said to sit tight.

The text said:

Want to hang out?

So not Chambers.

And it didn't sound like Scarlett.

Because it wasn't.

Avery?

Did he want to hang out with Avery?

Or did he want to stay here waiting for Chambers and answers?

Yes, as a matter of fact.

He *did* want to hang out.

Yes, with Avery.

Today, maybe *only* with Avery.

Avery was easy.

A friend.

Right?

Scarlett was . . .

Something else.

Something complicated.

He wrote back,

sure ! when?
where?

She said:

Now? Got wheels?

Ryan and Miranda were out.

But her car was just sitting there.

It was a bad idea, really.

But it was his only idea.

He went down the hall and into Ryan's room and looked for Miranda's overnight bag and found the key linked to the strap on a blue hook.

Back to his phone:

Yes.
Pick you up in five.

Then out the door.

Then back for his camera.

Then out again and into Miranda's car, where he had to push the driver's seat back and adjust the rearview, even for the two-minute drive.

Avery was waiting beside a pelican mailbox, wearing plaid shorts and a pink tank top and sunglasses with white frames.

"It has occurred to me," she said when she got into the car, pushing a stack of T-shirts aside and then tossing them into the backseat, "that I actually have no idea what we should do."

"Pick anything." He felt suddenly giddy. "Something fun."

"Fun," she said. "Like real fun or fake fun?"

"I wasn't aware there was a distinction," he said. "Possible to have both at once?"

"I don't know," she said. "Zoo? Or Zoomers? Mini-golf?"

"What's Zoomers?"

"Amusement park," she said. "So it would have to at least be *amusing* if not exactly fun, right?"

An amusement park.

He sat with the idea for a moment, just looking out the windshield.

CAROUSEL. BEACH. WHITE FIRE. HORSE.

A gardener was trimming hedges along the circular driveway. Lucas hadn't realized how rich Avery's family was before, but now it made sense.

The reward.

The house.

All of it.

This was the other side of the tracks, but there weren't tracks.

"I don't think there's a carousel," she said. "If it matters."

"Zoomers sounds perfect," he said. "I'm good."

They started on the Tilt-A-Whirl and the spinning was brutal, his gut surely disconnecting in there.

Round and round.

Looking for something each time.

Or someone?

To wave to?

No one there, of course.

No one who knew him.

No news vans thanks to Miranda's car.

But on that carousel?

Who'd *been* there?

At first he worked hard to avoid touching her. But as the car spun and journeyed around the rails, the force of it threw them together hip-to-hip and there was no stopping it and he stopped caring.

Her hair blew into his face and the scent of honeysuckle conjured images of tangled vines and bobbing bees. He had a feeling of remembering her even if it was ridiculous to think he'd remember a girl from the park or playground of his youth.

He felt his stomach drop out of him with each whip of the car, thought at least twice that he might lose his lunch, was probably turning green, but when they got off, she was steady, unfazed.

"What next?" she asked.

She seemed, somehow, complete. In a way he didn't feel and didn't know he'd ever be able to feel. Fully formed. Confident. At ease. Powerful.

"I'm not loving the spinning," he said, rubbing his stomach, though now that he was on the ground he felt perfectly fine again.

"I know just the thing," she said, and she took off. He followed her to the Go Karts track. A short line had formed inside a corral and they joined it.

Lucas watched as drivers got into cars and were strapped in by ride attendants. Dirty lights at the track entrance turned from red to green, and a car tore out. Loudly.

"You come here a lot?" he asked.

She elbowed him. "Are you trying to pick me up?"

He smiled.

Was he?

"You may have noticed there isn't exactly a lot to do around here." Avery adjusted her ponytail. "There are only so many times in one's life that one can play mini-golf."

"How many?" He smiled.

She gave him a look.

"No, really." Smiled wider. "What's a lifetime's worth of mini-golf, do you think?"

The line moved forward, so they did, too. This was nice. It felt normal. Hanging out with a friend. Just a few days ago, he'd never have imagined it possible he'd be having a day like this. "Wait. Shouldn't you be in school or something?"

"Starts up again on Monday."

"You probably had more fun plans for spring break than all this."

She shrugged. They were two people away from getting in cars.

"It was probably for the best. At least I've been able to be around for my parents. Well, my mom. And also, well. I've had a chance to get to know you again at least a little bit, and that hasn't been so awful." She leaned into him.

Was she flirting?

He'd read it all wrong.

Her feelings.

His feelings?

"You ever do this before?" she asked then, curious not funny or cruel or wiseacre-y.

"I doubt it?"

They gave their tickets, then got into cars, and the whole place smelled of burning rubber and he liked it.

The wheel of his car was hot, stiff.

The pedals heavy under his sneakers.

The light turned green for Avery, then red again, then green for him, and he tapped the pedal and the car jerked; then he pressed it more solidly and the machine zipped to life and out he went into the sun, taking curves, whole body vibrating, smiling, chasing after, yes, Avery with her hair like the tail of a kite.

AVERY

"It's always a tough call," she said, getting into the car again, her right leg almost numb from go-karts. Still. "Do you like your mini-golf with a side of pirates or a healthy dose of jungle animals?"

"I wouldn't know how to even begin to choose," Lucas said, starting the engine.

"Whose car is this?" she asked then, pulling a Strawberry Shortcake T-shirt out from under her feet.

"Ryan's girlfriend," he said.

"Okay, I guess. Whatever?" She tossed the shirt into the backseat with the others. "So the water features at Jungle Golf are arguably more impressive. But the pirates do have a way with rope bridges."

"What kind of water features we talking?" he asked.

"Fairly impressive waterfall thing that leads into a rocky river and then a large pool."

"I'm sold," he said. "Which way?"

"Left out of the lot," she said, and they were off.

Their date—no, not that!—their hang had extended into the evening. After go-karts there'd been bumper boats—they both got soaked, which actually felt good in the high heat of the afternoon—

then some arcade games, most notably Ms. Pac-Man. Then they'd driven to a Chick-fil-A and eaten, and now mini-golf.

Being with him was just . . . easy.

And torturous. It would be *easier* if he knew how she felt and felt the same.

Studying his hands and arms as he drove and scanned through radio stations, she wondered what the hell she'd been thinking texting him in the first place. Did she think she could win him over? With go-karts and mini-golf? Did she think she could compete with Scarlett? With years of history and the bond of trauma?

What if what she was feeling for Lucas was some twisted thing where she was treating him like a stand-in for Max? Like a brother? Did the way she felt so excited to be around him have more to do with The Leaving than with real feelings?

They paid and picked out clubs and stood in front of a tub of balls.

"What color?" she asked him.

"Doesn't matter."

"Doesn't matter?" Why had he even come? Boredom, maybe. Lack of anything else to do. "Where's the fun in that? Pick a color."

He laughed. "I honestly don't care. Just pick one for me."

"Fine," she said, and she picked out a pink ball and a black one. They walked to the first hole, a straightaway beside a large gorilla. She tossed Lucas the pink ball.

"Seriously?" he said.

"You said it didn't matter." She wrote their names on the scorecard. "You first."

He put the ball in one of the little holes on the rubber mat, then looked up at the course and tapped the ball. Sure enough, hole in one.

"So you're a ringer," she said.

"Beginner's luck?" he offered.

It took Avery two strokes to get the black ball in and, though she knew she shouldn't be, she was annoyed about it.

"Are you going to, like, go to school?" she asked on the next hole.

"I don't know," he said. "Nobody's really pushing the issue but . . . I guess? I have no idea."

He took his first stroke; the ball stopped about six inches short of the hole. She stepped up.

"What's it like," he asked. "Your school?"

"It's school. With all the usual BS. But I do all right."

"What are you into?"

"Yearbook. I did cheer for a few years but couldn't handle the practices. So many practices. I played soccer. Briefly. I'm thinking of trying out for the school play next week, but probably not."

They each took their turns hitting the balls into the cup and moved on, over a bridge. The waterfall below flowed an unnatural shade, like Gatorade. Electric-looking and saccharine.

The next hole had a sizable canyon between two sections of green. Avery knew the trick was to hit hard, to fly.

"What do you think you'd do?" she asked. "At school?"

"I can't imagine it. Like I hear people saying stuff about getting back to normal, but I don't have a normal. Or whatever my normal was blew up and got decimated into tiny pieces. So."

Avery's ball leaped over the canyon, practically shimmering from the lights lighting the course, but then it hit the rock border of the hole too hard and bounced back. "No, no, no," she said. "Slow down."

And off toward Frozen Slushy Falls the black ball went.

Lucas gave chase, but it was too fast—gone, bouncing down the rocky falls and landing in the pool below with a *ploop*.

"Black ball, I hardly knew ye," she said.

Lucas laughed and said, "You're funny."

"It's a coping mechanism," she said.

"Does it work?"

"Most of the time, yeah." She nudged him. "You should try it."

They stood there—the air still dense with heat—and she thought to say, "I broke up with my boyfriend yesterday."

He looked up, nodded. "Didn't know you had one."

She'd been leaning on a fence and now pushed off. "Well, now I don't." She nodded toward the front desk. "So do I go get another ball or not?"

"Do you have anything better to do?"

Nothing she could think of that she could tell him.

"Friend" is a horrible cover story.

She beat him in the end.

By a lot.

Scarlett

They had wanted to spend the afternoon on the beach. It was what you did when you lived in a beach town and had nothing else to do. And it was a decent way to kill time while waiting for a body to be identified.

But they had had to go shopping first.

For swimsuits.

Scarlett had stood in the fitting room, staring at her body for a long minute in between two suits she was trying on.

She still felt like a stranger to herself in some ways.

These are my hands.

These are my breasts.

My breasts are sore.

After she picked a suit—simple, navy—she went back out to pay. Kristen had chosen a black bikini and on their way out of the store, Scarlett said, "Have you gotten your period?"

Kristen had grabbed her breasts. "No, but I feel like it's coming."

"Me, too."

So they'd gone to a drugstore, and after that they were hungry, so they'd eaten—late—and then they'd gone back to Scarlett's house and found one of the old Leaving movies on some cable channel and couldn't resist. It was as bad as Tammy had said.

Finally, pretty confident they hadn't spent their lives in underground bunkers controlled by a madman with a tattooed face, they changed into their new suits and hit the beach. It was pretty much evening.

Kristen had brought magazines, so Scarlett had gone back up to the house for a book—*The Wonderful Wizard of Oz.*

But in the end, she didn't feel like reading.

She felt like staring at the water.

She still hadn't seen a dolphin, and it was starting to annoy her.

Kristen said, "I think I had a breakthrough with the hypnotist last night."

"Yeah?"

"Yeah. I haven't known how to bring it up all day. But we were talking about emotions. Could I remember a moment when I was feeling sad? Or afraid? Could I describe where I was and who I was with when I was feeling each of those things?"

"Okay," Scarlett said.

"I talked about you."

"When you were feeling which emotion?"

"Betrayed. Sad."

"Are you in love with Lucas?" Scarlett asked, not feeling too worried about the answer one way or the other.

Just wanting facts.

"I highly doubt it," Kristen said.

"I think I am." Felt weird to say it. "Or was." More accurate. "Do you think it's possible we were in some kind of . . ."

Kristen snorted. "Love triangle?"

"I guess?"

Scarlett said, "Do you not like me because maybe I was with him when you wanted to be?"

"Maybe."

She had the initials carved into the pier.

And the guard's memory of her and Lucas.

But anyone could have carved those; the guard could be wrong.

What *actual* proof did she have that they'd been together in ways they weren't *all* together?

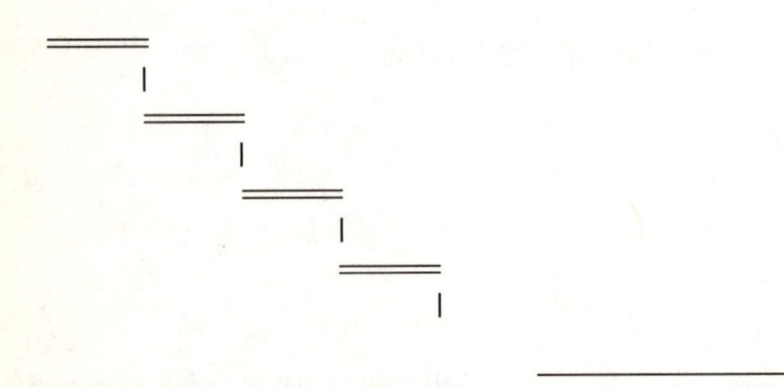

"This might sound weird," she said, "but do you skip the bottom step when you're going down a set of stairs?"

"I don't think so," Kristen said. "Why are you asking me *that*?"

"I think he and I used to sneak out or something. We both keep skipping a last step. Like maybe there was a noisy staircase where we were or something? I don't know."

"I heard about your penny, and someone recognized you?" Kristen flipped a page in the magazine she wasn't really reading.

"It was a crazy feeling." Everything about the guard's face—his stained teeth, his unruly brows—was now etched in her mind. She'd felt the spark of a new, amazing feeling when his eyes showed recognition of who she actually was. She was not just some missing child, newly returned, not some walking headline.

"And you're *sure* he didn't just see you on the news?"

"He described a jacket I used to wear," she said. "How it was homemade. And I went home and sat down at Tammy's sewing machine, and it turns out I know how to sew. Like, I think I made the jacket."

"Do you *remember* the jacket?" In spite of her questions, Kristen seemed to be losing interest; she looked at her magazine and flipped a few pages. She landed on a page with a row of models wearing formal gowns.

"I don't." Scarlett liked the fabric of one of the dresses, the color of another. "But I think you just gave me an idea. I should make it again."

It was, at the very least, something concrete she could do.

"But you *just said* you don't remember it."

"No, but I could just make a jacket that I'd like to make. My taste. See how it turns out. See if maybe it's the kind of thing more people would recognize or something."

"It's a stretch." Kristen closed her magazine.

"Everything's a stretch," Scarlett said back.

"So." Kristen lay back in her chair. "You can sew. Sarah can maybe draw, we think? Lucas has this camera and tattoo thing going on even though I have no idea how that might lead to anything. And you swallowed a penny. What kind of clue do I have?"

"You really can't think of anything?"

"I don't know. I've been writing a lot. Like I started keeping a journal. I saw a blank book and I just picked it up and started writing."

Fascinating.

But how would . . . ?

"Maybe you kept one when we were gone?"

"But where is it? And also what about Adam? What does *Adam* have? What if we need all these things to work together to even mean anything?"

"Maybe we only need a few," Scarlett said. "Maybe we had no idea what we would or wouldn't remember and were trying to cover our bases."

A girl walking along the beach, flip-flops dangling from her hands, stopped. She was flanked by two other girls. She had long blond hair and wore pink sunglasses, which she lifted off her face and perched atop her head. "Ohmygod, Scarlett?"

"No comment," Kristen said.

But it wasn't media. Just girls.

Normal girls.

Who looked like maybe they were on their way to a party.

The look of them made Scarlett self-conscious.

Were her eyebrows all wrong?

Hair all wrong?

She had no idea.

Thought she didn't care.

Maybe she did.

"I'm Vanessa," she said. "We used to be friends. You know, when we were little."

Scarlett recognized her from a photograph in her bedroom. She said, "I have a picture of us holding these ridiculously big stuffed horses."

Vanessa nodded. "My parents took us to the circus."

Kristen stood. "Do you remember *me*? Were *we* friends?"

Vanessa stiffened. "I'm sorry. I don't think so."

"Oh, don't be sorry." Kristen grabbed cigarettes from her bag. "I'm going to take a walk." She marched off toward the water.

"How are you holding up?" Vanessa took Kristen's seat and pulled her sunglasses back down. Her friends had lost interest and wandered off.

"As well as can be expected, given the circumstances."

"I heard your mom went off the deep end."

"Indeed she did."

"Is she back now? Now that you're back?"

"We're working on it."

"You think they're ever going to find Max? Figure the whole thing out?"

"I honestly have no idea."

Vanessa said, "You gave me a necklace right before. It was one of those best-friend hearts cut in half. I still have it."

"I'll have to look around upstairs."

She nodded. "For a long time my mother told me you'd just moved. I didn't understand why you didn't say good-bye. I cried a lot. Wasn't that an awful thing of her to do?"

"How else was she going to explain?"

"I don't know." Vanessa shrugged. "It just seems like the truth is always the better option."

"Oh, sorry, honey, your best friend and five other kids just disappeared without a trace tonight. Night-night!"

Vanessa laughed. "You're funny. You were always funny."

"First I've heard of it," Scarlett said.

"I should go." Vanessa stood and wagged a flip-flop down the beach, where her friends had stopped to wait.

"Sure," Scarlett said. "Have fun. Thanks for stopping."

By the water, Kristen was standing and smoking, her ankles buried in sand. Scarlett tried to let her gaze go fuzzy while she watched again for slick gray arched backs to pop up out of the water.

And watched.

And watched.

Down the beach a bit, there was some shouting, pointing.

"Two of them!" someone shouted. "Right over there!"

She panicked for a second. She'd seen on the news earlier that Adam and Sarah had been receiving death threats because they weren't cooperating with the investigation. Had she and Kristen been recognized?

No.

Two dolphins.

She got up and walked toward the woman pointing, a woman in her forties with two small daughters. "Look that way and maybe we'll see them again," she said, bending to share the girls' view.

"Wait for it," the mom said.

"Wait . . .

"There!"

"I see them!" one daughter shouted, and the other, smaller one, said, "Where? Where?"

"Oh, you missed them, sweetie," the mom said. "But we'll try again later!"

"But I wanted to see the dolphins," the girl cried.

Scarlett hadn't seen them, either.

What was wrong with her?

She felt a sliver of her heart

break

off

and

d r i f t .

• • •

Back by the house, Tammy and Steve were standing on the beach, looking up and down, looking *for her.*

"We got your book ending for you!" Steve called out.

"What do you mean?"

"They found the guy, Scarlett," Tammy said. "They found where you were."

Then Tammy kept talking about the Everglades and how they'd all go there in the morning and how there were photos and evidence they'd been there—clothes and stuff—and Scarlett felt her body seize up at the thought of seeing him, confronting him.

Her nerve endings vibrated.

He'd have to explain.

He'd have to fix them.

So they could retrieve.

Everything.

Get eleven years back.

Then Tammy said, "He's dead, Scarlett."

Seagulls halted midair.

Waves stopped midcrash.

And a breath caught in Scarlett's lungs and starting to congeal there.

Her mother came up to hug her and she felt her body go

limp,

accepting.

DAY FIVE

Lucas

He'd come alone.

Like in a dream state.

Hadn't been able to sleep.

Hadn't been able to stop thinking about Avery.

Had she been relieved that the body wasn't Max's? That it was a guy named John Norton?

Or was she disappointed?

They'd said they'd found evidence that they'd been here.

Photos of them as children.

But none of Max.

What did that mean?

He'd texted her.

She'd wished him good luck today.

Too late for good luck.

Scarlett had come with her mother.

Kristen with her parents.

Even Adam and Sarah and *their* parents had deigned to show up. Lucas couldn't bring himself to make eye contact with either of them. But then Adam walked up to him and said, "It's good to see you."

"Get away from me," Lucas said.

"Wow," Adam said. "Sorry. Don't know what I did to offend you."

"I asked you to get away."

"You told me. That's different."

"Listen, Adam. You let your parents turn you into a puppet and it's obvious you don't care about any of the rest of us at all. So seriously, get out of my face."

Adam said, "You should get help for that."

Lucas looked away. "Like you know anything."

"Can we focus?" Chambers said; he'd been speaking with the boat's captain.

Lucas nodded.

They were about an hour south of Fort Myers, standing on the dock of an airboat company—a business that John Norton's family had owned but he'd sold years ago, with the provision that he be allowed to come and go and keep a house on the property. "So that explains how no one saw you or knew where you were," Chambers had said on the phone. "This is twenty acres of private swampland."

"Well, what are we waiting for?" Lucas asked.

John Norton was dead, single gunshot to the head, and they were heading to a small cluster of structures he'd maintained—accessible only by airboat.

The airboat held just ten passengers, so Chambers's partner, Sarah's mother, Kristen's father, and Adam's mother would all follow in a second boat.

Lucas sat in the same row—on the same bench—as Scarlett, but with her mother between them.

Hated the look of the back of Adam's head.

The fan that powered the boat was as tall as Lucas and, when it turned on, louder than bombs.

The captain wore huge black padded earphones that surely blocked the sound.

Why hadn't they all been given earplugs?

Or at least a warning?

The boat moved with shocking speed and surprising grace.

Just whizzed across the surface of the water effortlessly.

Birds—some bright pink, some white—lifted off, their long legs dangling in flight.

Lucas swore he could feel the eyes of alligators on him, could close his eyes and feel his stomach shift with the turns of the boat and see their jaws opening and snapping.

They glided over long grasses and through archways of mangroves. They made hairpin turns through channels, the boat spraying them with briny water here and there. It was giddy-making—the speed, the roar, the way the boat seemed to be defying some of the laws of psychics—and Lucas wished he were experiencing it as a tourist, not as himself.

Wooly cloud cover made for a chilly gray day. The girls had borrowed thick rain slickers that smelled of swamp. Lucas didn't like the three of them in identical orange; it reminded him of how they'd all come back in the same clothes, like a uniform. Scarlett's hair leaped fitfully in the wind and seemed to be darkening in color from the weight of mist.

A group of six white birds danced in front of the boat, and when they passed, Scarlett pointed at something and Lucas looked.

Another pink bird.

Like fake pink.

Pinker than flamingos.

Pinker than any pink he could recall.

He felt like he'd remember having been here, having been on a boat like this, having seen that shade of pink in flight.

He'd have framed it all in his viewfinder.

Photographed it.

His hands itched for his camera.

But it was in his bag, which had been stowed in the back row.

He'd been afraid to have it out, afraid it would get wet.

Or broken.

Now, regretted it.

Around a turn, the boat slid into a wider channel, and a dock appeared up ahead.

A house appeared next—like an old shack but big.

Then behind it a series of smaller structures—almost hut-like—connected by a series of rope bridges.

A sort of mini-village.

When the boat's roar ceased and it pulled up to the dock, Chambers stood. He stepped out onto the dock, then turned to face them.

"Anything seem familiar?"

Heads shook.

"Well, let's go look around," Chambers said, holding out a hand to help Kristen off the boat. "We took the photos and personal effects away to bag them and tag them and dust for prints and run DNA, but you'll be able to see those later."

He led them to one of the structures, had to duck to go through the door. "This," he said, "is where you slept."

One room.

Five beds.

Not six.

Lucas walked down the center aisle.

He picked a bed, lay down on it.

The view out the window was nothing but sky.

What was Avery doing at that very moment?

Chambers said, "Anything?"

Lucas said, "No."

"Anybody?" Chambers tried, almost sounding irritated.

"Sorry," Adam said. "No."

Sarah shook her head.

"Kristen?"

"Nothing."

Everyone looked to Scarlett, who also shook her head.

"I don't know what to say, guys," Chambers said. "I was really hoping for some kind of epiphany for you all. I was hoping you'd get here and it would all flood back for you."

"It's just. It doesn't make sense." Lucas stood.

Chambers said, "It makes more sense than anything has in eleven years." He turned to face them all. "This was the guy. This was the place. You were here."

"Why only five?" Lucas asked. "Why wasn't Max in any of the photos?"

"Maybe he was never here," Chambers said. "Maybe his going missing was totally unrelated."

Lucas didn't like that idea.

Didn't like what it meant for Avery and her family.

That they'd wasted eleven years on the wrong search, the wrong type of grieving and hope.

He didn't want it to be true.

Didn't want any of this to be happening.

He wanted to see the photos.

Maybe that was the whole point of it, the tattoo.

"There's something you're going to want to see." Chambers ducked back out of the room. "Maybe it will convince you."

AVERY

The tip line headquarters was in the capital building of Blandville.

Well, not really.

But yes, it was the kind of building you'd never notice if you hadn't had reason to go there. In the kind of stretch of useless buildings that, if you were lucky, you'd never have any occasion to visit in your whole life.

Blandville Dry Cleaners.

Blandville Pizza.

Blandville Tax Accountant.

Blandville Florist.

Blandville Wines and Liquors.

The Blandville Tip Line's storefront might have been a bank once, or insurance office, or campaign headquarters for the Blandville mayor. It looked temporary, malleable. Just tables and phones and laptops and a coffeemaker and a tall water cooler with a stout blue family of empty jugs beside it.

Avery had been introduced around and her mother had put on quite an impressive performance in her leading role as GRATEFUL MOTHER OF MISSING CHILD.

A round of applause.

Brava.

Standing O.

Avery hadn't known that her mother had it in her, to pull out such a masterful performance. Maybe that was where she'd gotten her interest in theater and drama at school.

Last night, her mom had dropped to her knees and said, "Oh, thank god," when the call had come that the body was not Max's.

Avery had had quite a different reaction.

She'd been, well, disappointed.

Still was.

Because it meant that the waiting and wondering was going to drag on.

Did she want Max to be dead?

Of course not.

Did she want this whole thing to be over with?

Absolutely.

It meant she had to redouble her efforts.

She had to find another way to get answers.

She'd been ignoring texts from Emma all morning:

Any news?

You okay?

What's going on?

Maybe you lost your phone?

It had started to feel like a game:

IGNORING EMMA'S TEXTS.

FOR 1 PLAYER. AGES 14 AND UP.

Like, did Emma's brain have the capacity to think of maybe trying to call the landline or do anything other than keep texting?

The last text had been the one that really irked her.

Poor Sam. ☹

Poor *Sam*?

That was her takeaway?

This morning there had been a text from Lucas, too.

How are you holding up?

Did that mean he understood how she felt?

Because he hadn't said "Relieved for you" or "Happy for you."

Or was she reading into it?

She knew the cops were taking them all there.

So she'd texted:

Good luck today.

He'd written back:

Thanks.

They were here now with coffee and donuts, to say thanks, as well—to the tip line staff.

Yes, thanks, tip line.

Thanks for nothing.

Avery was eating a too-sweet jelly donut when she was cornered by a nerdy-looking woman in her forties with a long black ponytail.

"I remember you," the woman said. "I remember it all. And you, so little. On the news."

"Yeah?" Avery said. "I guess everyone who was around then remembers."

"Who could forget," the woman said—seemingly without any awareness at all of how ridiculous a statement that was. "I felt so awful for all you families. I joined a search party and everything."

"Well, um"—this was too weird—"Thanks, I guess."

The woman smiled sadly.

"So who was the tip from?" Avery asked, sounding upbeat. "Who made the call? Are they collecting the reward?"

"Oh." The woman waved a hand. "It was anonymous. When there's a dead body involved, they usually are."

Avery cocked her head. "You do this a lot? This kind of work?"

"Nine-one-one operator."

"Ah." Avery nodded. "Well, I'm glad it turned up a good lead. I'm glad they caught the guy. My father thought it was just all going to be crazy people."

"Well, we have those, too. They're *still* calling." She looked at her watch. "Speaking of which, I should get back to the phones."

"What are they saying, the crazy people?"

"Oh, you know. The crazy things." She smiled and walked off.

Scarlett

The color matching of memory and reality was striking.

The stripes, if measured, would have been equal down to the millimeter.

You couldn't see Scarlett.

Or anyone.

The photo had been taken from the ground, looking up at the balloon.

But she knew she was there in that dangling basket.

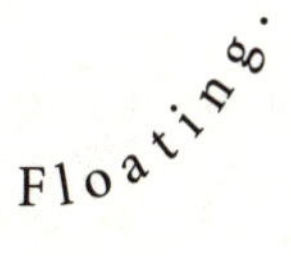

"This is it." She stepped closer to the large framed photograph on the wall of a big lodge-like room.

A singular cloud in the distance had the shape of an elephant mid-sneeze.

Felt calm just standing there.

Hypnotized.

"This is the puppy." Sarah broke the spell.

Scarlett turned to the voice, saw the puppy photo.

Beside that, a horse in a meadow.

Then . . . the crisscross hill of a roller coaster going up, up, up to the sky.

And a carousel horse in close-up.

Five large framed photos.

"This is the horse," Kristen said.

"This is the roller coaster," Adam said.

Lucas stood in front of the carousel horse, transfixed. "So we're remembering photographs?" he asked.

/

/

"Not necessarily," Chambers said. "These could be photos from things that you actually did. Just without you in them."

"These prints are big," Adam's father said. "They had to have been printed specially."

Chambers nodded. "I'll send people out to print shops. See if anything pops."

"Wouldn't they just do that online or something?" Kristen asked. "It's not exactly the kind of place where you'd get deliveries."

Scarlett turned back to her photo.

Her photo?

But something felt . . .

She took in the details of the room.

Lantern lights hanging from wooden beams.

A round window high on one wall, like a porthole.

Nothing but the photo familiar.

"I don't understand," Scarlett said. "This isn't anywhere near Anchor Beach."

"I know." Chambers nodded. "But the evidence is overwhelming."

"Did anybody near here ever see us?" she said. "Remembers us?"

"The nearest town is Everglades City and it's not much of a town. We're asking around." Chambers scratched his head. "This *happens*, this kind of stuff, and it's a shock *every time*. Women held in basements for years—babies being born while neighbors were only just fifty feet away—and no one around knew or even suspected anything was wrong."

Scarlett went back to staring at her hot air balloon.

Now that she was here, the memory felt . . . fake.

Chambers was still talking. "We found vials. Syringes. They're being tested. Some were labeled as a protein Sashor has talked about. A protein involved in memory formation."

"But who *is* he?" Scarlett asked. "Why did he do this?"

"Don't know," Chambers said. "Possibly just to make it easier to keep you here longer?"

"But *why*? And how would he have the skills to do it all?"

"We don't know yet."

Scarlett asked, "But who killed him?"

"We don't know," Chambers said.

She shouted, "You don't know anything!"

/

/

/

She was in the abyss.

Alone.

No, wait . . .

Tammy was there, too, chewing gum; she seemed to approve of her daughter's outburst. Something about the hand on her hip showed a bit of defiant swagger.

Kristen said, "Under hypnosis, I remembered something. A journal I hid near an owl. Did you find any . . . owls?"

Chambers shook his head. "No owls, no."

Like he was talking to a crazy person, pandering.

They all stood there for a moment, disappointment spreading like toxic invisible gas. Scarlett felt the urge to cough, resisted.

Then Chambers said, "Come on, I've got one more thing to show you back at the dock."

They walked back across one of the bridges. Police officers in chest-high rubber overalls were out scouring the property.

Scarlett fell in step beside Chambers and asked, "Did you find a gun?"

Lucas caught up with them and said, "What about a camera?"

Lucas

The ride back seemed faster.

The cloud burning off, the sky becoming blue again.

This time, he had his camera in hand the whole way.

Pink birds.

Click.

White birds.

Click.

Tall grass.

Click.

An alligator—or was that a stone?

The evidence said he'd been here.

He had no way to prove otherwise.

Back at the airboat dock, they followed Chambers through a field to an old garage.

Scarlett came over to Lucas's side as they walked. "There are no stairs," she said. "And like I said, it's nowhere near Anchor Beach."

He nodded. "It feels, I don't know . . . staged?"

"We have no way to prove it," she said.

"Not yet." He caught up with Sarah. "The house you see in your mind's eye. Is it here? Is this it?"

She shook her head. "Maybe it's just a house I drew. And a girl I drew. Imaginary."

"Maybe." Lucas had yet to come up with a good theory about the mystery girl Sarah remembered.

"Have you drawn them?" Scarlett asked. "So we can see?"

"I'm working on it," she said. "Soon."

Some uniformed officers were standing in front of a large shed and stepped aside as the group approached. They fanned out in a semicircle at the open door.

The mud was so thick that it was hard, at first, to even see it.

The yellow-orange paint of a small school bus.

"There's a white van, too," Chambers said. "Like the one you described. Broken taillight and all."

Lucas stepped into the shade of the structure to get the sun out of his eyes, to better see. He lifted his camera, took a few shots. Let it drop to hang around his neck on its strap.

Chambers looked at his phone, read a message, looked back up. "We have a gun," he said. "Listen, I'll be in touch with you all after we go over every inch of this place. And I'll come see each of you with some of the items we found."

He ushered them back to the parking lot, and Lucas couldn't take his eyes off Chambers's weapon, holstered in his belt.

Thought about grabbing it.

Aiming it.

Firing it.

When Chambers started to walk off toward his car, Lucas called out, "Wait!"

Chambers stopped and turned.

Everyone else turned, too.

And Lucas felt that dizziness return, for the first time in days—

HORSES, TEETH,
ROUND AND ROUND

—and steadied himself by thinking about the cold metal of the gun, the weight of it in his fingers, a feeling of calm, of release.

"The gun you found," he said. "You're going to find my fingerprints on it."

AVERY

Avery sat at the kitchen island eating chicken enchiladas that Rita had brought—right out of the dish. She couldn't remember the last time an actual meal had been cooked in this house.

God bless Rita.

Each bite brought Avery closer to tears.

The doorbell rang and it was UPS.

The book from Wisconsin.

So Avery went up to her room and lay down on her bed and started reading. Which was something she generally liked to do.

But this book was painful.

The same way old movies sometimes were, with their incredibly long opening credit sequences and slow starts.

She started to skim.

Then tried to get herself to stop, to focus.

Then started to skim.

Then focused.

Then finally hit the meat of the story and powered through.

And then set the book down and just lay there.

What would her life have been like if she'd been sent away? If she'd been able to just skip all the boredom and awfulness of the last eleven years and then just been returned to her parents as this happy, well-adjusted, fully formed person.

Because, really. What did she have to show for herself? For the last eleven years?

What had she done that was worthwhile?

What had she accomplished that meant anything?

She got up and walked over to her desk, above which a bunch of certificates of merit hung on a corkboard. French competitions. Math competitions. She started to take them down, one by one, and toss them into the trash can. Then, remembering a trophy she'd won by doing basically nothing that one year on soccer, she opened her closet, pulled it out, put it in the trash, too.

Then she just kept going.

Dumb art projects.

T-shirts from charity events she barely remembered.

Shoe boxes full of friendship bracelets.

What friends?

Posters from concerts and plays at school.

Old class photos.

She slowed her movements, started searching until she found her kindergarten class photo.

Went face by face.

Named names.

Sure enough, she had no idea who some of these people even were. How was that possible?

Setting the photo aside, she saw her handmade calendar.

Her countdown to going away.

And she flipped through until she found today's date and saw there were approximately 898 days left until she would be able to go to college.

How had she ever thought it was a good idea to make this calendar, when the truth was the idea of leaving home was terrifying?

Who would look after her mom?

What would she do without Emma?

What would she do after college?

What if she never found a job? Or a boyfriend? Or husband?

What would happen when her parents died and she had no one?

Something soft and brown caught her eye back there in the closet, and she reached out tentatively—dead mouse?—and then felt fuzz and pulled and it was Woof-Woof.

She hugged his floppy, dusty body tight to her neck and tears came and sobs followed, and when she was done she tossed the calendar into the trash, too, wanting nothing more than to just be able to stay.

Stay forever.

"Rita!" her mother was calling out. "Rita?"

The response came: "Yes, ma'am."

"We're running out of tissues in my room." Her mother's voice in the hall. "Can you restock them?"

Scarlett

Scarlett's nap dreams were ripped from the day's events.

Airboats.

LOUD.

Pink birds and gators.

Lucas with a gun.

And also came from other days and nowhere.

An airport.

A school cafeteria.

Zombies in a nursing home.

Then Scarlett, with a pain in her legs, on a hill, crawling up toward a power plant with four smokestacks.

She woke up and her stomach growled and she got up to go eat.

Tammy was vacuuming.

The whole house looked . . . cleaner, yes, but also . . . lighter?

In the fridge, she found leftover pizza and started to eat a piece cold, standing at the kitchen island.

The cat was in a corner, cowering, like maybe it had never seen Tammy vacuum.

Then it hopped up onto an end table that had once been covered with . . .

That was it.

No more *UFO Insiders*.

No more ET magazines.

Whole piles of back issues . . . gone.

"Mom??"

It just slipped out.

Tammy hadn't heard.

The vacuum too loud.

Louder: "Mom?"

She turned, used a foot to switch off the machine.

Looked like she might cry.

"You okay?"

Her mother sat on the couch, wiping away tears. Shaking her head. "When you have little kids, people are always saying it goes so fast. Blink and you'll miss it. And I remember feeling like it wasn't fast enough." She reached for a tissue box, pulled one out, dabbed her eyes. "Now I just want it all to slow down. I want to rewind and play the whole thing again but with you in it. I'm not ready to be this old. I'm not ready to have to let you go again so soon."

"You won't have to."

"I will! I can't keep you here forever."

Scarlett sighed. She couldn't argue with that. She said, "What happened to all your magazines and stuff?"

Her mother looked around the room, seeming satisfied. "Oh, I figure it's just time for us to be moving on with things, don't you think?" She stood and threw out her tissue and took up the vacuum again.

"I'm pretty sure it wasn't him," Scarlett said. "John Norton."

Her mother shrugged. "Either way, I'm pretty sure now it wasn't aliens." She turned the vacuum back on and finished the job.

Lucas

"Do we have any old family photos?" Lucas asked when he got back to the house and after he'd explained everything—about the Everglades, the photos on the walls, the gun, his sense that it was all too . . . neat.

Miranda, for once, wasn't there.

Ryan turned off the TV. "Yeah." He got up and went down the hall into their father's room. He came out with a box and walked past Lucas with it and into the kitchen. He sat. Lucas sat, too.

"Looking for anything in particular?" Ryan asked as he opened the box.

"Not really," Lucas said. "It's just that I don't really remember, you know . . . *Mom*."

Lucas reached in and took a stack and started to sift through a pile of sepia-toned prints.

Women in skirt suits and old, square swimsuits.

A dog—not Walker—on the front porch of a house—not theirs.

There were no names or dates on the back, nothing to go on.

A bunch of people swimming—a double exposure so that some of them looked like ghosts.

Nothing of use to him at all.

"Here." Ryan handed over a print. It was one of those long, skinny sheets of four pictures, each frame featuring a woman making a different silly face. "That's her."

"And here"—he handed over a regular-size print—"this is you as a baby."

At first, the disconnect seemed so wide that Lucas didn't think it could possibly be true.

That *that* baby in that photo in *that* woman's arms could possibly be him.

But Ryan just kept pulling out photos and started telling stories.

You got stung by a bee that day.

I loved that bike but I outgrew it and had to give it to you.

I think this is Mom's mom.

This was Mom in high school, I think.

Oh, this was you . . . that morning.

Lucas took that one, his hand shaking.

This was what he'd looked like just hours before his life had become the stuff of headlines and movies.

He wore a striped polo shirt and khaki shorts and white socks and sneakers. He had a Superman backpack at his feet. Behind him was a classroom wall, with signs and letters and numbers. Beside him were two boys.

"Do you recognize either of them?" he asked Ryan, who took the picture back to look.

Ryan looked at them, then said, "No, sorry."

Lucas looked again.

SHINY FLOORS. STACKS OF TOWELS. SHOPPING CARTS.
AISLES OF TOYS.
POPCORN AND HOT DOGS AND COFFEE.

"I remember buying that backpack. Like at a Kmart or something?"

The memory annoyed him. If he could remember that—something so long ago, from before he was taken—why *couldn't* he remember things that maybe mattered?

He listened with awe as Ryan continued to rattle off stories.

Such a gift his brother had—memories—and he didn't even know it, would never understand what it was like to be without.

To not even know who you really were.

This is you and mom on your birthday.

Three candles on the cake. A cone hat on his head. His mother smiling, pointing at the camera. Him looking at the cake, ready to blow. He felt like maybe he remembered but couldn't fill in anything around it.

Maybe he remembered only the photo.

Maybe he'd seen it before.

"What about photos of after? You know. You and Dad."

"We pretty much stopped taking pictures." Ryan shrugged. "Mom was always the one with the camera. Dad lost interest."

"Any videos?"

"Not that I know of. People take videos of happy occasions, right? We didn't have many of those."

They both turned at the sound of a key in the front door, and Miranda came in, carrying a stack of T-shirts. She tossed them onto the couch, came back to the kitchen, and sat down. "Whatcha doing?"

"'Reminiscing' isn't the right word, is it?" Ryan said.

"Not exactly, no."

"You were cute kids," Miranda said, studying a photo. Then she smiled. "What happened?"

"Hardy har har," Ryan said.

"Aw, look at this one," she said, picking up a picture. "Is this Walker?" She showed it to Ryan, who smiled but then looked at her a little funny and said, "Yeah, that's him."

"What?" she said.

"I don't remember telling you about him."

"Well, you did."

Lucas was looking at another picture, this one of him and a girl. And for a second he thought it was Scarlett but no.

It was Avery.

They were squeezed onto a single swing together.

On a beach.

Sand at their feet.

Surf behind them.

His arm around her shoulder.

Her grin wide.

"Where's this?" he asked Ryan.

"Oh, those swings were death traps. They got taken down years ago."

Ryan said it like it wasn't anything at all.

Lucas absorbed it like a fist to the gut.

AVERY

He texted that night when she was watching TV alone in the den:

I'm outside

She got up and went downstairs and out the front door and then down to the car. "My parents are out," she said. "Want to come in?"

"You sure?" he asked.

When she said "I'm sure" back, she said it in a way that was meant to be doubly meaningful, but of course he wouldn't notice.

She'd never been more sure of anything than her wish to be with him.

She led him through the house and out to the pool, and sat in a lounger. He took the one beside her.

"So?" She tucked her hands into her hoodie pockets.

"Well, they found clothes and stuff there. There were huge framed photos of the things we remember. Like the carousel horse I've been picturing. Scarlett's hot air balloon."

"Really?" Avery had certainly never imagined *that.*

He nodded. "They think it was really him. But I don't know. Nothing was familiar at all."

"I'm sorry," she said.

"They found a gun there and I feel like it's going to have my prints on it."

Not at all the conversation she'd been expecting.

She said, "Why would you think *that*?"

"It turns out I know how to load a gun."

She tried to picture it.

Couldn't.

"I'm confused," she said. "If you don't think it was the place—"

"I think the gun is going to have my prints on it but that it's a setup. I think the whole location was staged."

"Who would even be able to do that, though?" He was suggesting some kind of crazy conspiracy theory. And people who believed in all that were, well, kind of crazy, right? Backward Beatles records about Elvis. Smoke on the grassy knoll.

"I don't know," he said. "I know it sounds crazy. Maybe I'm wrong."

She didn't know what to say, so she didn't even try. The surface of the pool shimmered like fish scales.

"What do you remember most about your childhood?" he asked.

"I wouldn't even know where to start." She recrossed her legs, switching which ankle was on top. Her bones hurt.

"Try."

She closed her eyes. A few eager memories were already there, shouting pick-me-pick-me. "Playing with my neighbors, drinking nectar huckleberry blossoms. Riding our bikes. Playing at the beach. I remember being bored a lot. I remember sleepovers with my cousin . . . or actually I remember looking forward to them more than I even remember what we did. I remember having to get picked up from kindergarten because I fell during recess and hurt my knee really bad and couldn't stop crying. I remember a lot of daydreaming. Wanting to be famous.

Like a rock star or an Olympic figure skater. I think I only gave up on that last one last year."

He sat up and sat sideways on his chair, smiling. "But what's your single most vivid memory of your childhood?"

The memories quieted; none stepped forward. "I don't know. I feel like I've been asked that before and wondered why it would matter?"

"It matters because I'm asking."

"But what would it mean?"

"Just try. Most vivid."

"I remember going to Mexico with my parents. They let me buy a piñata. It had its own seat on the plane home."

"That's not it. Try again."

That panic started to peek around the corner again. This shouldn't be hard. She had to remember. She said, "A vacation in Maine where I played video games in an ice-cream shop. It was the first time my parents let me go out on my own with my cousin."

"Not it. Try again."

"Why?"

"Just do it."

Racing around her mind, grabbing at anything of value, like a Supermarket Memory Sweep. "Getting stung by a bee. I felt something on my leg and went to scratch it and got a handful of bee. I screamed."

"You could just keep going and going, couldn't you?"

"I don't know. I guess?" It felt like they were having a fight and she wasn't sure why. But yes, memories were lining up at the checkout now, waiting their turn.

That time she made a massive sand castle with her father, the way he'd taught her to drip sand to form towers.

The night her parents had a party and she and Max crept halfway down the stairs to peek at the dancing, at the wine being poured.

The time she fell down the back stairs, slid on her back, couldn't breathe; the panic in her mother's eyes.

The first time she went off the high diving board at the pool where she'd learned to swim, the way she'd felt like she'd never make it back up to the surface in time and might die.

If he hadn't asked her, would she have remembered any of that ever again?

And if not, wasn't that terrifying?

Lucas said, "You really can't think of your *most vivid* memory?"

And something inside her snapped. "I remember The Leaving, okay? Is that what you want me to say?" It felt like she'd pulled a muscle she hadn't even known she'd had. "I remember standing at the bus stop for like an hour. There was a tree there that I was trying to climb and I thought it was fun. But then the crying started and then my mom sobbed for days and nothing was even *allowed* to be fun for a long time. I remember being on the news in my pajamas. I remember that more than any good day or Christmas or birthday, okay?"

"You don't even know how lucky you are." He shook his head. "I want my life back."

"So start living it."

"That's easy for you to say."

"It *is* easy," she said. "All *anyone* is trying to do is to move on from their own crappy situation or baggage."

"There has to be more to life than that."

"Says who?"

He looked at something far away. "On the way here, I was thinking these crazy things, like how we're going to find some pill or magical cube. Something that will bring it all back, like my whole childhood will come rushing into me and I'll feel complete again, like I can move on."

"I think you're going to need to find another way."

"To get my memory back?"

"No, to move on." *With me, you idiot!*

"Ever since we came back," he said, "I've had this thought about killing the person who did this. That that would be how I'd be able to move on. Now, with the gun and the body, I'm wondering whether I already did that and still haven't moved on."

"You don't seem like a killer," she said, and she reached out and took his hand and held it, hard. He didn't refuse.

"I know. But you don't know me. *I* don't know me." He pulled his hand away. "I shouldn't have told you any of that."

She was about to tell him that he could tell her *everything*—that she wanted to know his every thought, every flaw—when he said, "I shouldn't have come here."

"Why not?"

He stood. "I don't know. Because of me. I'm messed up. Because of Scarlett. I don't know. I just need to figure this out. It needs to be with her."

So this was what life was.

A series of events in which things you care about—the only good things around you—get taken away one by one.

She wouldn't just allow it.

She stood and got within inches of him, face-to-face. "But you and I are just old friends," she said, and waited for him to try to deny what was between them. In some mirror universe they were touching, and in this universe their bodies knew it, had some muscle memory of it.

"Avery," he said. "I can't."

She nodded, then walked inside, leaving the lanai door open behind her. She said, "You're right that you should stop showing up here like this. It's creepy."

DAY SIX

Scarlett

Scarlett drifted through aisles of bright colors and sparkly displays and bold prints before ending up in a far corner of the fabric store, drawn to a number of vintage prints in muted tones.

She ran a finger across a roll of light-brown fabric with pale-pink stripes running in both directions, like oversize graph paper. She pulled the bolt out of the stand and set out in search of buttons.

And debated between purple and blue before selecting an almost neon aqua.

By the registers, she handed over the fabric and asked for two yards and spun a display of patterns but found none she liked. She'd make her own pattern, maybe using the jacket she'd bought at the outlets with her mother for a guide.

The guard hadn't mentioned a hood, but she wanted one.

He hadn't mentioned a subtle pleated fringe down the front but she could see it in her mind's eye and knew her fingers could make it work.

"Will that be all?" The woman was done cutting.

"And these buttons, please." Scarlett put them on the counter.

"What are you making?"

"A jacket."

"You can post pics on my website when you're done. If you want."

"Okay," Scarlett said. "I will."

"You've been in here before, right?"

"No."

"Really?"

Confused silence that Scarlett then filled: "I'm one of the returned kids. You know, The Leaving."

"Oh. Right." She slid the fabric into a bag. "You know how to sew?"

"Yes, we forget where we were, but apparently the part of the brain where you learn things—they call it procedural memory—is intact."

"I'd like to forget my whole first marriage." She held up a bag and receipt.

"Wish I could help you with that." Scarlett grabbed the bag and left.

She was parked a ways down the street and felt a weird sense that someone was following her. Footsteps in pace with hers? Something?

So she turned.

Just people going about their beach business.

No man carrying wrapping paper.

Nothing that looked like wrapping paper.

Nothing.

So she kept walking.

Then stopped and turned again a block later.

Compared the crowd.

Yes, that girl.

Definitely following her.

So she walked straight at her, surprised that the girl stood her ground, didn't run. "Why are you following me?"

"I was afraid to say . . . I just."

"You just what?" Scarlett stepped closer.

"I wanted to see you with my own eyes, I guess," she said.

"Why? Who are you?"

But the girl's voice was so familiar that Scarlett realized she knew the answer. She'd seen her before, on the news.

The girl said, "I'm Avery. I'm Max's little sister."

Lucas

"I wasn't expecting I'd hear from you again." Sashor shook Lucas's hand, and again Lucas didn't want to let go. But did. They walked down a long hall to his office together. "So, what's up?" Sashor asked.

They sat—Sashor at his desk, Lucas in a chair in front. A sign on the wall that Lucas hadn't noticed last time read,

THERE'S NO TIME LIKE THE PRESENT
AND NO PRESENT LIKE TIME.

"Have you ever heard of a memory scientist named Daniel Orlean?"

"First I heard of him was from Chambers."

"His research had to do with erasing trauma, curing post-traumatic stress."

"Yes, I read up on him a bit. The science has come a long way since he was working in the field, but it's still a minefield of moral issues."

"It seems like maybe whoever did this was influenced by him, by the book. Because our traumas have been erased."

"You remember the scene of your mother's car crash, Lucas."

"But not the shooting. That must mean something."

"It could mean everything or nothing. Chambers and I, well—Lucas, I'm not sure I'm free to talk about it yet."

"About what?" Lucas asked.

Sashor just pressed his lips together.

"You're seriously not going to tell me."

"I'm really sorry." Sashor looked it, at least. "Soon," he said. "I'll have something to tell you soon."

"I kissed Scarlett," Lucas blurted, and Sashor looked surprised and interested. "And I knew it wasn't the first time. But I've been trying to will myself to remember and I can't. Can I will myself to remember things she and I did together?"

"Well, certainly there are memories we have and never access until someone else mentions them." Sashor sat back in his chair, swiveled a little one way, then the other. "Like someone will say 'Remember the time you did the "Thriller" dance in your underwear,' and you won't have thought of it in years but you'll remember it."

Lucas said, "I don't know that dance."

"You get my point," Sashor said. "There's also stuff that your subconscious hangs onto—like a buffering or savings effect—so if you memorize a list or something, then wait a long time until you're sure you've forgotten. Like if you tested yourself. Then if you try to memorize the same list again it'll take you less time than it did the first time around. So the memory of the sequences was stashed away somewhere in your brain and then reactivated."

"How do you remember everything that you know about memory?" Lucas asked.

Sashor laughed.

Lucas worked hard to phrase the next question just so. "So if I can remember loving someone, would I remember hurting someone?"

"I wish I had clearer answers for you, Lucas."

"I wish you did, too."

"I just wonder if there's a point at which you should just stop trying to remember. If maybe what you need is the opposite of trying to will yourself to remember. Maybe you need to intentionally forget about remembering."

"I'm not sure I follow." Lucas shifted in his chair.

"Imagine each memory of these past eleven years, imagine each one as, well, a penny. Say the reality of each moment is the penny. Now imagine them all stretched like Scarlett's penny—because your recall, if you had any, of what happened wouldn't necessarily be accurate anyway. So why fixate?"

"There was a woman in the nursing home. Where Orlean is. She couldn't remember anything. Not from one minute to the next. You leave the room and you go right back in, and she had no idea who you were."

"I've read about her."

"Who is she?"

"Her name, you mean?" Sashor shrugged. "I don't remember."

"No, I mean, how do you form and maintain your identity if you have no memories?"

"*You* have the whole rest of your life ahead of you to make memories."

"But how do I know how to be?"

"How does anybody? Most people only come into adulthood with a handful of vivid memories of their childhood anyway. There's a forgetting curve that has been researched and documented. The longer you live, the less you remember. Don't overvalue what you've lost."

"You can't be serious."

"I'm just thinking out loud. People aren't shaped by conscious memories so much as they are by their overall life experience and bonds. The important thing is arriving at adulthood feeling secure, and even though there are a lot of questions about what happened to you, you seem pretty secure."

"I have barely suppressed homicidal rage," Lucas said. "How does that make me secure?"

"Your rage is justified. You're feeling rage toward someone who did something awful to you, not just some random guy who cut you off on the highway." A beat. "I really am just trying to help."

"What's up with the sign?" He nodded at it.

Sashor turned. "Oh, that." Then turned back to Lucas. "A memory science in-joke of sorts. And by in-joke, I mean it's funny *to me*."

"I don't get it."

"We may not remember this moment," Sashor said. "And we might be happy we've forgotten it."

"Dancing in your underwear."

"Exactly."

AVERY

So she'd been caught. Maybe she'd wanted to be.

"What do you want?" Scarlett demanded.

"Nothing. I just wanted to say hi, I guess. I remember you."

"Yeah?" Scarlett laughed in disbelief.

Poor choice of words.

Scarlett said, "What do you remember?"

"I guess I remember being sad that you were gone. Maybe in a way even sadder, at first, that you were gone than that my brother was gone. I think I worshipped you. In a kid way, you know. You were always nice to the littler kids. And making up stories about wizards and fairies and stuff. I felt like there was something . . . magical about it. About you."

"Trust me," Scarlett said. "There is nothing magical about me at all."

Avery shrugged and then her phone vibrated and she wanted to take it out, read the text, see if it was from Lucas.

She didn't want to be rude. She just wanted something more from all this.

"Well," Scarlett said, "I guess, nice to meet you. Again."

"Yeah," Avery said. "Sorry. For the following thing."

"It's okay," Scarlett said. "I hope they find him."

"Yeah, thanks."

Scarlett turned to walk away.

No.

No.

No.

"Wait," Avery called out.

Scarlett turned.

"Do you think he did it? Do you think Lucas killed that guy?"

Something in Scarlett's eyes turned darker. "Why would you think that?"

"He told me," Avery said. "That he thinks they're going to find his prints."

Scarlett tilted her head, took a step back toward her. "I would say that the Lucas I know would only have done that if his—or our—lives depended on it."

Avery felt her face tighten into something fake-feeling when she asked Scarlett the question she hadn't been able to ask Lucas. "Are you a couple or something?"

Scarlett was unflinching. "I think we used to be, yes."

He'd said he needed to figure it out. With her. But where was *Scarlett's* head in all this?

"What about now?" Avery dared, like her life depended on it.

Scarlett

Chambers put the brown paper bag on the dining room table and pulled out a large manila envelope. He slid a stack of photographs out of it, sifted through them as he spoke to Scarlett and her mother.

"All the photos are from an instant camera. I guess Norton didn't want to risk any of you being recognized if he had prints made somewhere? I'm assuming that's the reason the blown-up shots didn't have you all in them, as well."

He pushed a square photo across the table to Scarlett, who had to move the fabric she'd been cutting, having already ruined some with weird stitches.

She picked it up,

looked—

"That's me"—

/

/

Maybe twelve years old?

And felt the world tilt.

And stood there with an ache that made her knees buckle.

Her mother and Chambers were still talking, but she couldn't process the sounds of their words—

they might as well have been speaking **另一种语言**

—and then she started to cry.

At first, a leak from the eye.

But . . .

. . . the gap in her teeth where she'd lost one,

the ribbon in her hair,

the picture of Rainbow Dash on her shirt,

the color of the ice-cream cone in her hands—her favorite, green chocolate-chip mint.

She couldn't hold back the force of it.

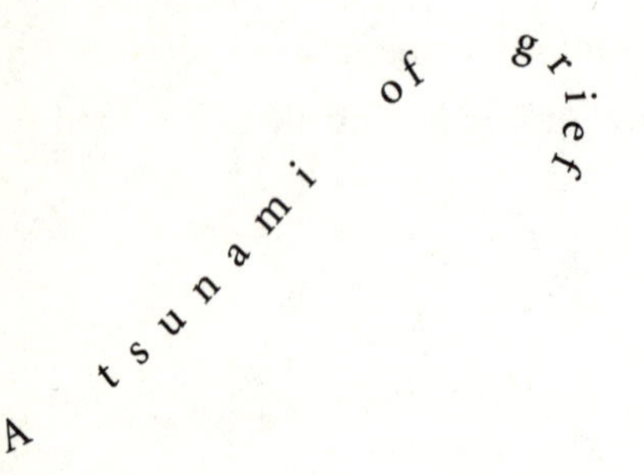

crashing on her shores.

Her mind set about filling in the edges of the photo . . .

Making it bigger . . .

Remembering?

Or making it up?

Did it matter?

How much of anything anyone remembered was real anyway?

WE ARE ALL STRETCHED PENNIES.

Damaged.
Manipulated.
Dinged this way and that.

"Why would this sicko take pictures at all?" her mother asked.

"I don't know," Chambers said. "He saved a lot of stuff. Drawings the kids made, that kind of thing. He appears to have been a bit of a sentimentalist. Or he was keeping everything because he was afraid if he threw it out it would be found and lead the police to him? I have no idea."

"But what about Anchor Beach?" Scarlett asked as she set down that photo to look at others:

Riding a bike with a banana seat and handlebar streamers.

Wearing a pale-pink bodysuit and tutu, arms arched overhead.

"I don't know what to tell you, Scarlett. I guess it's possible you figured out some way to get there? I spoke with the security guard, and he seems legit, but beyond that, I'm not sure what to do. We showed your photos around but didn't get any other hits."

"I *swallowed* that penny," she said. "It must be important."

"I know you're frustrated," he said. "But look—" He indicated the photos. "This is real."

Scarlett gestured to the brown bag. "You said you had clothes?"

Chambers took a clear plastic bag from the brown one, opened it. He started to unfold a few things, but Scarlett reached to the bottom of the pile, for the jacket.

She nearly gasped.

It was mostly pale gray with sections of aqua and lavender.

Sort of quilted but in large patches so not overly busy.

Not particularly well made—a few stray threads knotted off poorly, and a lot of weird extra stitches—like those rectangles she'd made—on the inside back, but at least you couldn't see all that when you wore it.

Chambers held forward a photograph of her wearing the jacket.

She looked like who she felt like she was in it.

"You recognize it?"

She slid the jacket on and it felt right, too. "Can I keep it?"

"Sorry," Chambers said. "Not yet."

When he left, her mother sat down at the dining room table and started to cry. Comet came out of hiding and hopped up onto the table, then gingerly climbed down to her lap.

"You okay?" Scarlett asked.

Her mother shook her head, moved Comet, got up, and went to the kitchen. She got a glass out of one cabinet and a bottle of vodka out of another. She put them on the table in front of her and sat down again.

"I don't think—" Scarlett said.

"I never got to play Tooth Fairy. Or teach you how to ride a bike. Or how to jump rope. I never got to take you shopping, like for a fancy dress. Or go to a ballet recital. Or tell you about the birds and the bees. Or have your friends for a sleepover and yell at you all to go to bed. Or tell you you were too young to date."

Scarlett nodded, not sure what to say.

"I used to drink when you were really small because you needed me *so badly* that I couldn't handle it. Couldn't handle the fear, like of something happening to me or to you." She poured an inch of vodka into the glass, put the bottle back down. "Now that you're back, these past bunch of days, I feel like drinking because you don't need me anymore."

She put her hand on the glass, stared at it, but then started to cry.

"And I missed everything in between. Everything in between is supposed to be the good stuff. I just," in between gasps, "I just. I can't believe it's really over."

"Me neither," Scarlett said, looking away as mascara started to fill wrinkles around her mother's eyes.

Realized she meant it a different way than the way it sounded.

She couldn't believe it was over.

Because it wasn't.

Something still wasn't right.

Letting go of the glass, her mother yanked a tissue from a box, seemed to declare her cry over. "We need to move on." She stood and took the glass and bottle back to the kitchen. "Steve wants to take us on a vacation. Wouldn't that be fun?"

And dumped all the vodka down the sink, the bottle glugging empty.

"Yes," Scarlett said. "We should do all that."

The doorbell rang and Scarlett assumed it would be Chambers, having forgotten something?

Opened the door and was surprised, instead, to see Kristen.

"Hey," Scarlett said.

"Can we talk?" Kristen said, then looked at Tammy, who said, "Nice to see you, too, Kristen," and left the room.

"Sorry, did I interrupt a moment?"

"It's okay." Scarlett stepped out, and they sat on the bottom steps together. "What's going on?"

Kristen leaned back on two elbows. "I remembered something else under hypnosis this morning."

"About your journal?" Scarlett asked greedily.

"No, not that. Well, actually yes, I remembered more about the owl. It was carved in wood or something. But that's not why I'm here. It's, well, you're really not going to like it."

Scarlett took a deep breath, exhaled it.

It was a collage art day. Ridiculously blue sky. Cotton-ball clouds. A sailboat in construction-paper colors on the horizon.

It seemed a shame to ruin it with . . . whatever it was.

And yet . . .

"Tell me."

Kristen smiled some. "You're *really* not going to like it."

"Just tell me!" Nearly shouting.

Kristen pushed up off her elbows, then wiped sand off them. "I remembered seeing you kissing someone," she said, now brushing sand off her hands, "but it wasn't Lucas."

Lucas

The map of Opus 6 on the kitchen wall was hand drawn on graph paper with black ink; clearly showed six main paths leading to the center. Lucas thought his own capital *O*s, when he wrote, had the same angle, and he admired his father's weird small cap/script hybrid where he'd labeled the lower reflecting pool and upper pond.

The urn with his father's ashes sat on a high shelf in the next room.

Miranda was in the shower, water running like rain.

"Let's finish it," Lucas said to Ryan, who was attempting to cook spaghetti, reading the box. "Let's finish Opus 6. Let's put a stone there."

"That thing has to weigh like four hundred pounds."

"Wait," Lucas said. "He *has* the stone?"

Ryan put the box down, set a timer on the stove. "It's out behind the RV."

Lucas had never gone around the back, through overgrown shrubs. "How was *he* going to move it?"

"I don't know." Ryan stirred the water.

"So let's figure it out." Lucas went for the door. "Maybe it's on a dolly or cart or something?"

"Now?" Water dripped from the wooden spoon in Ryan's hand.

"Why *not* now?"

"Because I'm cooking." Stirred the pot again. "And it's going to rain any second now. And you're not even convinced they caught the right guy."

It was true that the sky was bruised and menacing, true that he didn't buy the John Norton theory. But right now it didn't feel like it mattered. "Maybe I'm wrong. And why should Dad have to wait? We'll just have to be quick before the storm. Let's go."

"Lucas," Ryan said. "Just calm down, okay?"

"Uh." Miranda came into the kitchen, hair in wet pigtails, wearing a Smurfette shirt. "Are you okay? 'Cause you sound like you're losing it."

"Already lost it." Lucas felt it to be true; the sight of Smurfette—the thought of Avery—might surely send him over the edge. "But it's time to move forward with my life, right?"

"I don't understand why you won't believe they found the guy." Miranda peered into the pot to see what was there.

Lucas removed the tacks holding the map up and put it on the kitchen table to better study it. "Maybe he was the guy. Maybe I'm wrong. I mean, it makes no sense that one person could do this. I must have gotten sick at least once in my entire childhood. So what doctor did I go to? What about the other four . . . or five? We're supposed to believe that one guy pulled all this off? Raised five kids and no one else helped? But whatever, I guess. Everyone else seems satisfied. "

"Well, maybe they'll figure it out *now.*" Ryan dumped the contents of a jar of tomato sauce into a pot. "Put together more pieces now that they know who he is. Maybe people will start coming forward. Maybe they'll find who he was working with."

Miranda picked at the polish on her fingernails. "Have you considered the possibility that you maybe had better childhoods than the ones you were going to have?"

"We're not living in a science-fiction novel," Lucas said, and had a pang of guilt about not having gone back to see Orlean again. And useless Chambers had, of course, turned up nothing related to *that* at all. And now he had a body, so why should he?

"What if you were?" Miranda pushed. "Would it make you feel better? Would you be able to move on then?"

"I don't know, Miranda. And I really don't feel like I have to explain myself to you."

"Fine." She got up and took plates from the cabinet. "Lash out at one of the few people in your life who actually cares about you."

"Why *do* you care?"

She stood at the table, holding the plates. "I don't know, Luke, why do I?"

He slid the map out of the way and she started putting plates down, loudly. He tacked it back up to the wall and, out the window, saw Scarlett's mother's car coming up the drive.

He opened the front door, went out.

"Everything okay?" he asked when Scarlett got out.

Then Ryan was beside them, saying "Scarlett" and looking awestruck, like she was famous, some idol of his, and she said "Ryan." And smiled. "Hey."

And Miranda cleared her throat, and Ryan turned but barely. "This is Miranda," he said.

"His girlfriend," Miranda added.

"Nice to meet you," Scarlett said. Then she turned to Lucas and said, "Can we talk?"

"Sure." Lucas headed toward the RV.

And she seemed anxious—this nervous look in her eye—so he reached for her hand, but she slipped away and said, "There's something I have to tell you but I'm scared to," and she looked more like a stranger than she had since they'd come back.

"You can tell me anything," he said, and felt it to be true.

"Where are we going?" she asked, looking around.

"I need to see something," he said. "It's not far. We'll talk there."

They walked in silence until they got to the RV and Lucas pushed through tall weeds behind it, stepping on dry branches with his boots.

It was propped up on cinder blocks and caked with dirt. Lucas brushed away and cracked some of it off to see:

OPUS 6

— A song of stone for the missing, to keep their memory alive on this earth. —

Adam Acosta	Max Godard
Kristen Daley	Sarah Madson
Lucas Davis	Scarlett Waters

He squatted down to better see. "It reads like a joke now."

"He couldn't have known how it was all going to play out," Scarlett said.

He shook his head, put his hands on his thighs, and pushed up to stand. "How do I keep his memory alive if I can't remember him?"

"I'm so sorry, Lucas," she said.

"I know." They walked back toward one of the reflecting pools and stopped. "So what do you need to tell me?"

Thunder rumbled, and she looked off toward the direction it had come from. "Kristen remembered seeing me with Adam."

A drop of rain landed on his nose, had to be wiped. "What does that mean, 'with Adam'?"

"*Kissing* Adam." She looked away. "And I don't know, when we kissed—you and I—when we were in Anchor Beach . . . I felt happy on the one hand but there was something underneath it, too. Like guilt? And I think I thought or hoped it was just a weird feeling about us being there together and not knowing our past. But . . ."

The rain was starting to feel personal, like it had some kind of grudge against him.

"I think I was remembering feeling suffocated." She seemed not to notice or care about the rain. "I don't know. Maybe I was cheating on you? Maybe you found out? I think I wanted out and you weren't happy about it. At all."

He wanted the storm to just get on with it, to really let loose and get it over with, but it seemed liked it was already stopping. They weren't in its path after all. He said, "I would never try to pressure you into anything."

"See, I feel like we've had this conversation before."

Him wanting more than she wanted from him?

Him caring more, or about the wrong things?

Yes, maybe that did feel right.

He went and sat on a low stone wall, pulled a weed that had sprung up between two rocks, releasing the smell of dirt into the air. Drops from trees shimmied the water in the pool, stirred some of its murk. "I'm starting to really not like this picture of who I was," he said. "Jealous and angry?"

They turned at the sound of footsteps and voices.

Chambers was walking toward them, this time with his partner in tow.

"I'm really sorry, Lucas." Chambers stopped a few feet away. "It wasn't my call on this one. I'm sure you can argue self-defense, but the feds, well . . ."

His partner kept coming.

"You were right about the fingerprints on the gun . . . ," Chambers said.

". . . and there's gunshot residue on a jacket that also has your DNA all over it."

". . . and the coroner put John Norton's time of death as the day you all escaped."

Escaped?

They didn't escape.

"Lucas Davis," Chambers's partner said. "You are under arrest for the murder of John Norton. You have the right to remain silent . . ."

AVERY

Her cell phone rang during episode six of a web series she'd decided to binge-watch to kill time. At long last, Emma had remembered that her phone was a phone.

"Hey."

Emma: "Are you watching the news?"

"No. Why?"

"Just turn on CNN."

So now even talking sounded like texting.

Avery got up to stop her show and switched over to regular TV, then found CNN.

". . . arrest made in the case of The Leaving . . . but perhaps not the arrest people expected or hoped for. The perpetrator of the crime has been identified as one John Norton, and he has been found dead. A gun with fingerprints belonging to returned Leaving victim Lucas Davis is alleged to be the weapon used and Davis has been taken into custody."

Another guy said, "*Now, I understand there is some speculation here, as to whether Davis might have also played some role in the death of Max Godard.*"

Then the original guy: "*I'm not sure there's much to that theory but . . .*"

Avery said, "I gotta go," and hung up and turned off the TV and went up to The Shrine and looked through a desk drawer until she found the picture of herself—Smurfette—and Max and Lucas as pirate and sailor. She looked for signs. Signs that Lucas was not who she thought he was. Something maybe in his eyes that would reveal some dark side he had spent his life learning how to disguise.

She couldn't see it, but also didn't want her memory of Max to be tangled up with him, just in case.

She took the photo and went back downstairs and out to the lanai and to the grill, where a trigger lighter hung from a side hook.

She clicked it a few times before it lit, and then she ignited the corner of the photograph and watched as the image started to melt away.

There was no point in keeping a photo like that, in keeping a memory like that.

Not with him in it.

There would be no happy ending for any of them.

Maybe murderers *could* have soft hair.

And anyway: memories of ridiculous things like princesses and ballerinas and superheroes and pirates, all that nonsense? What place did they even have when you grew up? And what was *wrong* with people—parents—for even allowing kids to dream about all that, for *encouraging* it?

She'd never be a mermaid or ballerina or magical fairy. No boy would ever fly or scale walls and swing from bridges. Growing up was about crushing every dream kids had—nonsense, empty dreams that we'd given them.

Burn, Smurfette, burn.

You too, Tink.

Throw Santa in there on a stake while we're at it.

The flames were too fast.

She pushed open the screen door and dropped the flaming photo onto the dirt, startling a salamander, which scurried away. She picked up a nearby rock and hit the embers a few times, not wanting to burn the whole house down, though, really, it wasn't the worst idea.

DAY SEVEN

Scarlett

A woman in a pale-pink dress holding a feather duster answered the door. "Can I help you?"

"Oh." Scarlett hadn't been expecting . . . the help?

Thought about just walking away.

Back down the marble steps, past those two pillars.

Down the long path, past that Jaguar and that BMW, past the gardening crew pruning the flowering trees by the front gate, back to where she belonged.

But . . .

No.

"Is Adam home?"

A happy smile. "Can I tell him who's calling?"

"Scarlett."

"Come!" She waved Scarlett in. "You can wait in the sitting room."

Scarlett stepped into the main hall—a curved staircase like for women in ball gowns—feeling small and even more poorly dressed than usual, and followed the woman into a room off to the right.

Couches the colors of coral—peach, turquoise—and large houseplants. Trees, really.

Walls of books.

An antique-looking globe on a whitewashed wooden table.

Large windows with sheer white drapes held back by golden sashes.

"Scarlett?"

She turned.

Adam wore an ivory linen short-sleeved shirt and plaid shorts—red, white, and blue; his shoes looked like they were intended for boating.

"Everything okay?" he asked.

"Yes." She hadn't called before turning up because she figured he'd just put her off somehow. "Can we talk?"

"Come on," he said. "I hate this room."

So she followed him down a few hallways, this way and that, and ended up in a more casual sunroom that looked out at the yard; a few foam noodles and a pair of pink inner tubes floated lazily in a massive in-ground pool. He sat in a cozy-looking white armchair and indicated another one for her.

"So," he said. "What's up?"

He seemed so . . . normal . . . that it irked her, and yet something about how at ease he seemed put her at ease, too. She felt like she could relax for the first time maybe since coming home. As she sat, she said, "Kristen said she remembered something under hypnosis."

"And?"

"You and me." She hesitated at having to say it out loud, but there was no way around it. "Kissing."

He tilted his head for a second, then righted it. "How do you feel about that?"

"Confused. How do you feel?"

"You want lemonade?" He stood and crossed the room to where a pitcher and some glasses sat on a tray.

"Uh," she said. "Sure."

He poured. "My mom's gone all atheist New Age-y on me and she keeps saying this thing, 'It is always now.'"

He turned to her with two glasses, handed her one, and sat. "'It is always now.' Some guru of hers says that. And that's what I've been clinging to. I'm not going to spend the rest of my life trying to figure out what happened to the last eleven years."

"Don't you want to know if it's true that you and I were together?" She sipped her lemonade; it was too bitter. "More importantly, don't you want to know who did it and why?"

"Why does it matter if we were together if we don't remember?" He drank, too. "And John Norton did it."

A girl about seven years old walked into the room; her light-brown hair was in a wet ponytail, her sundress showing bony shoulders and a pale-pink leotard underneath it. Behind her trailed another girl with darker brown hair and skin, also wet ponytails and ballet gear.

"Well, hello, dancers," Adam said.

"Hello." The first one crossed her ankles and took a strand of her hair and pulled it toward her mouth, a nervous tic.

"Hello," the other said, mimicking.

"This is my friend Scarlett," Adam said.

"You have *friends*?"—from the darker-skinned girl, with a tickle laugh. Genuine curiosity. Not a sarcastic bone in her body.

Adam laughed. "Yes, I have friends." He turned to Scarlett. "These are my sisters—Belle and Nadia."

"Hi, Belle," Scarlett said. "Hi, Nadia."

They both said hi shyly, then went to another part of the room and started playing with ghoulish dolls—Goth clothes, oversize hair, red lips scowling.

"My replacements," Adam said. "The wonder twins."

"No," Scarlett said, when the meaning of the words sank in. "Don't be like that."

"It's true." He didn't seem upset by it. "My parents were so miserable for like four years after I disappeared that they decided to have another kid. And it wasn't happening, so they adopted Nadia from Costa Rica and *then* they got pregnant with Belle."

"Wow," Scarlett said.

"I think it was smart." He nodded. "What else were they supposed to do? Spend their whole life mourning and wishing they still had a kid? Build some crazy stone monument? Blame it all on aliens?"

"Nadia!" A woman was calling from the other room. "Belle!"

"What?" Belle said back.

"Where are your ballet shoes?" from the hall.

"In the bag!" Nadia shouted.

"Come on or we'll be late."

Belle dropped the dolls on the rug, stood, said "See ya," and left the room. Nadia followed, giving Scarlett a smile and a wave.

Adam just watched them go, then said, "They're pretty much my favorite people on the planet right now."

"Mine, too, I think." Scarlett smiled. "Speaking of which, why have you been avoiding us?"

"I don't know, Scarlett." He leaned forward in his chair. "I definitely sensed there was something maybe not great between Lucas and me. I felt tension that first night back and figured I should trust that. Now maybe we know more about why I felt that. If it's true about you and me. Did you tell him?"

"He deserved to know. We remember so little. It seems unfair to hold back anything we actually know."

He got up and went to a window, looked out. "Do you really trust hypnosis? Or Kristen?"

"I don't know," Scarlett said. "I think so. What do *you* trust? Who?"

He said, "I've started to trust that maybe it's okay—maybe even better than okay—that we don't remember."

"That sounds like giving up."

He got up again and picked up a guitar Scarlett hadn't noticed in the corner. It looked comfortable in his hands. His fingers knew what they were doing when they found strings and frets. He sat and started to play.

She recognized the chords right away.

Knew some of the words before he started singing them.

And started to feel ill.

Started to feel her world tilt again in a way it hadn't in days.

The song tugged at her, and not in a nice way.

It was an aggravating tug, an unwanted pull.

And after a few more lines, she felt herself burst open, like a confetti cannon.

Joy, pain.

The things you can't forget even if you tried.

Drizzling down around her, blurring the air she breathed.

With each new note, she remembered running.

Fighting.

Aching.

For their lives.

Then snapping back.

Repeating.

Aching again.

Fear.

Running.

Snapping.

Struggling.

Failing.

Giving in.

He finished the song and looked up. "It's the only song I can play full from beginning to end and it makes me want to throw up."

"Who's it by? Did *you* write it? What does it mean?" she asked. "It's a message for us, right? A clue? One we left for ourselves?"

"Is it?" He put the guitar down. "Because to me it feels like a warning. It's telling me to stop digging because I won't like what I find."

"We have to figure it out. What if it could somehow help explain everything and clear Lucas? You *have heard* that he was arrested, right?"

"Of course." He stood. "I haven't played that song for anyone else and I'm not going to."

She stood, too.

"Most people never know why bad things happen to them." He folded his arms. "John Norton did it. I've moved on."

She moved on, too, by getting up and leaving. When she was tempted to skip the bottom step out front, she caught herself, grabbed the railing, and took them one at a time.

She tried to hum the song to herself.

It was already gone.

Lucas

The local jail felt like something out of the Old West. Basic slammer. Keys on silver hoops. Lucas would be sent off to a proper prison farther north tomorrow if Ryan couldn't secure a bail bond—ten percent of the $1 million price tag the judge had put on Lucas, who was only even allowed bail and pretrial release at all because he was under the age of eighteen. Ryan was going through the motions, making calls to their father's lawyers, but Lucas wasn't hopeful. Overnight, he'd shared his small cell with a few drunk college students and a lone prostitute who'd grumbled loudly the whole time about entrapment.

An officer came down the hall in the late morning, handcuffs in hand, and told Lucas he had a visitor. That didn't take long, Ryan running out of options. Since there was no real visiting room, he was escorted to an interview room.

Chambers met him outside the room, unlocked the handcuffs the escorting officer had put on him. "Ten minutes," Chambers said, and he opened the door. "I'll be back and we'll all talk."

Sashor sat at a metal table.

"What are you doing here?" Lucas stepped into the room.

"I felt bad about our last chat," Sashor said. "And I wanted to see you before you, well . . ."

Lucas took the chair across from him; it shrieked across the floor when he moved it. "Do you think I did it?"

"No." Sashor folded his hands on the table in front of him; a thick silver band on his right ring finger. "But what I think really doesn't matter. Do *you* think you did it?"

"No." Lucas smiled. "But what I think doesn't really seem to matter, either. This theory that I killed him and we escaped? It makes no sense. Was his corpse driving that van? Or wait, no, it was his ghost, I bet."

"I think they're still working out the details of that theory." Sashor shrugged. "I get the sense they thought an arrest might shake something loose."

"A patsy!"

"That's a word for it," Sashor said. "But in the meantime, I was talking to Chambers. He told me they analyzed the photos they found—the hot air balloon and carousel and all. And they found *other prints* from those sets, some photos of you all doing those things. Those things *really happened*."

Lucas had seen some of the pictures; a detective had brought them by the holding cell that morning and Lucas—at that point the only one left in there—had asked for time with them, to study them, to see if they'd help make sense of things in a more satisfying way. But hadn't been allowed. "I'm not even sure I care."

"Better to come back with a happy memory than a traumatic one, though." Sashor released his folded hands in a sudden burst.

"So I rode a carousel by the beach one day. So there are pictures of me riding a bike and holding a soccer ball and blowing out ten candles on a cake. So what?"

"Well, at least now you know it wasn't *all* bad."

"These people. Or John Norton, if you believe that theory. He doesn't deserve the benefit of the doubt."

Sashor sat back in his chair, then had to swipe his dreads out from behind him. "How are things with you and Scarlett?"

How best to say it?

"I was mostly remembering good things—only feeling good ones; she was remembering bad."

Sashor smiled. "Sounds like me and most women I've dated."

"When one of your girlfriends did the 'Thriller' dance in her underwear," Lucas said. "Was that good or bad?"

"Ah, you assume it was *her* in the underwear."

"Now I'm sorry I asked."

Sashor smiled. "I have some serious moves."

"I'm sure," Lucas said. "Apparently Scarlett kissed Adam? Or at least Kristen said she remembered that happening. Under hypnosis."

"Does Scarlett remember?"

"No," Lucas said. "Anyway, it's a relief that we don't have to try to make something between us work now. It's like being freed from inheriting a legacy I wasn't even sure I wanted."

"Fair enough." Sashor nodded. "So listen, I came here to tell you what Chambers and I have been doing; and he'll join us in a minute, like he said. What we've done is gone back to find other kids who were at the school shooting, kids who were only four, who were at the open house, to see how many of them remember the shooting."

Lucas sat up straighter, leaned forward. "And . . . ?"

"And they all remember it. I could only find a sample, but it's a significant number of kids, significant enough to give me pause."

"Go on." Lucas wanted the information to come faster, wished he could speed-read Sashor's thoughts.

"It's been bothering me from the beginning, that you could remember certain things from early childhood but not this huge event. And we were thinking, well, maybe you were there but didn't see anything specifically horrible so it didn't register. But there are at least a few other kids who can ID some of you from photos we showed them of you when you were young. They say you were there. All of you. They all remember the shooter, the principal, screaming, blood, awful stuff. *You* saw awful stuff."

Lucas felt a darkening in his mind, spotted the distant glow of an idea.

"And the six of you were *taken from school*," Sashor said. "Not from a playground. Not from home."

This time a different kind of *click-hiss* and *snap*, like an image appearing on photo paper in rippling water in the darkroom of his mind. He said, "Erasing the shooting was the whole point to begin with?"

AVERY

School had been a disaster. Matt Rogoff had asked her how her spring break had been and she'd asked him if he ever read the news. Emma had signed Avery up for auditions and then snatched the pen away when Avery went to cross her name out. Sam had said "hey" and acted too-cool-for-school. The halls had been plastered with signs for the junior prom; she'd voted in favor of "A Time to Remember" as the theme months ago and now cringed. Alongside those signs were flyers about the shooting anniversary memorial next week. Worst of all, a note appeared in her locker: *Welcome back, you evil cow.*

She'd had no choice but to duck out before facing the prospect of Mr. Knopf prattling on *en français* for forty-five minutes.

At home, she heard her father; he was in his office with the door open: "Yes, I suppose it's run its course. So yes, shut it down."

"What were you talking about?" She popped her head in when he hung up. "Shut what down?"

"The tip line." He looked at his watch. "Why aren't you in school?"

"But we haven't found Max yet." Avery's tongue burned.

He rubbed his eyes. "I know you *really* wanted to find him, Ave, but we need to start facing facts."

"There *are* no facts. Not about Max." She seriously felt like she could breathe fire.

"I'm sorry, hon. It's done. They found the person who did it and they didn't find Max."

"But Lucas doesn't even believe it's the right place. And if the call about John Norton's body was even legitimate, why not leave a name? They didn't even claim the reward!"

"Avery, we need to move on."

"You've been saying that for *years*, Dad." She was shouting now. "Has it worked?"

"Keeping the tip line open isn't going to change that. They've sent me all the recordings. And at this point Chambers says it's just the same nut-job calling. Cryptic nonsense. I'm not going to pay to staff an answering service indefinitely when Max was probably killed and his body was probably dumped in the Everglades or who even knows where?" He looked at his watch again. "I have to head into the office. I'm sorry. We'll talk later, okay?"

He left.

Fine.

She'd move on.

She went and got a few large trash bags from the kitchen and grabbed a few empty Amazon boxes from the garage, where the recycling hadn't been broken down yet and *obviously her flip-flops were never going to arrive.*

She went back upstairs and into Max's room and put her supplies down. She took a good look around, closed her eyes for a moment, opened them, and picked up a trash bag. She started with Max's dresser drawers, emptying them of clothes. Tiny shorts and socks. Superhero shirts. She'd put it all in that drop box behind the VFW hall. They'd find new, good homes. They'd be worn by real, live boys.

Next, she set about boxing up toys.

X-Men.

Plastic toy soldiers.

LEGOs.

So. Many. LEGOs.

Transformers.

Plastic dinosaurs.

Pirate this, pirate that.

Matchbox cars.

She filled two boxes without having to pause. But paused at:

Daphne

Velma.

Fred.

Shaggy.

Scooby.

But they had to go.

She turned to face the framed photos on the wall. This time, a smaller box. This time, more care in the packing. This box she'd keep.

Her and Max on that carousel at Disney.

Max at his first soccer game.

Max as a baby, leaning on a big blue rubber ball at some indoor play space.

Christmas. Santa's lap. Her on one side, him on the other.

He was dead.

Her parents were going to have to accept it.

She'd have to accept it.

The world would always see her as an only child, but she'd always know better.

Down the hall in her room, she hid the box where no one would ever find it but her.

Back in Max's room, she stripped the bed, folded everything neatly before putting it all in another bag, another one for the donation dump.

She made four trips down to the garage. Hiding the stuff in a corner. She'd have to get rid of it fast, or else her mother would find it, say it was too soon, put it all back, make a scene.

There was no point in telling anyone about the newest note. The writing was different, anyway.

And maybe she *was* an evil cow.

Maybe she deserved the hate being sent her way.

Scarlett

She stood on the center pier at Anchor Beach, squinting out at the water as clouds gossiped on the horizon.

It had been foolish, maybe, to visit Orlean again. But she'd left Adam's house feeling like she had to do *something*—and Orlean was the last possible lead they hadn't gone back to follow up on. A lead that might point to the real who, the real why. But of course he hadn't remembered her, hadn't read *The Leaving*, hadn't been able to tell her once and for all what the stuff was that you couldn't forget if you tried.

She'd visited Goldie again, only now they were calling her by her name, Margaret. They'd talked about the painting on the wall, which was named *Christina's World*.

"Do you like it?" Margaret had asked.

"I do," Scarlett had said. "Her body positioning projects such desire for movement. Do you think she ever gets there? To the house?"

Margaret had said, "Yes, I think so. I think someone comes to help."

Scarlett had texted Sarah—**Any progress on the sketches?**—when she'd left, but had gotten no reply. A text from Ryan had said, **Going to bail my brother out. He asked me to let you know.**

Now Scarlett closed her eyes and tried to picture the sky in

Christina's World—was it blue? Gray?—and wondered what a painting of this moment—her on this pier, this sky—might look like.

Would the artist be able to capture the pull she felt to the water?

To anywhere but here?

But to where?

The world was so big.

Her life story so huge in it.

The stuff of movies!

And yet her part in it all felt so small.

One tiny stitch.

Something blubbed in the water, and she looked down trying to find what it was, hoping for a manatee who'd maybe turned up early for the winter party.

Then imagined herself

diving in, fully clothed.

Imagined how her clothes would fall away like a skin she was shedding, or maybe float like wings.

How her hair would swirl around her like mermaid hair as her lungs got tight, or how it might get knotted up, strangling her.

She imagined someone coming to save her from drowning

—could she even swim?—

Or no one.

She looked to the skies again and tried to imagine what it would feel like to be the sort of person who'd see something up there and think it was a UFO.

What would it be like to be that free to believe?

To cling to something—a memory, a trick of the eye, the same thing—even in the face of logic and reason.

The afternoon had turned chilly and she wished she had her jacket with her. She'd stalled in making the new one several times now but felt like if she had the original one, if she were able to put it on, she might feel like herself again.

She walked back to where she knew the initials would be and ran her fingers over them—the prick of the splintered wood on her thumb—and had a physical memory of what it had felt like to kiss him, how amazing and terrifying to connect with another human being, with him.

He'd loved her once.

She'd loved him.

What was love if not a kind of forgetting?

A forgetting about the inevitability of loss.

Or was love more a kind of remembering?

Remembering how badly we need to be needed, understood.

Remembering that maybe it was the whole reason we were here.

Had she been the one to x those letters out?

Had Adam?

It didn't matter.

She'd save herself.

It turned out she very much liked being alone.

So she planned on doing that for a while.

When she was alone she felt free and in control, even if the only thing she was in control of was herself.

Maybe the remembering and forgetting of love would come later, down the line, when she was ready.

Her phone buzzed with a text from Sarah.

This is the house.

There was a sketch attached.

Scarlett opened it, zoomed in on it.

Nothing familiar about it at all.

Then another photo came through.

A face.

A remarkable likeness of Ryan's girlfriend.

Younger, sure, but definitely her.

Miranda, was it?

Why was Sarah sending her a drawing of Miranda?

Did Sarah even *know* Miranda?

The text followed:

This is the girl.

What girl?

Oh.

No.

/

/

/

Lucas

The guard unlocked the gate and let Lucas through. Ryan had hands in his shorts pockets, looked tired around the eyes.

"You actually got the money?" Lucas said.

Ryan nodded but looked baffled. "It turns out there's a fair amount of savings. Like Dad had applied for all these artist grants and had won a bunch and made some good investments and it adds up. I'm not sure what'll be left once we're done paying a lawyer for you. But—"

"It won't come to that," Lucas said.

"I wouldn't be so sure."

"I'm *not* sure. I just—I need to go over everything again. We're missing something."

Miranda was idling in the car just out front and switched over to the passenger seat—climbing across the center console—so that Ryan could drive.

"How's it going?" she asked.

"Better now," Lucas said. "Sashor actually came to see me and said they have a theory they're pursuing now that the whole thing started with someone trying to erase our memory of the shooting."

"What?" Ryan said.

Miranda said, "That's crazy."

"Apparently it's not that crazy. Chambers pointed to a bunch of studies where scientists have successfully erased traumatic memories."

"Maybe you should try hypnosis," Ryan said. "Kristen did, right? Maybe you'll remember something that will clear your name. Maybe you'll remember what your tattoo means."

In the backseat, Lucas rolled his eyes. "Kristen remembers a wooden owl. Not the most useful information."

"Maybe you should try it anyway," Ryan said.

"Why are you suddenly all fired up about all this?" Lucas asked when Ryan stopped at a light.

"Why aren't *you*?" Ryan shouted. "You've been charged with murder."

"I didn't do it!" Lucas shouted.

"How do you know?"

"I just"—How did he know?—"he's not the guy. I'd *know*. We'd know. This guy, there's no connection to Anchor Beach or to anything."

"You don't *know* anything," Ryan said.

That SUN'S OUT, GUNS OUT shirt was still hanging there in the shop window in town.

They weren't that far from the house.

He could walk the rest of the way.

"Thanks for the support." He got out of the car at the next light and headed for the gift shop.

Inside, he wound his way through overstuffed racks, lost in a hedge maze of T-shirts and baseball hats and gnomes on beaches and seashells with googly eyes.

This was what people wanted to help them remember? Flamingo snow globes? LIFE'S A BEACH coffee mugs?

The only souvenir he had from his whole life was inked into his skin. It had, over the last week, healed nicely.

And yet . . .

"Can I help you?" A girl with fake blond hair with a purple streak in it sat perched on a barstool by the register reading a magazine. She barely looked up.

"That shirt in the window," he said. "'Sun's Out, Guns Out.'"

"What size?" She moved to get up.

"No," he said. "I don't want to buy one. I just want to know . . . what does it mean?"

"It's like a muscle-head thing," she said.

"Muscle head?"

She bent her arm, made a fist. "Like when it's warm enough out to show off your arm muscles."

He couldn't help but feel disappointed. "That's got to be one of the dumbest things I've ever heard."

"Agreed," she said, and he turned to go and started the long, hot walk home. He would head for the RV—regroup. He'd take a run at everything again.

Sure, they'd erased the shooting.

They'd erased eleven years.

But he still had his inked skin.

He still had his trained eye.

It *had* to be the thing that would help him prove he was innocent and that they'd gotten it all wrong.

Maybe Sashor and Chambers were onto something with regard to why. But the more important thing, the thing that had always mattered most to Lucas, was who?

Nothing had changed.

AVERY

In her father's office, she sat at the computer and rooted around through his e-mail and figured out where the audio files were and started to listen to every call that had been recorded since the tip line went live. After a while she started to recognize the voice of the "nut-job" her father had been referring to.

"*He didn't do it. You have to dig deeper. It's not over.*"

"*How do you know this? Who are you?*" the tip-line guy asked.

"*I'm a dead man.*"

Click. Gone.

Later, the same voice again:

"*It was only supposed to be for a few hours, you see.*"

And again later,

"*I was only there once. I don't know where it was, but it wasn't that place.*"

"*Sir, can you be more specific?*"

"*I can't. They're probably watching me. They're probably listening.*"

And the last one:

"*They were going to pin it all on me if I talked. They buried him in my backyard, for Chrissake.*"

Maybe everyone was right.

The guy was just crazy.

Or he wasn't.

She had to go back to the drawing board.

With Lucas in jail, she'd have the RV all to herself.

Scarlett

Drove like a lunatic, then pounded on the door until her fists hurt.

Lucas still hadn't responded to the texts she'd sent from Anchor Beach. And that had been several hours ago.

She'd forwarded the sketch of Miranda.

Wrote, **This is the girl Sarah says was with us.**

Then, **On my way to you from Anchor Beach.**

"Is Lucas here?" she asked when Ryan answered.

"No," Ryan said, sounding annoyed. "We had a fight *after I bailed him out of jail.*"

"Is *Miranda* here?"

"She *was.*" A look of confusion. "But she ran home to get some stuff she needed. Why?"

"Sarah said she remembered another girl being with us. She sent me a picture she drew of her." She pulled the picture up on her phone and held it out.

Ryan shook his head. "I don't understand."

"Have they ever met? Miranda and Sarah?"

"I don't *think* so. But if Miranda's . . . that would mean . . ." Ryan sat down, dropped his head. "That she *targeted* me?"

It was the conclusion Scarlett had come to on her drive, as well. "How did you meet her?"

"She came into the hotel where I work one night with some friends."

"She could have known who you were before she turned up." Scarlett's thoughts were in sharp focus. "It means they knew they were going to let us go . . . because when was that?"

"A few months ago."

"They wanted someone here in place to watch him . . . or us."

What if there were more like her?

What if someone closer to her was also watching her?

What if they all had someone watching?

How long had her mother known Steve again?

How long had Adam's family had that housekeeper?

What if Kristen's hypnotist was somehow . . . ?

"The other day," Ryan said. "Wow. When we were looking at photos. She knew our dog's name but I couldn't think of a time I'd ever told her we'd even had a dog."

"I'm so sorry, Ryan."

"She called him Luke the other day, too. He didn't seem to notice, but—it seemed weird." Ryan got up and took off down the hall. "She keeps some stuff here."

Scarlett followed him, but by the time she got down to the door of his bedroom, he was already coming back out.

"She's gone." He ran his hands through his hair and let out a guttural moan. "All her stuff is gone."

The phone on the coffee table buzzed.

"Is that yours?" she asked when he didn't move for it.

"Lucas's. He left it in my car."

She slid down onto the couch under the weight of exhaustion. "She saw my texts. She knows we know."

Lucas

He'd fallen asleep against his will and now struggled to rouse himself in the bedroom compartment. Then heard movement in the RV's main room and grabbed an empty bottle by the neck. Moving quietly toward the hallway, he then burst into the other room with a loud "Who's there?"

Avery.

The relief he felt at seeing her caught him off guard. He dropped the bottle. He wanted to rush to her, take her in his arms, inhale the chlorine and honeysuckle of her hair. He wanted to pretend he'd never told her he couldn't be with her.

"You're out?" She shook her head. "Obviously." She stood. "I don't understand. I should go."

"Avery, wait." He grabbed her by the arm and stood in front of her. "I didn't kill John Norton. And I know what crazy theories are being thrown around, but I didn't kill *anyone*."

"But you can't *prove* it." She sounded equal parts sad and mad. Was there a word for that?

"Can't prove that I'm a good person?" He looked around like the proof might be there, in his father's writing on the walls. "No, but who can? Can you? I was wrong, Avery. You *do* know me." He stepped closer, stood right up against her the way she had with him on the lanai, when it had been all he could do to pull his body away from hers, like she'd been magnetized.

"I don't." She backed away, clearly not feeling the same pull.

"You do." Moving closer still, but then backing away, giving her space. "And I'm going to go through everything in here again and I'm not going to stop until I get to the truth *and* find Max."

"You sound like your father," she said, not in a kind way.

"Good!"

"Everyone thought he was crazy."

"Maybe I am, too. It doesn't matter." This was wasting time. "You can help me or you can leave."

He'd brought his father's laptop out here and now sat down at the desk to get to work, going through every file in a folder marked "Videos." He heard her leave and had to stop himself from going after her. But then the door clicked open again and the floor creaked under her as she sat beside him. He took her hand, squeezed, then released.

They sifted through pages and pages of notes while playing videos of anniversary vigils and more. Most of the notes had been transferred to the whiteboards, and many of the news reports were repetitive, nothing actually new in the news. No connection to the shooting that they could directly see.

They went backward chronologically, working their way through the clips, one after the other, occasionally pausing to study a face—"Chambers was so young," Lucas said; "My mother loses it during this one," Avery said—then moving on.

Finally, they were back to the night of the day it had happened, the first national report. Watching it, Lucas felt panic, like he was back there, reliving the whole thing as a kid but not as one of the missing kids. What must it have felt like for Ryan? And for Avery. Not having any idea what was going on. Being shoved away from TVs and pushed out of rooms while her parents spent hours on the phone and crying.

And his father? What had gone through his head before he'd picked up a chisel and stone and committed himself to someday uncovering the truth?

"Chambers and the memory specialist are working this theory that what happened to us has to do with the shooting. Like trying to erase the memory of that."

"That's why they were asking if Max was there?"

"Yes."

The next clip played. A woman holding a girl toddler. The toddler holding a stuffed dog. She wore pajamas; she looked cold.

"That's me," Avery said.

And the whole scene came into focus alongside Lucas's feelings for Avery.

"I could only ever bring myself to watch this one once," she said. "Years ago."

"I'm sorry." Lucas paused it. "We can stop."

"No." She leaned closer, to study her own image. "It's okay."

He slid his arm around the back of her chair.

"It's so weird." She shook her head. "I can't believe that was ever . . . *me.* That I was ever that small. And just, like, clinging to my mother like that. And Woof-Woof—the dog—it's just so . . . different, I guess. It all went away that night."

"We *really* don't have to watch." He started to navigate away.

"Play it." She nodded, and leaned back into her chair, into his arm. He felt the connection like a lifeline.

A reporter shouts out, "Has the school made an official statement? Has the bus been traced?"

Another man steps up to the mike. "We're doing everything we can to help with the investigation. We have every expectation that the children will be returned safely."

"Everyone looks so naive," Lucas said. "They had no idea what was actually happening."

Avery's whole body stiffened, cold like a corpse, and he couldn't think of what he'd said wrong. "Avery, are you—"

"'It was only supposed to be for a few hours,'" she said, like reciting a line, in a trance.

"What?" He paused the video.

Again: "'It was only supposed to be for a few hours.'"

"What does that mean?" He felt irritation at not understanding.

"He's still alive." Her eyes lit like fireflies.

"But—" How could she have figured that out just now? How could she know? "Max? How do you—?"

"Not Max." She pointed at the screen, tapped twice. "The principal."

AVERY

Only the whole world coming together and cracking open.

"He's been calling the tip line." Avery got up and paced. "Saying all these cryptic things. Except that maybe they're not that cryptic once you know who he is?"

"We need to call Chambers," Lucas said. "He needs to review the calls."

She reached for her phone, then remembered. "I don't have his number in here."

They buried the body in his backyard.

Was *that* what he'd said?

"I left mine in Ryan's car," Lucas said. "I got out in a hurry. Come on."

Avery followed Lucas and they peered into the backseat of the car with cupped hands at their eyes, but it wasn't there. As they walked up toward the house, Chambers's car appeared, rolling loudly over gravel.

How on earth—?

How could he have—?

"What are you doing here?" Lucas asked Chambers when he got out of his car.

"Your brother called me," Chambers said. "Said it was urgent."

"We were just going to call you," Avery said. "We've been watching old news reports and—"

Ryan opened the front door of the house.

Scarlett appeared beside him.

"What's going on? What are you doing here?" Lucas asked Scarlett.

"You have to find Miranda," Ryan said to Chambers.

"She was with us," Scarlett said. "She's been here watching us."

"And she took off," Ryan said.

"The principal is still alive," Avery said, and even though she felt like she was screaming, no one seemed to hear.

"Everybody inside," Chambers said. "Now."

In the living room he said, "One thing at a time. What's this about Miranda?"

Scarlett showed everyone Sarah's sketch, and Chambers turned to Ryan. "Anything at all that seemed off about her? Anything at all she may have said that might be a lead? She ever say anything about her family?"

"Nothing out of the ordinary," Ryan said. "She said her childhood was boring. That her parents were control freaks. She said they wanted her to get a real job. That kind of stuff, the stuff everyone says. I never met them."

"Any suspicious phone calls?" Chambers asked. "Habits?"

Ryan looked bewildered. "No," with a sad emphasis that made Avery want to throttle him.

"I need her address," Chambers said. "Her friends' names."

"I don't actually know any of her friends."

"What is *wrong* with you?" Avery screamed. "How could you not have *seen*?" She rushed at him, pushed him on the chest.

"Avery, please," Chambers said, touching her arm. "I've got this."

She clenched her teeth so hard that her jawbones shifted.

Chambers let go of her arm and turned back to Ryan. "What did she do for work? Did she go to school?"

Avery couldn't stand to listen—some Etsy/eBay nonsense. If they'd figured this out sooner, maybe they could have found and rescued them all months ago. They could have known the truth about Max and been done with it.

"So I'll look into it," Chambers was saying. "And we'll have a team come here to dust for prints." Then he turned to Scarlett. "You said there was another sketch?"

Scarlett nodded—"A house"—and held her phone out to Chambers again. "Maybe it's near Anchor Beach."

"I need you to send me both of those," Chambers said.

"Can I talk now?" Avery said, not hiding her impatience well and not caring.

"Yes," Chambers said. "Of course."

"The person calling the tip line that everyone wrote off as crazy is actually the principal. I recognized his voice." She was running out of air, slowed down. "He said they were blackmailing him, burying a body in his yard. And how it was only supposed to be for a few hours that they were gone. How the place where you found that body wasn't the right place. He sounds terrified. He said they're watching him."

Miranda had been watching, too? How did she even fit in?

Chambers said he needed the transcripts or recordings immediately and offered to drive her home. When they got up to leave, she caught Lucas's eye and he walked them out, followed her to the squad car.

"Good work," he said.

"Thanks," she said. "You, too."

Chambers had already started the car, was calling ahead to her house.

She watched out the window as they passed the psychic's storefront, a candle flickering beneath the neon sign:

Know Your Future.

As if.

Dad was waiting at the door.

Scarlett

"Do I look like him?" Scarlett asked her mother. "My father?"

Chambers had dropped off her clothes and photographs earlier that day, while she'd been at Anchor Beach. Now she sat at the dining room table in pajamas—her hair wet from a long bath—studying her younger self. She held a photo out to her mother and said, "I really don't think I look like you, so . . ."

"He's not the answer you need," Tammy said, taking the photo.

"Answer?" Scarlett said.

"I know you feel like you don't belong here . . . with me." Her voice shaky.

"It's not that . . ." Scarlett ran out of steam.

"No, it's okay." Her mother waved a hand. "When you were little I was like, where did this kid come from? 'Cause you were so smart—smarter than me, and I didn't know what to do with that." She put the photo down. "So I'll give you his name and address, even, and sure, you have his eyes and something around the chin that's similar, but I'm tellin' ya. He ain't what you're looking for." Looking up, finally, she said, "It's late. I'm turning in." She got up and came over and kissed Scarlett on the forehead.

The warm, damp spot on her head became so distracting.

The whole day such a jumble.

Miranda's betrayal.

The principal's role in the whole thing.

The revelation that she'd witnessed the shooting.

"Why didn't you tell me about the shooting?" Scarlett said. "That I was there."

Tammy shrugged one shoulder. "Didn't seem like a happy thing to remind you of if you didn't remember it yourself. And the truth is, I don't really remember it, either."

"You must." This time it was Scarlett who Comet came to visit. Scarlett reached out to pet her, for the first time.

"I remember I got blood on me, and you asked me if I was going to die, and I said, no, of course not, but you said, 'But everybody dies, right?' And you started to cry and said, 'Promise me you won't die.'" She ran a hand over Scarlett's hair. "That's when I realized we were stuck with each other, you and me. Maybe that was the first time I got terrified—that you needed me so bad—and then, you know the rest, the drinking got real bad after that. I remember it the way you remember a dream, and that's fine for me."

Scarlett nodded and Tammy smiled and padded down the hall. "He brought that weird jacket, by the way. It's in the closet."

Scarlett got up and went to the closet and gently pulled it off a hanger. She turned it around in her hands, inhaled it—some familiar perfume—and then was about to put it on when her eye caught on some stitching on the inner lining.

Rectangles, like the ones she'd sewn absentmindedly a few times now.

Only here they had little circles of stitches on top of them.

So not rectangles.

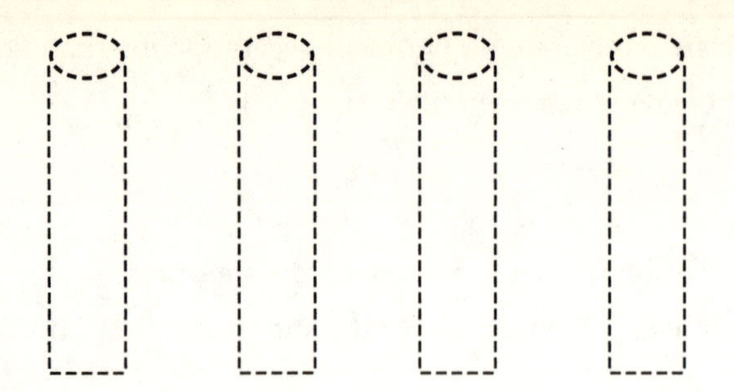

Cylinders.

Four of them.

Smokestacks, to be precise.

She laid the jacket flat on the table, best she could.

Her fingers tingled as she ran them over the bumps of thread.

Near the smokestacks, spotted stitches that took the shape of a

. . . pier?

The entire inner lining was stitched with lines, maybe indicating streets?

And up by an armhole . . .

Stitched thicker than all the rest.

Thread upon thread to form:

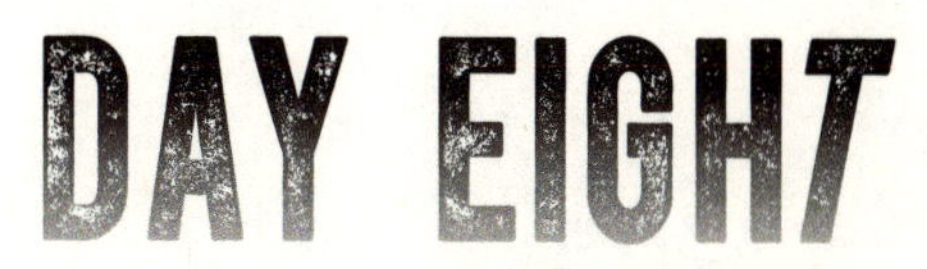
DAY EIGHT

Lucas

Rain turned roads to rivers. Frantic wipers failed. Ryan put the hazard lights on and slowed the car to rowboat speed.

They were on their way to an address Chambers had given them. Using Scarlett's jacket as a map, he had sent officers out looking for the house Sarah had drawn, and they'd found it overnight.

It all seemed too long in coming and sudden at the same time.

Lucas didn't feel . . . ready . . . even though he'd been waiting and waiting.

They were the last to arrive—just as the rain eased to drizzle—at a house that looked exactly like Sarah's sketch: a boring two-story, shingled ranch with a two-car garage. A house you'd drive by and not even notice. Chambers stood on the front porch with Scarlett, Sarah, Kristen, Adam, and various adults who had come. He and Ryan got out of the car and, closing his eyes for a moment at the bottom of the path, Lucas tried to imagine himself on that porch, walking up those steps. His brain conjured images of shoes—smaller shoes, beat-up sneakers—but he could have been imagining them.

"Everybody ready?" The raindrops clinging to Chambers's black jacket looked like snow.

Inside, everything was new, clean, modern. The opposite of what Lucas had imagined it would be like, based on the exterior.

The five of them fanned out in a large living room, forming a semicircle looking out large windows. Wet glass garbled the view, but Lucas lifted his camera from where it hung on his chest and snapped a few shots anyway. A row of palm trees in the yard were being battered by wind and looked like witches with wild hair on bent brooms. Turning back to the room, he looked at Chambers, who seemed to be waiting for one of them to say, *Now, this place, I remember*, but none of them did.

"Let's go upstairs," Chambers said, and turned.

Up a wooden split-level staircase, they arrived in a main hall, where Lucas's gaze latched onto the third doorway on the left and wouldn't let go. He went and stood in it and lifted his camera again.

He fired off a few shutters from the doorway, then looked up and down the hall.

Each of the others had gone to stand in front of a different door.

Chambers stood at the one none of them had claimed.

Adam stepped through his doorway and then Sarah went through hers. Scarlett was next. Then Kristen.

Lucas felt he had no choice, so he inched in.

One window.

A small closet.

Walls newly painted white, the scent of paint still detectable.

The only evidence he had that maybe this had been his room was that he didn't like the feel of it.

Back out in the hall, he found just Chambers. "Did you find clothes and photos here, too?"

"This place is completely wiped clean," Chambers said. "Like nothing I've ever seen before."

"Like *us*."

Lucas started down the stairs again, felt a pull toward the backyard.

"Lucas, wait!" Chambers called after him. "I want us all to stay together."

Too late.

Lucas skipped the last step.

Then stopped and turned back and put a foot on it, pressed.

It groaned.

Chambers appeared on the staircase's halfway landing, Scarlett right behind him.

"This is the place." Lucas pushed on the bottom step again. Another groan.

Scarlett pushed past Chambers and Lucas and headed for another staircase. Lucas followed her down and out.

And the air smelled like dirt and ocean.

He felt free, but also . . .

There were no electrified or barbed-wire fences.

No fences at all.

Why had they stayed?

Scarlett cut across the lawn to the right, down toward a small barn, and he followed, wet grasses licking his feet and ankles.

"Scarlett! Wait!"

"I don't want to wait." She disappeared through an opening in the brush beside the barn.

Chasing her, his feet found boards over swamp, springy beneath him. He caught glimpses of her blue hoodie up ahead and thought he heard her laughing—like this was a game they were playing. Or had been?

Coming out of the woods and onto a road, he stopped. Across the way was the back end of some fenced-in industrial property. Scarlett had her eyes up as she moved down the road to the left, like she was tracking a bird.

No, she hadn't been laughing.

So who?

He reached her just as she stopped moving, followed her gaze. Steam billowed from the power plant's smokestacks in white swells and got absorbed into lingering storm clouds.

"We used to sneak out down that path," she said.

"Seems so." Had it been a memory of laughing?

"But we weren't trying to escape?"

"I guess not." His fingers twitched. "But I knew how to use a gun? Taught myself?"

"So maybe we tried to get away," she said. "Once. Like if we somehow figured out who we were?"

"But it didn't work."

"And they erased the memory," she offered. "And all the memories involving how we figured out who we were?"

"But it happened again?" he said.

"And again," she said. "And so eventually we started to figure out ways to remember."

He nodded. "But what about my tattoo? The journal?"

"The penny, the map, the drawings. They brought us here, to *where*, but nothing has bought us to *who*."

"Or why."

"Lucas!" Chambers's voice was far away, irritated. "Scarlett!"

"Coming!" she called out.

Back through the pathway and over the planks, Scarlett went and Lucas followed, not liking the feeling of following. Had it always been like that between them?

"You need to stop running off," Chambers said when they came back out into the yard.

"Sorry," Scarlett said. But she didn't sound sorry.

Lucas wasn't, either. He was only sorry he wasn't finding his own answers. What did the tattoo mean? Were there hidden cameras here? Buried film?

What?

"The others are in here," Chambers said, indicating the barn.

The barn was pulling the same trick as the house. From the outside, it looked like it might house a farm animal or three on a good day. Inside, it was a slick lab. Empty fridges and freezers lined one wall; cages where mice might have been kept lined another; a large video monitor hung on a third.

"We've been working on the principal angle," Chambers said as they gathered around him, and Lucas had a moment of feeling *so proud* of Avery. "When you piece together all his calls, they start to form a narrative. That he was approached by this group who wanted to take a few kids for a few hours and try to erase the memory of the shooting."

"You're serious," Adam said.

"I am." Chambers nodded. "The principal facilitated the abduction after interviewing you all during those first days of kindergarten. The idea was that if it worked, they could treat *all* the students."

"That's completely insane." Sarah rubbed her own arms.

"We believe this is a serious group with unlimited resources," Chambers said. "We believe they're interested in military applications of the treatment."

"Military?" Adam's father asked from across the room.

"Postwar, yes." Chambers nodded. "Treatment for PTSD."

"But how did a few hours turn into *eleven years*?" Sarah looked like she might literally fall to pieces, leaving only a pile of jagged flesh on the white concrete floor.

"I can't explain that," Chambers said. "Not yet."

"And what about Max?" Lucas asked.

"We don't have clarity on that yet, either," Chambers said. "But it sounds like there was an incident, possibly an asthma attack. We're still working on all that. So unless you—"

"Where's *Kristen*?" Scarlett interrupted.

They found her back up at the house, in one of the bedrooms.

"Here." She pointed. "This one."

"This one what?" Lucas stepped toward her.

"An owl. In the knots of the wood." She knelt down. "Can you give me a hand?"

Lucas bent down to look and, sure enough, the knot in the floorboard really looked like an owl. He and Kristen both worked with fingertips to try to pull the board up. But it wouldn't come and so Chambers went and found a pocketknife and joined in the quest.

When the board finally surrendered, the others all gathered in. The small blue leather journal made Lucas think of babies—helpless, waiting to be lifted out of cribs.

Kristen reached for the book and stood and started to flip its pages.

"Well?" Lucas stepped toward her and Chambers did, too. "What does it say?"

"I need a minute," Kristen said, backing away from them, and she kept flipping.

She was probably feeling vindicated and Lucas envied her for it.

Then she looked up and said, "It's all over the place. There are huge gaps. Years with nothing, it looks like." She looked back down to read more.

Scarlett said, "Maybe you'd forgotten where it was? That you even had it?"

"Yes," Kristen said, turning pages. "Here." She read, "Found this journal again today."

"What about the last entry?" Lucas asked.

Kristen flipped ahead and read aloud:

> *"We have decided to trust this journal.*
> *We found it again today, after more than a year.*
> *We're planning to leave tonight before we forget again.*
> *We've read back in these pages and must believe it all to be true.*
> *We have set our traps, tried to bring clues.*
> *Wish us luck."*

She looked up. "We all signed it. But it was dated months ago."

Chambers said, "You must have tried again to get away, and they stopped you. They let you go when they thought it was best for them, when they could control it."

"Did you write names anywhere?" Lucas snapped at Kristen. "The name of who kept us here?"

"I must have," she said, flipping through pages frantically. "Right?"

"I'm going to need to take that into evidence, Kristen," Chambers said.

She looked like she might never let it go.

AVERY

Waiting was dog years.

Again.

Chambers was following up on any and all leads from the tip-line recordings, which Avery was told meant yes, looking to see if anyone or anything had been buried at the house where the principal had lived eleven years ago. But now that they'd found the place where Lucas and the others had been kept—for real this time, by the sound of it—that had probably taken up a good part of Chambers's day and who even knew when they'd know anything?

So even though she'd skipped school, Avery went to the auditions that afternoon to support Emma. They sat in squeaky seats in the back row and waited for Emma's name to be called.

But then Mr. Louska called Avery's name.

She'd never crossed it out on the sheet.

Would she regret not doing it?

Be jealous if Emma got the lead?

Louska called her name again.

She stood.

Emma looked up at her.

All doubts fizzled on the spot.

Avery didn't need to be the star of anything.

Preferred not to be, really.

Tragedy had made her famous for a time and now it was time to do things differently, to be, different.

"I'm sorry," she said. "That was a mistake. I'm not auditioning."

"Well, that's disappointing," Mr. Louska said. Then, without missing a beat, he looked at his list and called whoever was next in alphabetical order.

When it was her turn, Emma sounded nervous at first, but by the chorus, she was soaring, like she *really believed* things were going to be better when she grew up.

Maybe she was right. Maybe for her, they would be.

Avery's phone dinged but she ignored it.

Emma sounded way better here than she had that day on the lanai and now Avery thought her friend might actually get the lead, which she hadn't before, not really. But it had been the right thing to say and to hope for.

People in the audience clapped when she was done and Avery put two fingers in her mouth and whistled, loudly. Even from the back row, Emma's smile beamed.

She rejoined Avery in their seats and Avery high-fived her. "Nailed it!"

"You think?"

"I think." Avery gathered her things. "I'm heading out."

"Okay. Talk later." Emma hugged her. "Thanks for coming."

"Of course." Avery got up and went out into the hall, then out the doors of school.

The text from Dad said,

Hi hon. You should come home.

In-person news was bad news.

That was the rule.

Sure enough:

"I'm so sorry." Chambers stood facing her and her parents, who were seated on the living room sofa; Rita puttered in the kitchen. "We found remains at the former principal's house. We're still waiting on the confirmation from the lab, but all signs point to the remains being Max's. He appears to have died quite a long time ago. Possibly the same day as the abduction."

"An asthma attack," Avery said.

"Most likely, yes."

"Did Max even *have* asthma?" She turned to her parents.

"The onset can be unpredictable, and sudden," Chambers said. "I mean, if he wasn't diagnosed?"

Her father shook his head.

Chambers said, "It's possible there'd never been a strong enough trigger before . . ." Then he and her father stepped away to talk further and Avery moved closer to her mom on the couch.

"What did I ever do to deserve this?" her mom wailed.

"It's not your fault," Avery said through tears that had started to form. Because it was finally and truly over—the tiny bit of hope they'd all been clinging to had been chopped off, like with a hatchet, taking the whole hand with it.

Just *gone.*

"Oh, Max. My poor Max. I don't think I can get over this"—her mother was all panicked-sounding—"I don't think I'm going to be able to get over this."

The feeling of wanting to take that severed limb of hope and hit her mother over the head with it, just to snap her out of it.

"I don't think I can. I don't think I can."

"You have to, Mommy."

"I can't! I won't! My Max!" Her mother moved far enough to grab a tissue and blow her nose.

"But you have *me*." Avery's voice got deep. "*I'm* here. I've *been* here. I've *been here* the whole time."

Her father came in and said, "Let's give her some time, Ave," and sat beside his wife.

The doorbell rang maybe twenty minutes later and Avery was grateful for the excuse to leave the room. Her dad had just been sitting by her mother's side, stroking her hand. Avery wasn't sure he'd even looked at her, though he'd called a few friends, relatives.

She opened the door expecting her mom's friend Patty to be there, holding some useless casserole.

Lucas said, "I just heard."

He reached for her hand and she stepped out onto the porch and into his arms. With her chin against his chest, she started to sob.

"You did it, Ave," he said softly into her hair. "You found him."

DAY NINE

Scarlett

Kristen had taken down the puffy princess mobile, and Scarlett had purged the jewelry box of plastic beads and clip-on earrings—everything except the Anchor Beach penny and the half of the best-friend heart she'd split with Vanessa.

Together they'd bagged up clothes and books for donations.

They'd tossed most of the toys and peeled My Little Pony decals off the wall.

They'd gone through a sizable stack of kid artwork—photographing a few nice pieces and chucking the rest.

That left Glinda, which Scarlett decided she was going to burn on the beach.

It would feel cleansing, symbolic.

Perhaps not as symbolic as it would if she had a life-size cardboard cutout of the Great Oz, but close enough.

It was a good evening for it.

A little bit unseasonably cold.

She took a lighter she'd found in a kitchen drawer down to the beach just past the back fence and lit Glinda at the hem of her dress. A moment later the flame went out.

"Brilliant plan," Kristen said.

"Why are you here again?"

"Moral support."

"Exactly." Then Scarlett pulled her into a hug and squeezed. "I don't care that you think we didn't like each other."

"Yeah," Kristen said, "I'm over it." She looked serious, then said, "It was never about Lucas, you know."

"Adam?" Scarlett tried to light Glinda again.

"No, Scarlett. It was *you*. I think I was in love with you."

/ / /

"Oh."

The flame caught.

"Apart from the ridiculous horseback-riding thing, it was the one thing I remembered right away." Kristen had her own lighter out and lit Glinda at another point. "Feeling different than all of you. And then when the memory guy asked me about kissing Lucas and Adam . . ."

"You said Sashor was hot!" Scarlett remembered.

"Objectively!"

Scarlett elbowed her. "So you *do* like me."

Glinda finally *swoosh*ed; they jumped back.

"I guess I was hurt or angry or something. But I'm done with that." She nodded. "You think they'll ever find him?"

There was still so much up in the air.

Charges against Lucas for the murder of John Norton had been dropped, at least, but Miranda was still in the wind.

Scarlett said, "I'm not counting on it."

"And you're okay with that?"

"I want to be?"

Kristen nudged Glinda farther away from them with a booted foot. "Why didn't I write their names down? Why didn't we keep better notes?"

The fire popped and they watched as Glinda's face became consumed. Scarlett tracked the flames as they made their way to the very tip of Glinda's magic wand, which lit, then blackened and converted to embers. Tiny, blowing orange bursts of magic that burned until they couldn't burn anymore.

I'm melting, Scarlett thought. *Melting.*

Lucas

Ryan and Lucas were on a way-high bleacher bench at the high school football field; the elementary school sat silent and empty past buzz-cut soccer fields.

A marching band had just heel-and-toed out onto the field. Black pants with stripes running down the side. Tall, hot-looking hats.

The members of the color guard were all carrying enormous bouquets of flowers and the instrumentalists made a block of long lines, right at the center of the field. They played a mournful song Lucas didn't recognize.

There were speakers, then, with shaky voices at a microphone on a small podium by the fifty-yard line.

Some students who spoke about gun safety.

Some parents who spoke about depression, the shooter, the counseling services available locally to anyone with thoughts of harming themselves or others.

Then the school principal—a woman in a red suit—talked about no lives ever being wasted.

Of young people as an inspiration to us all.

Of the heroism of teachers.

The strength of those left behind.

The cause that they all, as a community, could not forget.

Near the makeshift stage and microphone, a woman was holding up a large photograph of one of the victims of the shooting. Probably her daughter. The mother looked so sad and hollow, even now, that Lucas wished that someone could erase her grief, erase her memories—of hearing about the shooting, of hearing there were casualties, of not being able to find her daughter, of having to ID a body, of having to tell her husband, her other children if she had any, of waking up the next day and the day after that into that same bad dream.

The man beside her had one arm around her and a sign in the other that said, NEVER FORGET.

Why *not* forget?

Why *not* just black out something awful?

Like a shooting.

Or war.

Childhood, even.

Sure!

Oh.

Forgetting meant not knowing, meant ignorance, meant maybe making the same mistakes again and again.

Lucas's phone buzzed and he looked at it and didn't recognize the number. "Hello?"

"You won't find him," Miranda said. "He's long gone."

"Who?" Lucas asked, turning away from the proceedings and looking out toward the baseball field behind the bleachers. "Who is he?"

"My father," she said.

Lucas met eyes with Ryan, who raised his brow questioningly. "Why were you watching me?"

"He needed to see how re-entry would impact the results of the treatment."

"It was only supposed to be for a few hours?" Lucas asked.

"Yes, but then Max died, and you were all traumatized again, so *that* had to be erased, and it took a while and then he had to erase your memory of him and the house and it just got messy, so it dragged on."

"For eleven years?" he near-screamed.

"Well, the nature of the thing changed. It was working but not consistently—and they really wanted him to get it right, and then he saw this opportunity to raise you all . . . *completely* without trauma. Building on some work he'd already done on me."

"What kind of work?"

"This isn't about me."

"Why were we let go?" he asked.

"Couldn't keep you forever. The plan was always to release you in your sixteenth year. It was more rushed than he'd wanted, but that was because you'd figured out who you were a few times and had somehow found a way to figure it out every day, so it was all a bit out of control at the end. You'd found the gun and all. You always were the fighter. That's why he picked you for me to keep an eye on. Figured if anybody was going to start remembering, it'd be you."

"*How* did he do it?" Lucas said. "How did he erase . . . everything?"

"Now, that even *I* don't know," she said.

"Why did you call me?" he asked.

"To make sure you knew that it wasn't *all* awful. We were like a big family. Except he only ever took a few of us out at a time. He always said you were foster kids if anyone asked."

"I'm going to find him." Lucas felt his disgust like a foul taste in his mouth. "I'll find *you*."

She said, "I won't remember you if you do."

• • •

Back home, in the RV, Lucas sorted all the photos of himself Chambers had given him into piles according to groups or general age range.

Then, when nothing jarring stood out, he set about hanging all the large photos that had been brought from the faked location of their kidnapping on the walls of the RV's main compartment. Chambers had agreed to lend them out to him.

He started to study every inch of them.

Not this again, Miranda had said when he'd taken her photo.

He understood now.

He had taken *these* photos, too.

There was a clue here.

That was what the tattoo meant.

He just had to find it.

Wouldn't sleep until he did.

He went over every inch of each of them.

Then did it again.

And again.

He'd done it probably twenty times by the time Ryan came to check on him.

He started to do it again anyway.

He was missing something.

He had to be.

The hot air balloon turned up nothing.

Puppy, nothing.

Horse, nothing.

Roller coaster, useless.

He always left the carousel for last. It was the most complicated, the most dense.

So much to look at.

The scratches on the teeth.

The burst of sun off the water in the distance.

Reflections in mirrors on the carousel's cylinder.

He'd already gone over this one maybe twice as often as the others.

Still, nothing.

He went back to the photos Chambers had given him and picked up the small stack he'd made of the photos from the same day.

One of him actually on that carousel horse, long arms holding on to the pole. So someone else had to have taken that.

One of the carousel from a distance.

Then a dozen more shots of the same horse as the one in the blown-up shot.

Why so many pictures of one horse?

He spread them out on the kitchenette table and started to compare.

And saw a blur of sorts in one that wasn't in the others.

A reflection in the mirror behind the horse.

He picked up his camera and took a close-up shot of that section of the photo. Then zoomed in on it on the camera display screen.

A man's face took shape.

Lucas said, "Gotcha."

The skin on his hip pulsed.

DAY ELEVEN

AVERY

The funeral was fast, small, and private. Avery thought Max deserved more, bigger—some actual fanfare—after waiting so long for a proper good-bye.

She'd grabbed Woof-Woof when they'd left the house, shoved him in her purse, not even knowing why until they were in the church, the first five rows of pews filled with family and friends she hadn't seen in ages. Now it was the part of the service where people were coming forward and taking a flower from a basket and placing it on top of the coffin. She couldn't will herself to get up, had to let people past her in the pew, brushing against her knees.

It would look bad, her not putting a flower on.

Emma did it.

Sam, too.

All the returned kids did their part.

She didn't want to be ornery or melodramatic.

She just didn't want to do it.

Flowers? What was the point?

She slid Woof-Woof out of her bag and waited until the line was gone, most of the flowers resting in a scattered pile on top of the casket. Then she got up, walked over, and put Woof-Woof on top.

Feeling her insides crumble, she turned and walked down the long aisle—whispers, whimpers, wails from the people there—and past Lucas and Ryan, two dark suits in the back pew—and out the church doors. Lucas had found a clue last night; and Chambers had told him that with some luck, some digital finesse, and some facial recognition software, they might actually ID their captor. So that was something, at least.

Lucas had followed her out.

"I thought I'd feel better," she said. "Closure and all. I thought my one greatest wish was to find Max."

"And now?" He stood beside her on the church steps.

"Now I want what you want," she said.

"To find *him*," Lucas said. "To find *me*."

"Those are different things," she said. "They have to be. Anyway, *I* found you. You're right here." She started down the remaining steps. "Come on. There's someplace I want to go to honor Max way better than what they're doing in there."

They were the only teenagers on the pirate tour boat, *and* they were overdressed. At first that felt kind of ridiculous but then it seemed no one else noticed or cared—maybe just assumed their younger siblings were there among the (mostly) boys and (handful of) girls, gathered around the pirate who was teaching them some basic pirate vocabulary. A few kids were lined up to get bandanas and scars painted onto their faces.

"Is it me or are those scars a little too realistic?" Avery said as they sat on a sunned-hot black leather bench along the side of the boat.

This ship's flag had a winking pirate face on it of the Big Beard variety. The pirate dude had the kids all saying *Arrgh* and was telling them it wasn't loud enough. They tried harder and Avery laughed.

All the kids were roaring "Yo ho ho!" when Lucas kissed her.

Scarlett

With her first funeral under her belt, Scarlett felt strangely alive.

Maybe it was morbid but all through the service she hadn't been able to fight a nagging feeling of—

It couldn't be excitement.

No.

Maybe just *awareness.*

Of the blood in her veins.

The air in her lungs.

The synapses firing in her brain every second of her existence.

There *was* something magical about her.

Something magical about everyone.

The scene itself—the small coffin, the way Max's mother just locked eyes with the coffin through the whole Mass, like staring down an enemy—had been borderline unbearable.

Tammy, who'd foolishly worn mascara, had wept silently the whole time.

Then Avery and that stuffed dog . . .

Scarlett had had to look away.

But none of it could stop her from looking up at the stained-glass windows—angels on high—and thinking about how Max, at least, had been loved.

That was what mattered.

When her phone lit up in the church parking lot afterward, it seemed right that there'd be news. She called Chambers back and he filled her in.

They'd arrested the old principal. They'd found him—disguised but not by much because who would even think to look for him?—among the crowd at the memorial yesterday; they'd spent twenty-four hours trailing him, to see if he might lead them anywhere interesting.

He hadn't.

Now he was in custody and they'd gotten at least a few more answers—were able to explain a few more things.

Like how he'd selected the six of them, specifically, because he'd been right there with them—showing them a mural of a zoo scene on the cafeteria wall while their parents did paperwork—when it happened. He'd seen exactly what they'd seen—blood, fear, mayhem—when they'd huddled with him by that slightly misshapen giraffe on the wall. He'd seen it in their eyes that they would never be the same.

He'd had a copy of *The Leaving* in his office when the kids had been vetted during kindergarten orientation. He'd wanted to read it after he'd been told that it had inspired the scientist running the experiment, a man he thought was named David Kunkel, but who had used an alias. Of course. It had never occurred to the principal how closely what would eventually happen would mirror the book.

Scarlett must have seen his copy of *The Leaving* and read the description. And her five-year-old imagination had taken it and run with it.

I'm going on a trip.

To the leaving.

Maybe it had sounded exciting!

Fun!

Maybe even back then she was fantasizing about getting away from her mother.

Now they drove home together, then went their own ways off the hall to change. When Scarlett came out in a tank top and shorts, her mother was already out in the yard, sitting in a bright-green plastic Adirondack chair with another beside it. Beyond her, in the water, Scarlett saw the quick bump of a dolphin's arched body and almost gasped.

She smiled and opened the door. "What's with the chairs?" she said, going down the back stairs.

Tammy uncrossed, then recrossed her legs. "Thought those old loungers were looking kind of ragged and saw these on sale at the Home Depot."

"Not too shabby," Scarlett said, and she sat, head resting comfortably back. The parasailing people were at it again, the sail dragging slowly across the sky.

Maybe Scarlett would brave it someday.

Maybe it would feel sort of like riding in a hot air balloon.

Maybe it didn't matter if it did or didn't.

She'd start redecorating her room tomorrow, maybe order a poster of *Christina's World*, so she'd never forget how a single moment—any one, really—could be so perfectly its own.

"It is always now," she said, and her mother said, "Huh?"

Scarlett closed her eyes and the sun warmed her lids. "Oh, nothing."

Lucas

Ryan had finally gone back to working regular hours at the hotel, and Lucas met him there for his dinner break. They sat on the roof deck, at a canopied table on coasters that swung, and ate fish sandwiches and fries. Below, on the beach level, a live band had just started playing.

"We should be down there," Ryan said. "The girls coming in so far today have been hot."

"You rebound pretty quickly," Lucas said.

"Trust me. I'm reeling on other levels from the deception and all that. Feeling like an idiot in general. But I am not, by any stretch of the imagination, heartbroken." He looked down. "She gave me this shirt."

"Who is that, anyway?" Lucas asked. His brother's valet shirt was hanging on the corner of his bench.

"Mr. Magoo," Ryan said. "Some old cartoon character. She made me watch a bunch of clips on YouTube when I told her I had no idea who he was. He's this old nearsighted guy who keeps getting into sticky situations because he can't see and won't admit he can't see. But it always works out. She gave me another one, too. The Pink Panther."

"Who is . . . ?"

"He's this cartoon pink panther who was in the opening credits of these old movies about an incompetent detective." He shook his head. "This whole time she's been here, she's been mocking me for not seeing it."

"I'm really sorry."

According to Chambers her identity was entirely faked. She only started to exist a few years ago. But with the combination of the photo Lucas had flagged—and ones that the others had, with the same man also in the distance, or reflected in mirrors or hidden in plain sight—they'd found the name of the man in the photo and identified him as Louis Immerso. He'd published a few papers in obscure journals years ago, about his success erasing his young daughter Lola's memories of abuse by an uncle, but then he'd gone off the grid.

Chambers was now in touch with Orlean's daughter-in-law, hoping for evidence that would connect Immerso with Orlean, confident Immerso fell under the category of obsessed fan.

Hoping, still, to find him.

Hoping he'd lead them to whatever organization had orchestrated it all.

Hoping, of course, to shut it down.

Kristen's diary had been similarly unhelpful. A chilling tale but not the best record of what had happened.

Ryan shook his head. "I feel like such an idiot for being so duped."

"Don't beat yourself up too much," Lucas said. "How could you even imagine that someone would do that?"

"Still." Ryan picked up his Coke—in a large red frosted plastic cup—and drained about half of it in one long pull off the straw.

"Onward and upward!" Lucas ate a french fry. He was going to have to learn to cook ASAP.

"Yes, indeed." Ryan attacked his sandwich, then, while chewing, said, "College for me. Senior year for you."

"Will I be able to stand it?"

Avery would be there, one year behind him. That would help.

"It's just one year," Ryan said. "It's better than, you know, getting a job."

"Is it?"

"I don't know, man. But you can meet girls and make friends and get drunk and do something dumb like be in a marching band and go to football games and pep rallies and prom and live it up a little, right?"

"What do I do? Just walk into the office and ask to register?"

"I'm pretty sure they'll know who you are." Ryan looked at his phone. "Break's up. I've got to go." He took one last huge bite of his sandwich and stood. "So we're good, then. This weekend?"

It felt right to scatter Will's ashes at Opus 6; even if Immerso hadn't been caught, the mystery had been solved.

"We're good," Lucas said.

Men with know-how were coming to move the stone in the morning.

DAY FIFTEEN

AVERY

Spring breaks across the country ended, and town emptied out. Her flip-flops arrived in a beat-up box, and things got back to normal. Emma got the lead and grew instantly obsessed with the school play; the media stopped being obsessed with the returned kids and were now focused, instead, on Louis Immerso, who was alternately a monster and a genius. Photos had been released of him and his daughter, Lola, but so far . . . nothing.

Avery's mother had had a breakdown after the funeral and was now in an outpatient grief management program. Her father had taken the week off to drive her mom there and back daily in order to guarantee she was actually going, and her mother had actually asked her about the school play auditions, while straightening papers on the fridge.

"Oh," Avery said. "I missed the auditions."

"Well, that's too bad," her mom said. "I always enjoy the plays."

This, Avery decided to take as progress.

Casseroles had, in fact, started arriving—even Sam had brought one. "Sorry," he'd said, "my mom insisted."

"What is it with moms and casseroles?" she'd asked.

"I have no idea," he'd said, holding it over the trash with eyebrows raised in question.

"Is it plastic? The dish?" she asked.

"No." He laughed. "Do you really care? I doubt she's going to come ask for it back."

She'd stepped on the lid pedal and opened it. He'd slid it in.

She was pretty sure he'd gone on a date with Emma and was pretty sure she didn't care.

Lucas had asked her to come today for the scattering of Will's ashes. So she put on a dark-gray dress and nice sandals and walked down by the bay, then past the fish market and psychic—again—and arrived at Opus 6.

Something was different.

It felt . . . complete.

Now, at the very apex, at the dead center, stood a tall stone with a long, flat face. It was vaguely head-shaped, in that Easter Island kind of way, and she wondered whether she'd ever go there, or anywhere—Stonehenge?—and whether she'd ever see anything as bizarre and spectacular made from rocks as Opus 6.

Ryan and Lucas stood near the stone, talking to Scarlett and Kristen.

Sarah and Adam had come, too. Avery had had to work hard to convince Lucas that it was right to ask them, pointing to the fact that their names were also on the stone, carved there by Will's hands.

She was the odd man out, or felt that way until Lucas saw her. His eyes ignited. He smiled. She walked to him and he kissed her by the ear and said, "Thank you for coming."

"Of course," she said. Then she said hi to everyone she knew and was introduced to those she hadn't met in person and it felt like she was part of some strange club and she neither liked it nor didn't like it.

It was what it was.

Lucas reached into his suit jacket and said, "I have something for you. I found it in an old box of photos."

He held out a print—an almost identical print to the one she'd burned. Lucas, Max, Smurfette. She grinned and kissed him.

Love was its own happy ending.

After a few more minutes, Lucas took the urn and went to stand by the newly placed stone and started talking about his father, his dedication to his sons, to the investigation, and to the creation of Opus 6 itself. He nodded at something beyond her and Avery turned. Detective Chambers and another man Avery didn't know but whose dreads were longer than her ponytail. Chambers nodded solemnly.

Turning back toward Lucas, watching his lips move, watching his eyes fill with emotion, Avery wondered what she'd remember about this day later, when she'd be home wiping mascara away in black smears in the upstairs bathroom?

And in the morning, how much would be left when she sat in the kitchen doing the maze on the back of the cereal box again?

How much of today would be gone by next week, and the week after?

What would be left next year when she'd inhale air enough to darken sixteen candles?

Ten years from now? What then? And twenty?

What was the exact percentage of this day that had already slipped away?

She wanted *this* moment, this half of a half of a percent, to stick.

She set out to capture it.

She chased down those vines by the reflecting pool, their orange blooms like bonfires for Barbies.

She caught that tree, the one that had been turned into a wise old woman by long gray braids of Spanish moss.

She scooped up Lucas—so vulnerable, so fully here now, his tie knot all wrong.

She took it all in with her net, knowing that so very much of it would slip through and fall away hard and fast.

That the curve of memory was steep.

Lucas opened the urn and the wind cooperated as he shook it and the ashes swirled high—like in a movie about spells—before settling and disappearing at their feet.

A return to form.

We are all dust.

All dying.

All losing.

All forgetting.

We are all leaving all the time.

David Dunton
at Harvey Klinger Agency
(our 10th book together!)

Adrienne Maria Vrettos
(first reader and ultimate writing dater)

Morghan, Paul, and Rachel
("my lawyers")

Harvey Fite
(for Opus 40)

Anne Ursu
(for the right lecture
at the right time)

Teeny Tiny Filmworks
(not so teeny anymore!)

Bob
(Of course.)

Nick
(Always.)

Ellie
(For the idea.)

Violet
(Just because.)

The amazing *Leaving* design team:
Donna Mark, Amanda Bartlett,
Jessie Gang, and Kimi Weart
(Because, I mean, **LOOK AT IT!!**)

and Sarah Shumway
(for always *push push push*ing for more)
(okay, sometimes less)

THE POSSIBLE

BLOOMSBURY

TARA ALTEBRANDO

Author of *The Leaving*

I REALIZED IN THE FOURTH inning that I hadn't given up a hit yet. The whispers about the possibility of a no-hitter started when I headed for the mound to pitch the sixth.

You think she can do it? I bet she's gonna do it.

Has anyone at school ever done that? No, not ever.

I shut down three batters no problem.

Now it was the top of the seventh.

The last inning.

Two batters had already tried their hardest to break my streak and failed, and the whispers were louder than ever.

If I struck out one more batter, I'd have our school's first ever perfect game.

And if we won—the score was 1–0—we'd be on our way to regional championship play-offs.

It was down to me.

Me and their best player, number 14.

I drew the strike zone in my mind's eye as 14 positioned herself at the plate and took a few arm-loosening swings.

I picked the top-right corner of the zone.

I stared at my chosen spot as I set my fingers on the ball.

When I had my grip right and the batter was ready, I stepped forward hard with my left foot and threw, and the world got so very slow as I watched the ball curve up and out and over and up a notch, heading for that corner I'd carved out of the air.

A smile stole its way onto my face maybe a second too soon, dirt dancing on my tongue.

But I knew the ball would sneak past and go exactly where I'd put it.

She swung.

And it did.

She missed.

The smack of the ball hitting the catcher's mitt.

Cheers.

Whistles.

High-fives as my teammates rushed the mound.

*Nice job, Kaylee*s and *Holy cow that was amazing*s.

I'd done it, like I'd known I would.

. . .

Bennett Laurie said, "Nice job" as I walked off the field. He wasn't actually talking to *me* but there was no question that he was into me. And I hadn't been so crazy for anyone ever before. Just the sight of him made me carnival-ride woozy. The sight of *her*—his girlfriend, whose sister, Evelyn, had scored our one run—made me burn.

She didn't deserve him.

He'd realize it.

I simply had to be patient.

Because this was what was going to happen:

Junior prom tickets were going on sale soon. And when they did, he'd realize he didn't want to take Princess Bubblegum. So he'd dump her. He'd take me.

If that didn't happen, no worries. He belonged to the swim club where I'd be lifeguarding all summer. He'd watch me twirling my whistle in my tall white chair. He'd see me up there in my swimsuit, limbs long and strong, and he'd want me the way I wanted him.

"That was off the hook," Chiara said as she came to sit next to me in the dugout. It always took a second for her dark-brown curls to stop moving after the rest of her had.

Aiden appeared from the bleachers, which were emptying of the small crowd who'd come to watch. "Seriously," he said. "That was amazing."

"Thanks," I said, ready to talk about something else. It was just a game. I watched Bennett and Princess Bubblegum talking to Evelyn. Then for some no doubt ridiculous reason, Princess Bubblegum did one of those trust falls, and Bennett caught her under the arms.

"They're so gross," I said.

"Open your eyes, Kaylee." He handed me a bottle of water. "They're *happy*. I saw them all lovey-dovey over the weekend actually. In the bookstore of all places."

"Why do you sound surprised?" I asked, half laughing, then drank some water.

"I guess I didn't think he could read." Aiden's smile was crooked, but the rest of him was all right angles. It was seriously like he'd been built with flesh on LEGOs and not bones.

"Nice," I said. "Real nice. Anyway, it's only a matter of time before he realizes he's in love with me."

"You can't make someone like you," Aiden said, and he brushed his bangs off to the side. They'd gotten long recently, and they made his head look permanently pensive, perpetually pondering something. Which he pretty much was.

"Just you wait," I said.

Then we all three watched Bennett and Princess Bubblegum walk away from the field, attached at the lips, arms around each other's waist.

Princess Bubblegum's actual name was Aubrey Hazelton, but she had this impossibly high-pitched voice—like she ate animated kids' shows for breakfast—and was always chewing gum. Thus my nickname for her. She was all Monster High–ed up today, with black knee socks and chunky shoes and fishnet tights and a black-leather miniskirt. Her shirt was purple and orange lollipop swirls, and she'd recently had lavender streaks put in her hair.

"Those shoes." I shook my head. "How can she even walk in those shoes? I mean, seriously." I faked a falling motion, circling my arms and making a scared face.

Chiara laughed. Aiden smiled reluctantly. I grabbed my bag, thinking about how Princess Bubblegum really ought to fall flat on her face. The laws of physics practically demanded it.

"You guys need rides?" I asked, and Aiden and Chiara both said yep.

A high-pitched *aaaaaaah* rose from the parking lot.

I turned. Princess Bubblegum had totally wiped out. Bennett was helping her to her feet as she brushed asphalt dust off her palms.

"Oh my god." I covered my mouth to hide my laugh and Chiara covered hers, too.

"You guys are awful," Aiden said.

Chiara and I looped arms.

Maybe it was true.

• • •

After softball games and even just after school, I'd gotten into a sort of gross habit of laying out a full baking sheet of tortilla chips covered with shredded cheddar cheese, I'd pop it in the oven, then stand there, peering in and wishing the cheese would melt faster. Then I'd pull out the tray, let it cool some, and eat every single chip while standing by the stovetop, starting with the cheesiest first.

A minute on the lips, people say, *a lifetime on the hips.*

But I didn't care. Nothing much stuck to me.

When the doorbell rang *that* day—that seemingly completely ordinary Tuesday—I figured it was UPS with an Amazon package for my dad. Probably a new router or thermostat or remote-control LED bulbs or some Sonos contraption or anything else that would make our house smarter, though at this point I was pretty sure the house was smarter than any of the three of us that lived there.

I opened the door.

Guess again.

A compact woman—maybe in her forties?—wearing a casual denim summer dress stood on the front porch with an orange tote bag looped over her right shoulder. She took off sunglasses with pale blue frames to reveal eyes that matched.

"Can I help you?" I'd noticed her at the game. Thought maybe she was a softball scout for a local college. When the time came I was sure I'd be enticed by at least two or three.

"It depends," she said.

"Is this is a recruiting thing?"

She looked confused and that made me confused, so I said, "Oh, well, there's no one home over the age of eighteen or whatever. Like if you're selling something or taking a poll."

"Oh, it's nothing like that." She held out a business card from our big public radio station. "You're Kaylee Bryar, right?"

"Um." I had cheese stuck in one of my molars. "I used to be."

"I was hoping we could talk about your birth mother."

. . .

She was producing a podcast, it turned out.

About Crystal.

Who had been in prison since I was four.

But she didn't ask me about the murder, or about my mother's persistent claims of innocence over the years, despite her plea agreement. No, this radio person—her name was Liana—wanted to talk about the first time Crystal had been famous, when she was only fourteen.

She asked, "Do you have telekinetic powers?"

I snorted. "Do *you*?"

. . .

Let's define ordinary.

Ordinary was late May, end of junior year.

Ordinary was driving around, newly licensed, with Aiden and Chiara in a town in Rockland County, New York, where the men had long commutes to the city that they complained about and the women mostly stayed home to raise the kids even after the kids were already raised.

Ordinary was softball and homework and test prep and violin lessons and yearbook committee and college visits and GPA freak-outs and everything-you-do-from-now-on-affects-where-you'll-go-to-college and daydreaming about Bennett Laurie and waiting for life to become something real and not something that parents and teachers and admissions boards and coaches were in charge of.

I could finally drive a car—so yay—but I was not remotely in the driver's seat in any other way. None of us were.

Ordinary was life with Christine and Robert Novell—my parents—who'd adopted me when I was four and helped me basically forget everything that had come before. Everything that had been, well, extraordinary.

Over time, my memories of Crystal and the murder of my younger brother, Jack, had faded like denim, taking on soft-white fuzzy edges. The Novells had liked it that way, and I guess I had, too. But then a bunch of years ago, when I was around twelve and got a phone, I'd started Googling more and asking questions. So they told me everything.

Like how Crystal had first become famous as a teen because of a photo that supposedly proved she was the focal point of some kind of poltergeist activity or telekinetic power. How the story had been picked up by the Associated Press and gone national. How she'd eventually been outed as a fake even though there were some people that still insisted it had all been real, that they'd seen some strange phenomena with their own eyes.

They told me how Crystal had had a sort of shit life after that, though not in those words. How it involved her getting knocked up by my father (again, not in those words) when she was twenty-one and then again (by Jack's father, who was not my father) when she was twenty-three. A few years later, Jack ended up dead—blunt force trauma—and Crystal, while claiming innocence, had taken a plea deal to avoid the death penalty when things weren't going her way during the trial.

She was sentenced to life in prison.

I reacted to all this the way I imagined most people would:

I shook my head in horrified disbelief.

I decided that my birth mother was either certifiably insane or somehow irreparably damaged by life in ways I probably didn't want to know about.

I felt bad for her.

I felt bad for me, too—I'd had a brother and he was dead; and my father had never been in the picture at all—but mostly I felt grateful that the Novells had rescued me. I boxed up the rest and put it away.

Of course I also started staring at objects for hours on

end—marbles, feathers, the Monopoly dog, the Operation funny bone—willing them to move. But nothing ever did, and after a while I outgrew such childish notions. Telekinesis was the stuff of movies and books and dreamers. It wasn't even real, let alone genetic or inheritable.

That was my story and I stuck to it.

. . .

"How did you find me?" I asked Liana, when she just stood there staring at me.

"You didn't answer my question." She put her hands on her hips.

"You first," I said.

"I found you because I'm resourceful and I'd like to interview you for the podcast." She looked at her watch as if she had better places to be. "Will your parents be home soon?"

Neither of them was due home for a few hours, no. So I told her I'd have them call her, and she left.

I stared at her card—her show was called *The Possible*—and my knee-jerk response was to call Chiara, who knew everything about me. Or, at least, everything *else.*

My parents had gently suggested, when I'd been twelve and asking all those questions, that I not tell anyone about my connection to Crystal, and I'd promised I wouldn't and had stayed true to that promise.

It had seemed like a good secret to keep.

But *now*?

With a *podcast* in the works?

. . .

"You have got to be shitting me," Chiara said.

To which I said, "I shit you not."

"Prove it," she said.

I did some quick Googling and sent her a link.

. . .

STRANGE HAPPENINGS PLAGUE LOCAL FAMILY

by Paul Schmidt

Columnist, *The PA Star*

March 6, 1993

A house in an otherwise sleepy neighborhood has become the center of some kind of unexplained phenomena—the sort of things more likely to happen in movies or books than in reality. At the home of the Bryar family, small objects have been flying across the room. Paintings and photos are falling off the walls. Lights and appliances are turning on and off on their own.

"I just want everyone to go away," said the family's teenage daughter, Crystal, when we visited.

But the phenomena seemed to follow her in particular. Right then, a telephone nearby leaped through the air. Again and again. Witnesses were understandably disturbed, especially when a glass vase flew off a shelf and shattered at the girl's feet. The family hopes that this report will help to attract the right kind of investigator to find an explanation.

. . .

"Un. Real," Chiara said. "And here I was thinking you were too boring to be my best friend."

"Nice," I said.

"Joking," she said. "Sort of. Now we just have to cure your RBF and we'll be in business."

Chiara was convinced that my "resting bitch face" was the reason we didn't have guys hanging on us all the time. Maybe she was right. I didn't care. Bennett Laurie was the only guy that mattered.

"So the podcast woman wants to interview me," I said as I typed Liana's name into a search field.

"You, my dear," Chiara said, "are about to become famous."

. . .

My search led me to the Free Public Radio website, where I learned that Liana Fatone was a graduate of Harvard University who lived in Queens with her husband and two young daughters. According to the radio station's page, she'd had an incredibly successful first podcast about a murder on a small college campus and now had selected Crystal as her season two topic.

A short bio on the preview page for the upcoming season said that she was born the same year as Crystal and had grown up in Connecticut. Below a photo of her holding a pen and notepad and looking investigative, her brow furrowed, she's quoted: “I never forgot about Crystal and how strange the whole story was. Then when I discovered that her life had taken this tragic turn many years later, I felt there was a story there. Did she fake the telekinesis? Will she cop to that now? Did she actually kill her own son? I want answers.”

A short Q&A revealed that she collected spoons and that her favorite book was, no joke, *Matilda.*

"How did she find you?" asked my mother when I explained about my visitor.

"She said she's resourceful."

Mom shook her head and sank into a chair at the kitchen table, looking tired. "I don't know, Kay. This doesn't seem like a thing to get involved in."

My mother was pretty much the opposite of Crystal. She had also grown up pretty poor—mostly in New Jersey with some time in Pennsylvania—but had made it her life's goal to be different, aka better. She'd gone away to a good college, where she met my dad, who'd grown up upper-middle class, and she ditched her accent and bad grammar and pretty much never looked back. Some of her cousins had gotten into a fight at her wedding, and she basically cut her family off and built a totally different kind of life with my father. She'd said there'd been a little bit of "look who decided to turn up" when her mother died, and then, a few years later, her father, but she didn't really care what they thought. She looked down on people who weren't the sort of achiever she'd become, so of course she wouldn't want to have anything at all to do with Crystal, who'd achieved notoriety but nothing more.

"Maybe," I said. "Maybe not. I don't know."

Because now maybe I wanted answers, too. Maybe I'd been hiding from the past—and from myself—for long enough. Just talking about it all with Chiara had felt like this big yoga kind of exhale. I'd been denying so much for so long, writing it all off as childish. Maybe it was time to face reality. Because if someone thought enough of Crystal's whole experience to talk to scientists and experts about it, maybe there was something to it?

. . .

Seriously.

What if?

. . .

Mom said, "Let's discuss it with your father when he gets home, m'k?"

That's how things were in our family, so there was no getting around it. I couldn't think of a single decision that had been made in our household without both parents having signed off on it. Mom ran *everything* by Dad, and vice versa.

I ran everything by Aiden.

So I went up to my room and called him and regaled him with the tale of Crystal—and the news of Liana's podcast.

"That is pretty crazy, Kay. I mean, I knew you were adopted but . . ."

"I know." My heart seemed to be beating slightly quicker than normal. "So what would you do? Would you do the interview?"

"I can honestly say"—he spoke slowly—"that I have no idea."

"Me neither," I said, lying down on my bed. "But I mean, I *think* I want to do it."

"What would you say? I mean, what does she want to ask you about?"

"Well, for starters, she asked me if I had telekinetic powers."

"Wait a second," he said. "You said she's from Free Public Radio? FPR?"

"Yes."

"You can't possibly believe in any of that. I mean. Do you? Does *she*? This podcast lady? Because you know it all had to be a hoax, right?"

"Right. I mean. Of course." I went to stand by the open window, the room suddenly stifling.

Of course.

Aiden breathed loudly. "I'm *so sorry* about your brother. I mean, about everything."

My throat constricted. Dried right up. No one apart from my parents had ever said that to me; no one else had had the chance.

© Peter Lutjen

TARA ALTEBRANDO is the author of several middle grade and young adult novels, including *The Leaving*. She lives in New York City with her family.

www.taraaltebrando.com
@TaraAltebrando